A Lady of
Hidden
Intent

LADIES *of* LIBERTY

A LADY *of*
HIDDEN
INTENT

TRACIE PETERSON

BETHANY HOUSE PUBLISHERS
Minneapolis, Minnesota

Published by Bethany House Publishers
11400 Hampshire Avenue South
Bloomington, Minnesota 55438

Bethany House Publishers is a division of
Baker Publishing Group, Grand Rapids, Michigan.

Printed in the United States of America

Library of Congress Cataloging-in-Publication Data

Peterson, Tracie.
    A lady of hidden intent / Tracie Peterson.
        p.   cm. — (Ladies of liberty)
    ISBN 978-0-7642-0472-2 (hardcover : alk. paper) — ISBN 978-0-7642-0146-2 (pbk.) — ISBN 978-0-0762-0473-9 (large-print pbk.)   1. Fathers and daughters—Fiction.   2. False imprisonment—Fiction.   3. British—United States—Fiction.   4. Women dressmakers—Fiction.   5. Philadelphia (Pa.)—Fiction.   I. Title.
    PS3566.E7717L327   2008
    813'.54—dc22

                                                                                                2007035138

To Judy Miller,
my dear friend and occasional partner in crime.
It is such a joy to work with you and to call you friend.
I cherish our friendship and thank God for you.

Books by Tracie Peterson

www.traciepeterson.com

A Slender Thread • *I Can't Do It All!***
What She Left for Me • *Where My Heart Belongs*

ALASKAN QUEST
Summer of the Midnight Sun
Under the Northern Lights • *Whispers of Winter*

BELLS OF LOWELL*
Daughter of the Loom • *A Fragile Design*
These Tangled Threads

BROADMOOR LEGACY*
A Daughter's Inheritance

LIGHTS OF LOWELL*
A Tapestry of Hope • *A Love Woven True*
The Pattern of Her Heart

DESERT ROSES
Shadows of the Canyon • *Across the Years*
Beneath a Harvest Sky

HEIRS OF MONTANA
Land of my Heart • *The Coming Storm*
To Dream Anew • *The Hope Within*

WESTWARD CHRONICLES
A Shelter of Hope • *Hidden in a Whisper*
A Veiled Reflection

LADIES OF LIBERTY
A Lady of High Regard • *A Lady of Hidden Intent*

SHANNON SAGA†
City of Angels • *Angels Flight* • *Angel of Mercy*

YUKON QUEST
Treasures of the North • *Ashes and Ice*
Rivers of Gold

*with Judith Miller   †with James Scott Bell
**with Allison Bottke and Dianne O'Brian

PROLOGUE

Bath, England
December 1850

"Catherine, my dear, I want you to meet Mr. Carter Danby of Pennsylvania in America." Nelson Newbury raised his voice to be heard above the stringed quartet providing dancing music for his guests. "Mr. Danby, this is my daughter, Catherine Newbury."

Catherine let her gaze sweep quickly over the dashing stranger before meeting his dark eyes. He wore an evening coat of some value; the cut and the materials were the finest available. His face was clean-shaven and his dark hair groomed to a meticulous point of fashion. He was, as her friend Elizabeth might have proclaimed, "Fit enough for Her Majesty's court."

"How do you do, Mr. Danby?" She gave a perfunctory curtsy.

"I do quite well, Miss Newbury. Thank you." He offered a bow and a charming smile that Catherine was sure had melted more than one young woman's heart. The twinkle in his eyes seemed to promise something more—maybe mischief, maybe understanding. Perhaps he could read her thoughts and knew how unimpressed she really was.

Having been called a handsome young woman since she was twelve, Catherine was used to men vying for her attention. She'd been promised the moon, given her share of silly trinkets, and endured more than one slobbering ninny twice her age begging for her hand in marriage. Perhaps Carter Danby was to be the next in line.

She couldn't help but smile at the thought. At least he was closer to her own seventeen years. She guessed him to be twenty and five, maybe a year or two younger. He had an assured air about him, however, that suggested he was confident of his position and personage. That alone put him head and shoulders above the rest. Not that he needed help in that department either. He was quite tall.

"Mr. Danby is studying architecture and has come to Bath to visit some of our finer examples," her father relayed.

Catherine smiled at her father. "I'm glad he could join our Christmas party. It would be quite dreary to spend the holidays looking only at stone and scrolling."

Mr. Danby chuckled, causing Catherine to once again extend him a glance. He seemed genuinely amused and did not appear to be putting on airs. But then again, he was from America, and what few Americans she had met were quite a mystery to Catherine.

"I assure you I am feeling far from dreary. I find the sights, especially in Bath, to be quite pleasing." He grinned, seeming to know she would catch his meaning. Yet rather than wait for her response, Danby continued. "I plan to be home before Christmas. In fact, this is my last stop. We travel in two days' time for Bristol and the ship that will bear us home."

"That's wonderful, Mr. Danby. Perhaps you will travel on one of my father's ships. He has the best fleet of passenger and cargo vessels."

"So I have been told. But, alas, I am not to enjoy that pleasure."

"Well, then, my good fellow, you must instead enjoy the pleasures of the evening and the hospitality we can afford you," her father declared.

Carter Danby eyed Catherine. "I intend to do just that."

Catherine felt her cheeks grow hot and quickly turned away. "If you'll both excuse me, I have other guests to see to."

She hurried off in the direction of her friend Elizabeth, who happened to be sharing a rather private conversation with another of their acquaintances, Mrs. Witherspoon.

"And that was the reason she could not be seen in good company. No one can be certain as to whether or not the poor soul was with child, but it is, of course, presumed so," Mrs. Witherspoon said with a tone that suggested grave concern.

"Of course," Elizabeth said, completely horrified. She looked up at Catherine and held her hand to her throat as if the entire matter were too much. "We were just discussing Lady Overton's youngest daughter."

"It appears the conversation is not a pleasant one," Catherine countered.

"Indeed it is not," Mrs. Witherspoon said, shaking her head and looking around suspiciously. "It is a sad day indeed when a young lady of good reputation ruins her chances in society by dallying with a man of ill repute."

"Sad, too, that society will be so judgmental of her actions."

Mrs. Witherspoon seemed taken aback. "My dear, we all live by the judgment of our society. There is no other mark by which we can base the value of a person's character than by their actions."

"Be they perceived or known," Catherine replied in a mocking voice that she hoped would put the older woman in her place. To her consternation, however, Mrs. Witherspoon nodded with great enthusiasm.

"To be sure. And that is why we must be very careful that we give no perceived offense. I cannot express enough the importance of that point."

Catherine then watched as the two women began to smile brightly, as though the sun itself had just burst through the clouds. She turned and saw Mr. Danby.

"Mrs. Witherspoon, Miss Merriweather, may I present Mr. Carter Danby of America."

The women curtsied and bowed their heads momentarily. Mr. Danby smiled and gave a crisp bow. "Ladies, I am quite delighted."

"What brings you to Bath, Mr. Danby?" Mrs. Witherspoon asked, her voice taking on a higher pitch in her nervousness.

"I am lately here on business, ma'am, but presently have come to ask Miss Newbury if she would do me the honor of a dance."

Knowing that duty was more important than her own personal feelings, Catherine said, "Of course. You are kind to ask."

She allowed him to draw her away, the wide expanse of her silk ball gown swinging in bell-like fashion as Mr. Danby moved her to the dance floor. The music began immediately as they stepped in line with the others.

Moving forward to the music, Catherine felt Danby take hold of her arm as he turned her ever so gently to the cadence. "You have a beautiful home, Miss Newbury, and I find your father quite congenial."

"He's a good man," Catherine replied as they came apart and circled with their partner to the right.

Coming back together, Danby took hold of her gloved fingers. "And what of your mother? I've not yet met her."

They performed the steps perfectly in unison, then again pulled apart as Catherine answered. "She passed on with my younger brothers some two years past. It was influenza."

As they rejoined after completing a series of intricate steps and turns, she found him quite sober. "I am sorry, Miss Newbury. That loss must have been quite acute."

"Yes," she murmured.

They went on in this manner, sharing little comments about the holidays and the weather. At one point Catherine was rather surprised when he asked for her impression of America.

"I have none, save that which I've experienced through her people or stories," she answered as the dance concluded and he led her from the floor.

"And have your experiences been good or bad?" He smiled as they stopped in a less-populated corner of the room.

"They have been good overall, I suppose." She looked at him and found his gaze intense. "Of course," she added quickly, "Americans do tend to be confused by the protocol and social structure of England. Perhaps it was one of the things they threw off in their independence."

He laughed, and she thought it delightful the way tiny lines appeared at the corners of his eyes. Perhaps he was a happy man by nature.

"I would prefer there be no social classes or divisions. I find charming company in most every circle. However, I assure you we have our social classes and taboos in America as well. It would have been nice to cast those aside with other archaic notions, but, alas, we have not so distanced ourselves from our mother country that we have allowed for that matter to be resolved in full. I am, however, working on a personal level to see it dismissed."

"Archaic notions? You think it wrong, then, for the classes to be divided?"

"I think people are people, Miss Newbury. Some are good. Some are bad. There will always be problems and issues to resolve so long as even one man remains alive and capable of thinking. Do you not feel imposed upon by the restrictions of your class?"

"Not at all," Catherine replied. "I know my place, and that is somewhat of a comfort to me."

"Perhaps that is only because you are at the upper echelons of society. Were you perhaps a scullery maid, you might feel differently."

"I doubt that. As a scullery maid, I would know my place—what was expected of me and what was out of my reach. I believe knowing one's place prevents a great many misfortunes."

The music started up again, and Catherine found herself growing increasingly uncomfortable. She wasn't sure if it was the topic of their conversation or the nearness of this stranger who seemed to completely captivate her senses.

"If you'll excuse me." She didn't wait for his response but gave a quick curtsy and hurried away. Her heart pounded rapidly as she imagined him watching her go. She forced herself to slow her pace, nod, and comment to those around her while escaping as fast as decorum would allow.

Among the things Catherine loved about her life in Bath was the beauty of the buildings. She thought Mr. Danby very wise to have come to see their architecture. Why, the Roman Baths alone were worthy of the trip, but so too were some of the other beauties, such as the Abbey and the Royal Crescent. She wondered if Danby had been instructed regarding John Wood the elder and his son John Wood the younger. The two had been quite instrumental in creating designs for Bath. Of course, there were others as well, but those two were often heralded above all.

Catherine accepted dances from two of her father's friends. They chatted briefly about the weather and the holidays to come, but nothing of significance. Despite having had her new satin slippers stepped on more times than she could count, Catherine was pleased overall with the way things were going. Their servants were well trained and eager to please, so there was no need to worry about the food running out or the liquor being depleted.

And yet for all her desire to forget him, Carter Danby re-mained present in her mind. He was quite handsome and clearly well-spoken. Catherine couldn't help but wonder about his life in America. Then, as if thinking on such things had conjured the man in the flesh, he suddenly stood before her.

"I wonder if I might entice you to take another turn with me."

Catherine looked up to find Mr. Danby smiling at her. The music that had just begun was clearly a waltz—that most inti-mate of dances. She hesitated a moment, but seeing Mr. Wooster heading her way, she agreed. At least Danby would not step on her feet.

"I do hope you get a chance to visit America," Carter Danby said as they turned into the flow of dancers. "I think you would find it quite entertaining—if not amusing."

"I have no intention of doing so," Catherine replied. "I have more than enough to amuse and entertain me right here."

"So you think us not worthy of your time or attention?"

She looked up at him and shook her head. "Hardly so. I simply do not think of you at all."

"Spoken like a true English patriot."

"And what is that supposed to mean?" She took great offense at his tone and stiffened in his arms.

Mr. Danby laughed. "Meaning only that for many an Eng-lishman it is far easier to forget our existence than to remember the loss. American independence is not that ancient of a history. If you consider the conflict little more than thirty years past when your country attacked and burned our capital, then it's even more understandable."

"I am not overly concerned with either your independence or our loss. To everything there is a season, and perhaps that season known as the American Colonies is best forgotten. The heartache comes from the sad way it divided families and destroyed livelihoods."

Danby nodded. "Perhaps you are right. Wrongs of the past are best forgotten."

She smiled knowingly. "So you admit America was wrong in rebelling."

He laughed so loudly that Catherine was immediately embarrassed as several couples looked their way. She wanted only to walk—no, run—from the room, but instead she forced herself to look at Danby.

"You're amused?"

"Only that you could so clearly misunderstand me. Of course, you are very young. I did not imply that America was wrong. Rather, that England was at fault for her poor management, abuses, and neglects. Those are the wrongs that I believe are best forgotten."

The music stopped and Catherine quickly pulled away from her partner. "Thank you for your explanation, Mr. Danby. At ten and seven, I do find that many things escape my understanding." She turned and left quickly, realizing that Carter Danby was the only man who had ever made her feel like running away.

She was still thinking about him later that evening as she lay in bed trying to sleep. It was nearly four in the morning, and while the party had been concluded for many hours, her desire to put the American from her mind was not as easily accomplished.

Getting up, she pulled on her housecoat and decided a bite to eat might settle her for the night. She'd eaten very little at the party, and prior to that had been much too busy in preparation to dine properly. Surely Cook had left something in the kitchen.

The warmth of the velvet robe embraced her as she did up the buttons. The coat had been a gift from her mother, and though no longer fashionable and suffering wear, Catherine had been reluctant to cast it off for another. She smiled as she pulled her long brown hair from the collar.

"I wish you could have been here tonight, Mother," she whispered in the chilled room. The night felt so damp and cold that even the small fire in her hearth did little to dispel it. Perhaps it would snow. Snow would at least keep Father home. He wouldn't risk a journey to Bristol if there were any threat of being delayed. It would be of great comfort to have him home. Especially for the holidays.

Catherine slipped into the hall and made her way downstairs. She paused on the first floor, seeing a light glow from under her father's library door. Could he have found sleep an elusive friend as well? Perhaps they might talk over the evening.

She decided to forgo the refreshment and instead went to her father's office, where she could now hear voices. Frowning, she recognized her father's business partner, Finley Baker. The man offered her nothing but misgivings about his gender.

"Consider it a final favor, then, Newbury. The truth is upon us."

"But it is a truth of which I had no knowledge." Catherine's father sounded very upset. She thought to interrupt as she reached for the door handle, then pulled back as Baker laughed bitterly.

"It matters not that you had no knowledge. Your name is on every ledger and invoice. You might as well have known from the start, for that is what will be presumed—if not proven—for the courts."

"This is an outrage, sir!" her father declared, and the sound of something being hit or thrown caused Catherine to nearly jump out of her skin. It wasn't like her father to lose his temper. "I have never agreed to deal in illegal goods, as you well know."

"Be that as it may, Newbury, there is no help for it now. The authorities will be fast upon my heels. I would expect them no later than this morning. Now I will take my leave, but you should credit me at least with having the decency to give you warning."

Catherine heard someone move for the door. As the handle began to turn, she quickly backed into the room across the hall and disappeared into the darkness. She could see from her hiding place that Baker now stood in the doorway, his back to her.

"Newbury, they will surely take hold of your assets. You would be wise to take what you can and leave the country. That is my purpose at this moment. Our ship *The Adelaide* is harbored at Plymouth. We can surely make it there and escape this matter. Why, in a fortnight we could be resting easy and sipping the finest of French wines."

"I don't mean to leave, Baker. This matter must be faced as an honorable man would deal with any unpleasant deception thrust upon him."

Baker laughed. "Be the scapegoat. It really matters little to me. They will confiscate your home and put you in prison. No doubt put that pretty daughter of yours there as well."

"Get out!"

Catherine backed even farther into the room's confines. She had never seen her father angrier. He lunged for Baker, but the man merely sidestepped his attack and headed down the hall.

"Mark my words, Newbury. You will find little comfort in the days to come."

Catherine heard the man's boots stomp on the stairs as he raced from the house. No doubt he would be gone even before one of the servants could be summoned to hold him for the authorities.

Creeping toward the hallway, Catherine watched her father shake his head and go back into the library. She knew he probably wouldn't wish her to have been witness to the affair, but she couldn't lie to him and say otherwise.

"Father, what in the world was that all about?"

Nelson Newbury looked up from the hearth where he now stood. "Catherine, what are you doing up?"

"I heard voices. I'm ashamed to admit I listened at your door."

"Then you know the worst of it," he said, hanging his head.

"No, I'm not sure that I do. I heard Mr. Baker say that the authorities would soon be here to take you to prison, but I do not pretend to know why." She felt a tight band wrap her chest, threatening to cut off her very breath. "Why would he say such things, Father?"

"Because my ships have been caught with contraband. Slaves from Africa."

"Slaves? Surely not. We've never traded in slaves. We do not believe in such things." She went to his side. "It must be a mistake."

"No mistake, unfortunately. Baker planned it all out and made a tidy profit for himself." Her father's tone left little doubt of his bitterness. "I can scarce believe the man would do such a deplorable thing, but to the authorities it will matter little what I believed of him."

Catherine took hold of his arm. "Father, this surely cannot be the end of it. You must send men to capture Mr. Baker. He has told you where he is headed. Let the authorities know this, so that they might keep him from leaving the country. You were a victim of Mr. Baker's duplicity. That is hardly worthy of imprisonment."

Her father straightened and met her gaze. "Daughter, you must get away from here."

"I will not. I will not leave your side."

"If you do not, I cannot focus on what must be done to clear my name. There is no telling what the authorities will deem necessary to resolve the matter. I will not have my estates confiscated and my daughter left to fend for herself. I will call Dugan. He and Selma may go with you. They have been faithful servants, but no doubt they will see their livelihood gone with this chaos. Go to Bristol. My dear friend Captain Marlowe will see you safely out of harm's way." Her father hurried to his desk and took up pen and paper.

"I won't go." Catherine shook her head. "Stop. I won't leave you, Father."

"You must. If you love me, then I beg you to do this thing for me. If the matter is easily resolved, I will merely send for you again. I will not have you bear the consequences of my mistakes. Captain Marlowe has family in America. I believe it would do you good to visit and see New York City, perhaps. It is quite fascinating."

Catherine could see his determination. "Is there no other way? No other hope for me to remain at your side?"

"No. I have not begun to tell you the full details, but let me say this much: Two men were murdered this night in Bristol by Baker's hand. There will be little rest for anyone until these issues are resolved." He dropped the pen and went to one of the bookcases. Pulling out several volumes, he placed the books on his desk, then went back to open a concealed compartment. "You will take this money and see to your needs. To the needs of Dugan and Selma as well."

The clock chimed from over the mantel. It was only a quarter until five. Soon the entire household would be about their duties. Catherine felt a chill permeate her body. Not even her housecoat could ward off the sense of doom that was now upon them.

"Here," her father said, thrusting a small leather satchel into her hands. "Take it and hide it well. The morning train would be the best way to get to Bristol, but I fear it will be watched. I'll advise Dugan to take the carriage."

Catherine hugged the satchel to her breast. "Why don't you come with us, Father? You can resolve the matter from America."

He looked at her sadly and gently touched her cheek. "I might be a poor judge of men, but I am no coward. I will face my mistakes, but I will not allow my only remaining child to do so as well."

She threw herself into his arms and held him as though she might drown if she let go. And truly that was what she felt might happen. How could she lose him like this? She'd only bid her mother and siblings good-bye two years ago. She needed him. He was her only connection to the past—to her mother and brothers—to her childhood.

Sobbing, she tried one more time. "Please let me stay with you."

"I love you too much to allow for that, kitten. You must be a good girl now. You must be brave and stand fast that I might also do the same."

She recognized the rough, desperate plea in his voice and knew her show of sorrow and despair was taking its toll on him. The thought sobered her, and straightening, Catherine stretched on tiptoe and kissed her father's cheek.

"I love you, Father. I will go to America, but even from there I will do whatever is possible to be at your aid—at your side."

"You will always be with me—at least in heart," he whispered. He kissed her forehead, then put her away from him. "Now go pack. There isn't time or the ability to take many things, I'm sorry to say. Take what will service you well. It will be cold on the Atlantic—I know it well. Take whatever will see you through the winter."

Catherine nodded and turned for the door. She wanted desperately to look back—to see his face and memorize every detail. A fear began to eat at her—tearing away her strength and resolve. She might never see him again. This might very well be good-bye.

CHAPTER I

Philadelphia
June 1855

"Catherine, where are you?"

Looking up from the bodice she'd just pinned, Catherine called out, "I'm here, Mrs. Clarkson. In the sewing room." Her employer, a stocky woman whose curly brown hair had been pulled straight back into a tight little bun, charged into the room like a general taking new ground.

"The news is very good. Your designs have been talked about all over the world."

"Excuse me?"

"Everyone is excited. Remember when I went to the Industry of the Nations exhibit in Paris? Well, I gave some of your drawings to my friends in the fashion industry there. *Catherine Shay* is a name they are now speaking with great reverence. They believe you will soon be known throughout all of society as the most reputable of American fashion designers for women."

Catherine straightened and put the bodice aside. She could scarcely believe Mrs. Clarkson was serious.

"Surely you jest. There are far too many credible French designers to worry about a silly . . . American woman." Catherine nearly stumbled on the description of herself. It had been five years since she'd come to hide in America. She couldn't risk losing that shelter now. Of course, if Mrs. Clarkson had her way, the entire world would be privy to Catherine's hiding place.

Mrs. Clarkson took a chair and pulled it up to the sewing table. "My dear, you are already greatly appreciated here. Why, every woman in Philadelphia is now demanding your fresh designs for their gowns. I cannot even allow you to take time away from your creative work to merely sew on garments of lesser value."

Catherine laughed. "You exaggerate, of course. Although, I appreciate your kind regard."

"It is not exaggeration. With the winter season beginning and holiday gowns in demand, you will soon see the truth of it. I had no fewer than ten requests for your personal attention and design. I've no doubt there will be at least another fifty before the end of the month."

"Well, I certainly hope for your sake that is true, but of course I cannot possibly design fifty or sixty new gowns in the time needed."

"But don't you see? That is what will make your creations even more sought after. Women will know that they will be among the chosen few, should they get a gown designed by Shay." She smiled and pulled off her gold-rimmed glasses. "I am quite pleased, my dear. You must know that."

Catherine heard the satisfaction in Mrs. Clarkson's voice as she added, "The business is doing very well, and you can be quite proud of what you have accomplished."

It was true. The business was doing exceptionally well. Only the day before a new sign had been delivered and installed over the door of the modest four-story brick building. It read *Clarkson's Dressmaking* in large lettering. Then in smaller print, *Specialized Designs for Women.*

"No one works alone here," Catherine finally offered. "We all do our part. Praise me if you will, but then allow that such praise must also fall back on yourself and the others."

"My dear, I will not be swayed. I know very well that your work here has brought about much of my success. Your designs are unequaled, except perhaps for those in France." She grinned mischievously. "I cannot discredit my own countrymen—no matter that I have been an American lo these thirty-two years. My, but it does not seem so much time has passed. Only yesterday Jean Pierre and I were working to tailor suits for fashionable men of means." She sighed and leaned back in the chair. "My brother is greatly missed. He was such a comfort to me after my own husband died; now I must comfort myself in knowing I shall one day see them both in heaven."

"I can very well understand," Catherine replied, not daring to meet Mrs. Clarkson's eyes. "At least I like to imagine that I can," she added, lest there be any question to her comment.

The longing to see her father again was something that ate at Catherine's heart daily. For so long there had been no word—no understanding of what had happened to him. She knew he had been sent to prison, but little else. With his assets taken by the Crown, there had been little hope of proper representation.

"Well, we must each bear our cross, no?"

"It is true." Catherine held up the bodice. "I think this will work nicely for Mrs. Stern." The low neckline was something Catherine had imitated after seeing a fashion plate in *Peterson's Magazine.*

"She does like to reveal more of herself than most," Mrs. Clarkson said, admiring Catherine's work. "You have made it perfectly."

Catherine smiled. "We shall see."

"Mrs. Clarkson?" A young girl of no more than fifteen entered the room. She brought a pattern to the older woman and frowned. "I cannot seem to remember how to enlarge the bust."

"Lydia, you cannot advance to Improver if you are slack in your work. Pay attention to the little things." Mrs. Clarkson got on her feet. "Come to the table by the window."

Catherine watched the girl begrudgingly follow. Lydia had been troubled since moving into the sewing house. She had apprenticed for a year before coming to live at Clarkson's, and the transition had not been easy. She missed her mother and sisters greatly and cried herself to sleep on many a night. Catherine had tried to befriend her, but Lydia seemed inclined toward Felicia, one of the more troublesome young women in the house.

Living at the sewing house had been Catherine's deliverance. It had been made even better by the fact that besides hiring Catherine because of her sewing abilities, Mrs. Clarkson had needed Dugan and Selma for their skills. Selma now cooked and cleaned for the house, and Dugan handled her yards and carriage.

Their time in America had been arduous, but finding work here with Mrs. Clarkson had been an answer to prayer. Catherine didn't even mind the long hours. Spending ten or twelve hours sewing each day gave her little time to feel sorry for herself. By the time the holidays came around, the hours increased to fifteen, and even then Catherine was grateful. It was a difficult task, but Catherine found that with some effort she was slowly purging the memories of better days gone by.

Catherine put the bodice away and made her way upstairs to her room. Her shoulders ached from sitting hunched over her work. It would soon be time to retire for the night, and there were still things she needed to tend to. Two blouses and several pairs of stockings would need to be washed by hand. Then, of course, she had tried to be faithful to read her Bible and spend time in prayer for her father.

"I hoped I might catch you before you went to bed."

Catherine looked up to find the ever-faithful Selma. "Of course. Shall we go to your quarters?"

Selma nodded. The woman had been like a mother to Catherine for these five long years. Yet Selma had always been special. When Nanny Bryce had died during the same influenza epidemic that claimed her mother and brothers, Catherine had sought solace in Selma's company.

"We've had a letter," Selma whispered conspiratorially as Catherine joined her.

"From home?"

"Yes. It's not much, but it will offer a thread of hope."

Catherine had great difficulty keeping her hopes up. Selma had told her over and over that God had not forgotten them, but that wasn't how it felt.

In their fourth-floor apartment, Dugan already had a fire lit in welcome. Catherine smiled as she came into their tiny sitting room. Apparently Dugan wasn't the only one who had anticipated her arrival. Selma had tea and buttered bread waiting to refresh them.

"Dugan, how are you tonight?"

"I'm fit as a fiddle, miss. You needn't worry about old Dugan." He smiled and pointed to the chair nearest the hearth. "You sit yourself right now."

Catherine knew better than to argue. The chair offered was Dugan's favorite, but he would not hear of her sitting elsewhere. "Selma said you'd had a letter."

"A short one," Selma explained as she retrieved the missive. " 'Tis from my sister Agnes." She extended the letter to Catherine. "You read while I pour tea."

Reading the contents was as refreshing as a glass of cold water on a warm day. There was the usual chatter about missing Selma and Dugan, as well as the exchange of pleasantries and news of the family. Finally there were a few lines regarding Catherine's father.

" 'We do not know,' " Catherine read aloud, " 'how our master endures his days in the prison. When we learned he was resettled in an institution nearby, Bradley tried to see him, but they would not allow for visitors. They assured us he was well and, in truth, Bradley felt the prison to be smaller and in better condition than most.' "

"At least we know where he is," Catherine murmured, then continued reading.

" 'Mr. Newbury was always of strong constitution. We pray that has followed him through his incarceration. The prison guard told Bradley that Mr. Newbury's sentence would see him there another twenty years.'"

Catherine felt the words cut deep. " 'There has come word that Mr. Baker was seen in France, but whether or not the proper authorities could be notified before he slipped away once again, no one can say. Then, too, this might well be nothing more than useless gossip.'"

Catherine looked up, letting the letter drop to her lap, "But surely there would be no reason to offer pretense on such a matter."

"I cannot think it would serve any good purpose," Selma replied. "But you know how people can be. Someone might very well have mentioned it simply to feel important." She handed Catherine a cup of tea. "Help yourself to the bread."

Catherine sipped the tea thoughtfully and glanced again at the letter. "Thank you. The tea is quite good."

"Something to warm your bones. The chill of autumn is upon us," Selma offered with a smile.

"I feel so helpless. I feel I have failed Father." Catherine reread the letter, hoping a second glance might offer something more. She shook her head and folded the pages. "I wish we could do something. I've saved as much money as I could these last years, but it is so little. It wouldn't even buy us passage home, much less buy adequate legal help or hire an investigator to hunt down Mr. Baker."

"You cannot blame yourself for that, child." Dugan reached for his pipe. "You and your father are innocent of the wrong in this matter."

"Yes, but we are the ones who suffer. Of course, Father suffers more than I, but Finley Baker goes about his business without retribution or consternation."

"I doubt that the man is free from worry," Selma declared. She took up a ball of yarn and plopped down in a rocking chair beside the fire. "He has had to remove himself from society and relocate whenever he is found out and questioned. We know that much to be true, for when the authorities first went in search of him, he moved no less than five times in six months."

"Yes, but I am certain that search has been forsaken long ago," Catherine said, reaching for a piece of bread.

"I'm surprised that he hasn't made his way to America," Dugan put in. "Seems it would be far easier to put himself out of reach by putting an ocean between him and England."

"America might offer the ocean, but the Continent allows easier and quicker transportation. The variety of transport, accommodations, and locations cannot be easily dismissed. Besides, you can be certain that he has friends there. Friends who have allowed him to escape while my father suffers and languishes in prison for five long years."

Catherine thought back to when they had traveled to America with the sympathetic Captain Marlowe, then been deposited at a boardinghouse run by the man's cousin. Shortly thereafter, the man's wife had helped them make the acquaintance of Mrs. Clarkson. A few short weeks later, the trio had moved to Philadelphia and settled into the sewing house.

Selma's knitting needles began clicking away as she rocked. "The good Lord will guide us, Catherine. He knows the injustice done and He will set things right."

"I only hope He doesn't wait too long," Catherine replied bitterly. "My father was a healthy man when I left, but no doubt prison has taken its toll—despite your nephew's report of him."

"And surely God cannot keep a man from ill health in prison," Dugan said with a smile.

Catherine realized he meant well. "Of course God can, but the question is, will He? He could have kept this from happening in the first place, but He chose not to."

"A hard thing to accept." Dugan puffed on his pipe and nodded thoughtfully.

One of her father's most trusted servants, Dugan had been injured in a carriage accident when he was young and bore a crippled leg that left him with a limp. Where other employers might have sent the man packing, Catherine's father had always seen to it that Dugan had work.

Father had been good about things like that. He noted the condition and abilities of the people around him. He sought to best fit them into service rather than merely dismiss them as beneath his concern.

"Oh, I miss him so much," Catherine whispered as she gazed into the fire.

"Aye, the master is a good man," Selma replied. "He would be proud of the way you've held up your head and put your hands to good work. He might never have wished for his daughter to do common labor, but I know he would delight in your choices."

"Situations thrust upon one are hardly choices," Catherine answered rather bitterly. "Nanny Bryce saw to it that I mastered sewing. I'm good for little else. And had it not been at Father's pleading, I would not be in this country at all."

"But America seems a good place," Selma countered. "I realize all we know of it is New York City and Philadelphia, but this
land has been good to us."

"True, true," Dugan offered. "We cannot be rejecting the goodness offered us. We would not have found it so in England."

Catherine nodded, knowing it was true enough. Work would
have been impossible, friends would have turned in fear of asso-
ciation, and relatives would have avoided her at all costs. Not that
there were many to be had, save some distant cousins. England's
hierarchy of society would have commiserated over her position
but offered her little else.

"Of course you're right. America has been good to us. I do
not mean to speak against her. There is, however, a longing for
the life I once knew. I cannot help but miss my friends and
our dear little home in Bath." She looked up and met Selma's
sympathetic gaze. "Your exile has been hard as well. I know you
miss your families there. I feel awful that you should be without
them on my account."

"Nonsense. We chose to come," Selma said as she continued
knitting. "Your father didn't force us. He very kindly asked."

"It was our desire to see you through these times," Dugan
admitted.

"I know." Catherine put aside her tea. "And you've both been
so very dear. I don't mind at all the pretense that you are my
mother and father, because in truth you have become so to me
in these years."

"We always wished for children," Selma said sadly. "Had
we ever had a daughter, we would have desired her to be just as
you are."

Catherine smiled. "Tired, dirty, and longing for what she had been denied?"

Selma laughed and Dugan offered a beaming smile. "Just so long as she was willing to sleep, bathe, and hope for what might yet be," the older man replied.

"That I am, Dugan. It's all that gets me through each day." She got to her feet and stretched. "I suppose I should go now. I have a few things to wash—besides myself."

"Take another piece of bread. You're far too skinny."

Catherine laughed but did as Selma instructed. "At least it keeps me from needing new clothes."

In the solitude of her room, Catherine tried to force despair from her heart. The image of her father wasting away in a hideous prison was a picture that would not leave her mind. It was the first thing she thought of when she awakened each morning and the last thing on her mind at night.

It mattered little that their fortune was gone—the ships, their home, and all of the furnishings that her mother had tenderly overseen. Catherine realized those things meant very little in light of losing her father to a punishment he did not deserve.

"Were I a man, I would have stayed and fought to see him free," she murmured.

But had she been a man, she would most likely have found herself imprisoned along with her father. Even now, she knew there were those who looked for her. Some even believed her to have run away with Finley Baker.

"Bah!" The man's name stirred rage in her as nothing else might. She had found herself expanding on the Lord's Prayer each night, praying that God might deliver her from evil and deliver Finley Baker to the proper authorities. She didn't believe God minded her personalized addition.

"Why is it that decent men may suffer such heinous injustice, while evil men go about their business wreaking havoc and pain?"

She went to the window and pulled back the drapery she'd helped to make. It was a privilege, she knew, to be in a private room. She was here because she now managed the sewing floor for Mrs. Clarkson. Having worked her way up after proving her ability with a needle, Catherine enjoyed many such privileges.

Turning from the window, she surveyed the room. It was only a fourth of the size of her room in Bath, but it was cozy and tidy. She hugged her arms to her body and felt the worn velvet of her housecoat. It was a little tight in the bodice but otherwise still served her needs faithfully.

Once again she thought of her mother's loving care in choosing it for her and embroidering the panels that ran down the front. The dark green material had been inset with black and embroidered with gold and silver, red, and lighter greens. The floral pattern her mother had created had come from her own design, and it was to her mother that Catherine credited her own creativity.

Designing had been easy enough for Catherine. Having worn glorious ball gowns and equally lavish day dresses, Catherine knew a thing or two about regal wear. She also knew, as a woman, what things she would like to see changed in fashionable garments. Catherine had instituted some of those ideas in the creations she made for Philadelphia's elite.

Taking a seat by the fire, she sighed and wondered where her life might take her next. How long before someone came to America and recognized her? Better yet, how long could she stay away from her father? Yet she knew there was nothing she could do. Even if she went to the prison, she would no doubt be turned away without ever being allowed to see him. Worse still, she might be taken into custody and given a similar fate—and then who would fight for her father?

"Lord, I do not pretend to understand that which has been thrust upon us. I can only pray for deliverance. As you freed your people from Egypt, I beg you to free my father from prison."

A knock sounded at her door and Catherine stiffened. It was not Selma's light knock or even Mrs. Clarkson's gentle hand.

"Who is it?" she asked as she went to the door.

"Felicia. Open the door, it's drafty out here."

Catherine did as the young woman requested, but she dreaded it. Felicia carried the title of Second Hand in the sewing house. That put her subservient only to Mrs. Clarkson and Catherine—a position Felicia greatly detested.

She swept into the room with queenly airs, letting her gaze quickly survey Catherine's possessions as if assessing for anything new. Appearing satisfied that all remained the same, she turned to Catherine.

"I saw your light was still on. I wondered what you could possibly be up to at this hour."

Catherine looked at her hard. "If it's such a strange hour to be awake, I might ask the same of you."

Felicia laughed and pushed back her long, loose blond hair. "I just finished my work for the day. I felt it important to complete the blouse I'd been given. So there is no foul on my part."

"I am glad to know it. Now that we have that clear, perhaps you will retire and allow me to do the same."

Felicia frowned. "You needn't be uppity with me. You have always taken on airs of superiority, and I resent it very much. Your English background does not give you any kind of preference here. The English have often been considered traitors and enemies of this country."

"I may well be English, but I am neither traitor nor enemy. I'm merely a dressmaker," Catherine stated, trying to sound indifferent. In truth, her anger was building by the second. Felicia had been nothing but trouble to her since coming to Mrs. Clarkson's.

"Well, as long as you know your place," Felicia said, moving to the open door. "It would appear that thought often escapes you. You might think yourself above the rest of us, but you aren't."

Catherine began to shut the door as Felicia passed through the portal. "I have never pretended to be other than I am." She closed the door and leaned against it, knowing her words were as far from the truth as anything she might have fabricated.

"Oh, what a liar you are," Catherine chided herself in a barely audible voice.

CHAPTER 2

*L*ee, you'll never guess my good fortune," Carter Danby announced as he strode into his best friend's law office. He shed his wet coat and hat. "Even the rain cannot dampen my spirits."

At thirty years of age, the two might have been mistaken for brothers, sharing not only a long-standing camaraderie but also physically mirroring each other in height and mannerisms. But where Carter's brown hair bordered on ebony, Leander Arlington's hair was honeyed brown. And while Carter's eyes matched the same deep hue as his hair, Lee's were twinkling blue.

"So what is it you've come to tell me, since I'll never guess," Lee replied with a grin.

"I have concluded the terms of the contract with Montgomery. He has approved the initial designs and now desires I draw up the detail prints for his new estate." Carter pulled off his gloves and placed them aside.

"Wonderful! Well done," Lee said, standing to reach his arm across the desk as Carter took a seat.

Carter shook Lee's hand, then leaned back into the chair. "It has been a trial, to be sure. The man and his wife have changed their minds on the details four times. I do believe I could have made better money elsewhere for all the time it's taken for this one estate."

"Still, the Montgomery name will bring you high regard. And that, along with your other designs, will surely send you on your way. I do wish you would reconsider your plans on leaving the area, however. Philadelphia needs good architects as well as Boston or New York City."

"True, but my family does not reside in either of those dear towns," Carter fired back with a smile.

"So things are as bad as ever?" Leander asked.

Carter put his hands behind his head and stretched back a bit. "It is certain to never change. At least my father and brother have accepted my desire to focus on a career outside of the family mills. Father has even offered to finance another trip abroad. I figure he means to get me out of his hair."

"Is this because of his mistress?" Lee settled back and eyed Carter.

"That, amongst other issues. The fact that he and my brother both have their wives and mistresses does little to help matters, but the fact that the men in my family are also given to cheating their customers and making profits on the backs of the less fortunate are also issues that divide us."

"Well, as your legal confidant, I, of course, will say nothing to anyone. But should they be caught, it will not bode well for the family—for your mother and sister."

"And don't I know that. Poor Winnie . . . she tries hard to keep the peace between our parents, but she's seldom successful. Father wants only to see her married off to a wealthy man, but the poor girl is so shy she is seldom seen in public. My mother doesn't make matters any better. She nags and pleads, constantly haranguing my father with accusations—granted, most of them true—and other nonsensical issues until not only does he want to be out of the house, but I want to be absent as well. Even now I'm steadying myself for the journey home."

"You could come home with me," Lee offered. "Share supper with us. At least delay your journey as long as possible."

"I do enjoy a good meal with such fine company," Carter said with a sigh, "but I promised my mother I would take supper with the family tonight. She wishes to discuss her Christmas preparations."

"Ah, the annual Danby Christmas masquerade ball." Lee chuckled. "I had nearly forgotten."

"I wish I could." Carter lowered his arms and leaned forward. "However, it does keep my mother much occupied for the latter half of the year, and that alone is well worth enduring the rest."

"You know, if it becomes too much, you have an open invitation at our house. My mother already considers you an extension of the family. Had I any sisters, you would have no doubt found an engagement imposed upon you."

Carter laughed. "Had you any sisters and were they of the same quality as your mother, an engagement would have been no imposition. I am wont to find a good wife, but I despair of there being any unattached woman of my requirements within one hundred miles of this place."

"True," Lee said with a sigh. "I have often thought the same. Mother suggested that I would find such a young lady at our church, but I see no one there to interest me."

"And my parents only consider attending any type of religious service to be for social purposes and financial gain. If others are of their mind, I frankly have no desire to look for a wife at church."

"Still," Lee said, moving a stack of books to one side, "there must be women of worth in this town."

"Perhaps, but I am certain they are either over fifty, under twelve, or already happily situated," Carter said with a laugh.

"I suppose we must trust that in time our hearts will show us where true love lies," Lee stated as Carter went to the window and pulled back the drape. "Have you come in your carriage today?"

"Yes. Do you want a ride home?" Carter let go the drape and turned. "I would be happy to have your company."

"I would appreciate that. It's still raining, and I have a stack of books to take with me. Father lent them to me a month ago, and I have been negligent in getting them back."

"The Judge won't like that—nor would he like it if they got wet," Carter teased. Leander's father was a retired judge, but he still commanded great influence in the community. People respected and loved him, unlike Carter's father, Elger Danby. People feared him, despised him, and mistrusted him, but still he managed to succeed. The contradiction of men left Carter somewhat confused. Where Lee's father was a good man who reverenced God and looked out for the oppressions of mankind, Carter's father was simply an oppressor.

The confusion was in why God allowed both men to do well—to profit and accomplish great things. Carter constantly worried that his father would bring ruin not only upon his own head but upon the entire family. He prayed that it might not be so, but at the same time he truly desired that his father leave off his illegal practices and illicit affairs and conduct himself more along the lines of Judge Kendrick Arlington.

They reached the Arlington house just as the rain lessened to sprinkles. Directing the horse through the narrow wrought-iron gates, Carter wished that this were his home as well. He could only imagine the joy and satisfaction he might have in sharing his accomplishments with Lee's parents. With a sigh he pulled the carriage to a stop and tipped his hat.

"There you are, sir. Safe and sound."

"Think about what I said, Carter. You are always welcome here."

"I appreciate that, Lee. I think the time has come for me to actually consider obtaining my own living quarters."

"People will think it strange for an unmarried man to leave his father's home for another in the same town."

Carter laughed. "They'd think it even stranger for that un-married man to strangle his father. No, I think it would do all of us good for me to leave."

Lee gave Carter a nod and opened the carriage door. "If I hear of a small place, I will let you know."

"And if I hear of a good woman . . ." Carter smiled and raised his brows before adding, "I'll probably keep that news to myself. At least until I see if it can prove useful to me."

Lee laughed and gathered his books. He'd wrapped them protectively in his coat and now stepped out into the weather. "I'd likely do the same."

Carter turned the horse and headed for home. He wasn't looking forward to the chaos, but he figured with any luck at all, his father would have taken himself out for the evening. Contending with his mother and sister would be much easier with Father gone. Sharing supper with Winifred alone would have been even more ideal. He was very close to his sister, who was ten years his junior—an unexpected surprise in the Danby family.

The rain picked up again and with it Carter's feelings of despair deepened. Why couldn't his family be a decent sort? They had wealth and social standing, but the respect given them was a mockery. Those who positioned themselves close to his mother and father only did so for whatever financial gain might be had.

A groomsman met Carter the moment he stopped the carriage near the front door. Usually he would drive back around to the carriage house, but in the rain the groomsman would expect him to stop at the front and take advantage of an easier, drier access to the house.

"Evenin', suh," the dark-skinned man said as he took the reins.

"Good evening to you, Joseph. Thank you for taking the carriage." Joseph was the only black man employed by the Danby family. Carter had found the man half dead on the road between Philadelphia and New York. Joseph had papers showing him to be free, but he had been robbed and left for dead when ruthless highwaymen crossed his path. Carter had brought him home and declared he would see the man restored to health and hired him as his own personal staff. His father had been livid, but Carter held his ground in a kind of private rebellion. Eventually his father had forgotten the matter and now considered Joseph an important part of the Danby work force.

"How are things today, Joseph?"

"Right as rain, suh," the younger man said with a glint in his coal-black eyes.

Carter smiled. "Well, that is sure to change when I make my way inside. Is my father to home?"

"No, suh. Left 'bout an hour ago."

"Good. Then perhaps things will continue to bode well."

Carter dismounted the carriage and made his way quickly inside. He thought it sad that he would have rather spent the evening drinking coffee and teaching Joseph to read than to endure yet another of his mother's emotional displays.

"Good evening, Mr. Danby," the butler announced as he took Carter's things.

"Good evening, Wilson."

"Oh, Carter. I thought I heard the carriage. I am so glad you are home," his mother declared as she scurried across the floor. "Your father has gone again—to her. I just know it."

"Good evening, Mother." Carter gave her a peck on the cheek and pulled back. "How go your plans for the annual ball?"

His mother's expression changed from fretful to excited. "Well, I was concerned at first of not getting the proper gown made. Everyone knows that Mrs. Clarkson's assistant, Catherine Shay, designs the best gowns in town. I, of course, insisted that

Winifred and I must have a creation from this woman, but Mrs. Clarkson argued that there were other requests ahead of mine. I told her that I could not be cast aside—that I would pay double what anyone else had offered."

Carter headed for the warmth of the smallest of the Danby sitting rooms. There he found a fire already blazing. He pulled up a large wing chair and settled in to hear his mother's tirade.

"I would like very much if you would accompany us tomorrow," his mother said, standing directly in front of him. Overdressed as usual in a gown more suited for an outing than a quiet dinner at home, Lillian Danby struck quite a picture. She was not a great beauty, but neither was she unpleasant to look at. Carter could not understand why his father had taken a mistress, throwing away his chance at true happiness with the woman he married.

His father had taken his first mistress some fifteen or sixteen years earlier, when Carter's mother had been considered quite lovely. She had also been far happier and less given to bouts of nerves and bitter musings. His father's dalliances with other women had aged her before her time.

"Did you hear me?"

Carter realized he hadn't been listening. "I am sorry, Mother. It's been a long day. A good one, but long. I received the final approval from Mr. Montgomery. He is commissioning me to design his estate."

"Oh, the Montgomery family is a thorn in my flesh," his mother said, offering no praise for her son's accomplishment. "Mrs. Montgomery believes herself well above the rest of us. She has declined my invitation year after year. I can only imagine she'll do so again this year, and what will that say to the rest of our friends?"

Carter gave only a hint of a smile. "That she doesn't like parties?"

"Oh, were that only true. But no. She will be seen at the homes of the Wellingtons and Duffs. Why, she was definitely present at the summer soiree that the Stanleys held. She even brought her nephew, who is a duke or some such thing. It was the talk of the town."

"Now, Mother. Those were all summer parties. Perhaps she fears the winter night air will be harmful to her health."

His mother gave a sniff and sank into a black-and-white striped chair. "I hardly believe that credible, but you are good to try to comfort my nerves. As I said before, I would like very much for you to escort your sister and me to Mrs. Clarkson's tomorrow. We are to talk to Catherine Shay herself."

"And what will this Catherine Shay do for you?"

"Why, she will design the gowns we are to wear to the masquerade. It's all very secretive, you know. It hardly does any good to have a masquerade if everyone already knows what gown you will wear."

Carter considered that for only a fraction of a second. "Of course."

"Well, your father is having a meeting here—something about the mills. I'm certain you will not mind being absent from the house."

Carter hadn't realized a meeting had been planned, but his mother was right. He had no desire to be anywhere around. "I can accompany you and Winifred."

"What about me?" Winifred asked as she swept into the room. Petite and sharing the same dark hair and eyes as Carter, she offered a sweet smile that seemed to brighten the entire room.

"I promised our mother that I would drive you both to the dressmaker tomorrow."

"That is kind," she said, kissing him on the top of his head. "Too bad Mrs. Clarkson's shop designs clothes only for women. You could use a new suit or two."

Their mother frowned. "Oh, it's true. You need new clothes, Carter. You must take yourself to the tailor as soon as possible. I won't have my friends looking down upon me because you're running about Philadelphia in threadbare, out-of-date clothing."

Carter laughed heartily at this. "I am hardly threadbare, Mother."

"Well, promise me you will go, nevertheless. If you do not go," she said, exaggerating the situation by waving her arms and fluttering her hands, "I am certain to hear about it. I only wish to keep the family from such negative gossip. Oh, it never fails to amaze me how innocent people can find themselves the focus of such twisted affairs."

Carter found it amazing the way his mother never seemed to draw air. She was like a little hummingbird flapping her wings furiously to stay in one place. The way her voice raised an octave when she was truly upset was even more birdlike.

To their surprise the front door crashed open, and they heard the muttered curses of the master. Elger Danby stormed into the house and entered the sitting room, as if knowing he'd find everyone assembled there. The butler hurried after him to take the hat and gloves he'd just thrown onto a nearby table.

Anger and tension emanated almost visibly from his form, but Carter knew better than to question his father's angry spirit. His mother, however, seemed to thrive on tormenting the man.

"What could possibly be wrong, my dear?" his mother asked in a sugary voice. "Was she not to home?"

Carter's father, a tall, broad-shouldered man, took a threatening step toward his wife, then stopped. "My affairs remain just that. Mine and no one else's. When is supper to be served?"

"Momentarily, sir," the butler said as he helped Mr. Danby from his coat.

"It seems nothing is ordered properly today."

"We hadn't expected that you would join us for supper," Carter's mother said sarcastically. "In fact, we are never certain when to expect that you might grace us with your company."

"Silence, woman! I will not be berated in my own home."

Winifred had taken a seat on the settee by this time and looked at Carter with such pleading that he couldn't help but feel sorry for her. She had never known a time when their parents had treated each other with respect and kindness.

"I have good news," Carter offered as his father ordered the butler to bring brandy.

"Oh, and what might that be?" his father asked out of obligation, not sounding as though he cared much for the answer.

"I have been commissioned to design the Montgomery estate. The new house will be over fifteen thousand square feet."

"Braggart," his father muttered.

Carter wasn't entirely sure to whom the comment was directed—himself or Mr. Montgomery. It wasn't until the butler had returned with the drink and his father had downed it that Elger Danby clarified his remark.

"The Montgomerys believe it necessary to build larger estates and more extensive grounds in order to prove their worth. It is hardly something I would want you involved in. I do hope when you tire of such play you will give yourself over to a decent living."

"I am hardly at play in my work, Father. You have even supported my desires in the past. You very kindly paid for my tours of Europe in order that I might more formally study architecture."

His father shook his head and said exactly what Carter had always suspected. "It seemed easier to send you on your way than to have your interference here."

Carter got to his feet, anger coursing through his veins. "I had hoped my news would be pleasing to you. I should have known better."

He stormed from the room, not waiting for a reply. There was no pleasing Elger Danby. Not if you were his youngest son, who had no intention of going into the family textile empire. Not if you weren't willing to act in as degenerate a manner as the man himself.

"Carter!" Winifred called after him. She hurried to catch up as he turned on the stairs. "Please don't leave. I need you at supper." Her voice was low and pleading.

Carter drew a deep breath and shook his head. "I'm sorry for the way I acted, Winnie. I fear if I remain in that man's presence for much longer, I shall become just like him."

Winifred smiled and extended her hand. "There is no chance of that, brother. You have a good and loving heart. You will not allow it to harden with disappointment and frustration."

Carter walked back down the steps and took hold of his sister's hand. "It wouldn't be that difficult to do," he said sadly.

"Perhaps, but then, I've never known you to settle for what is easy." She smiled at him, and he felt the last vestiges of anger slip away.

"Very well. Have it your way. I shall be your companion at dinner, but please do not expect me to be talkative."

Winifred laughed lightly. "You needn't worry. No doubt Mama will give everyone an earful."

CHAPTER 3

And here is Miss Shay," Mrs. Clarkson announced as Catherine entered the parlor. "She will interview you and determine the style of gown you desire. Catherine, this is Mrs. Danby and her daughter, Miss Winifred Danby."

Catherine observed the two women. Both were quite petite. It would be easy to design complementary gowns for these women. "Good afternoon, ladies." Catherine gave a brief curtsy.

"And this is Mrs. Danby's son, Mr. Carter Danby."

The name struck an immediate memory in Catherine's mind as she turned to face the man. If he recognized her, all hope was gone. She would have to leave immediately or be found out.

"Mr. Danby," she murmured with another brief curtsy. She forced her gaze to meet his. A thousand thoughts rushed through her mind. It had been five years since that evening in Bath. She was only a child then—a mere seventeen. She had changed a great deal in that time and, given her present station in life, couldn't possibly represent the wealthy shipper's daughter she'd been back then.

Mr. Danby smiled and gave a bow. There didn't appear to be any immediate recognition. For a moment he seemed to study her, as if knowing there was something he should remember, but just as easily he appeared to dismiss it.

"Miss Shay, I understand you are the much-sought-after authority on ladies' clothing." There was a hint of amusement in his tone, as though he were somehow mocking her.

"Our Catherine is indeed much sought after," Mrs. Clarkson replied before Catherine could. "And because of that, I must keep her on schedule. Mr. Danby, if you will come with me, I shall have you more comfortably arranged in one of the other sitting rooms. There, one of my girls will bring you refreshments. You will also find a good deal of reading material, including the newspaper."

"Thank you, Mrs. Clarkson. That sounds very comfortable."

Catherine breathed a sigh of relief as her employer led Mr. Danby away and closed the door behind them. It was obvious that he didn't recognize her and for now her secret remained safe. But the nagging thought that discovery could occur at any moment would not leave Catherine's mind.

"We are ever so grateful," Mrs. Danby began, "that you could work us into your schedule. I have heard nothing but high praise from my friends regarding your creations. I was hesitant at first, you understand. I was used to having my clothes made by only the best designers—mostly French, of course."

The woman continued to prattle while Catherine arranged her sketch pad and pencils, her thoughts still on Carter Danby. There definitely seemed to be something in his expression that suggested he might know her.

He's trying to remember where he's seen me. Of this Catherine was certain. The look in his eyes clearly indicated that there was something familiar about her. *Oh, I must let Selma and Dugan know. They'll have a better idea of what must be done.*

"And then we were most disappointed when that talented young man passed on," Mrs. Danby was saying.

Having no idea what Mrs. Danby was speaking about, Catherine turned to the mother and daughter duo and began to size them up in more intimate detail. "Let us discuss the type of dresses you would like to have made."

"Well, as you must know," Mrs. Danby began, "we host an annual masquerade ball. Not one of those annoying masquerades where everyone must wear a costume that they will never again wear, but instead one with magnificent ball gowns. We have held this ball for nearly twenty years. We are one of the only homes in town with its own ballroom, and because of this we find ourselves obliged to host at least two balls a year, and the Christmas ball is always a masquerade. Every year more impressive than the one before it."

She barely drew a breath before continuing with a frown. "Well, there was one year when a terrible yellow fever epidemic was followed by an equally bad one of influenza. That year the ball was much altered. It was all very sad." She halted, as if in respect for the sorrow of that time.

Her pause was all the time Catherine needed to regain the situation. "I have appointments throughout the day, so we would be wise to have you ladies measured. I'd like to take some notes as to the type of gown you would like. While one is fitted for measurements, the other can describe your likes and dislikes."

"I believe Winifred should have something quite low-cut. The bodice should show off her . . . assets," Mrs. Danby declared. "She is now twenty and must find a husband soon."

"And if she does not?" Catherine asked, rather annoyed that the woman would impose such a thing on the obviously shy young woman. Poor Winifred Danby had spent most of the time so far looking at the carpeted floor.

"If she does not, her father will surely arrange a marriage for her. My own marriage was arranged for the benefit of the family, and my husband will do no less for his own daughter. Winifred must look her best for the ball in order that the available young men who also attend can see what a good wife she might make."

"And they will tell this by the cut of her neckline?" Catherine asked, knowing her sarcasm was uncalled for. However, she didn't miss the slight giggle that came from Miss Danby.

"They will tell that she is . . . well . . . that is to say that her charms are many," Mrs. Danby replied. She seemed torn between rebuking Catherine for her comment and remaining in her new dressmaker's good graces.

Catherine nodded. It was easy to see that Mrs. Danby was a woman used to imposing her wishes on others. Catherine went to the closed door on the opposite side of the room. "Martha?" she called as she opened the door.

A young woman appeared. She was a pretty sort with a tight, trim waist and lovely brown hair. She wore gold-rimmed glasses, much the same as Mrs. Clarkson, and smiled broadly. "How may I assist you, Catherine?"

"Please measure Mrs. Danby. We will need a full accounting, and I am charging you to record the findings very faithfully." Martha smiled, understanding that Catherine meant for her to take her time so that she might draw out the younger of the Danby women. Mrs. Danby no doubt knew the type of gown that she desired, but Winifred probably had given it little thought.

With Mrs. Danby escorted to the measurements room, Catherine took a seat opposite Winifred. "Now, Miss Danby, if you would be so kind as to tell me what type of gown you would like."

Winifred looked up, appearing rather startled. "I . . . uh . . . my mother . . . ."

"I do not mean to be disrespectful, Miss Danby, but I am certain your mother will speak her mind on what she believes you would like. However, I would rather hear from your own mouth what this might be."

"Mother means well," Miss Danby offered. "She can be a bit nervous about these matters." She looked at the floor again.

"Miss Danby—"

"Please call me Winifred," the young woman suddenly blurted out. The look on her face told Catherine that she'd surprised herself as much as anyone.

"I would like that," Catherine replied, trying to sound as if the request were perfectly normal. The social classes demanded otherwise, but Catherine had learned to change her thinking about society and the separation of the classes since her move to America. "You must, in turn, call me Catherine."

"Thank you," Winifred whispered. She had gone back into her shell, as if embarrassed by the entire exchange.

Catherine wanted so much to put her at ease and considered the woman and her small frame for a moment. "I believe a skirt comprising a solid piece with perhaps tulle bouillons above the hem would serve your petite frame better than flounces. You would be rather lost in all of that frippery." She began to sketch it out on a sheet of paper. "See here what I mean."

Winifred leaned forward as Catherine's design came to take form on the page. "Yes," she whispered. "I like that very much."

"And perhaps we can create a bodice where the tulle puffing is repeated. If we can create a bodice in this fashion with the corsage cut low, then trimmed in the bouillons, it will allow for modesty. The same tulle can be drawn along the neckline, then be used in the sleeves as well. Do you mind baring your arms and shoulders?"

"No, not really." Winifred continued to watch. "I could not have drawn this better myself. Not that I have much talent for drawing. My watercolors are tolerable, but I have no skill with charcoals."

Catherine was glad to see the young woman revealing a bit more of herself. "I find watercolors to require a great deal of talent." Catherine put a few more details on the skirt sketch, then raised her gaze to Winifred.

"What materials and colors are you fond of? For a gown of this style, my thoughts would lean toward satin or silk. Your coloring would suggest something bright and feminine."

Winifred blushed, as if once again embarrassed. "I am told I'm fond of puce."

"You're told that, eh?" Catherine's tone suggested amusement, but in truth she felt very sorry for the girl. "Winifred, if you truly like that color, we can use it, but I believe it is much too dark."

"Well, what do you suggest?"

"You really need a more festive color." Catherine eyed her seriously for a moment. "I would not want you to choose a dark color, although we could trim it in something dark. I think lavender would be lovely on you. We also offer some wonderful shades of pink and dusty rose that blend well. Your coloring would also easily bear ivory, which could be decorated with any number of colors. Think about it. You needn't decide this moment."

"Mama will no doubt want to make the final choice," Winifred said. "We should ask her."

Catherine leaned forward. "I wish to know what you like. I find that I can quite easily influence overbearing mothers when I know what would be pleasing to their more modest daughters."

Winifred smiled. "I like you very much, Miss . . . Catherine. I have never had a dressmaker who was willing to stand up to my mother. I believe I would very much like the gown to be some shade of pink or rose," Winifred said rather conspiratorially.

Catherine nodded with just a hint of a smile. "Then it shall be."

"Winifred, they are ready for your measurements," Mrs. Danby announced as she came from the back room.

Winifred rose and headed for the door. Catherine felt sorry for her. The young woman was beautiful and refined, and there was certainly no sense in her mother pushing her at men.

"Now, I have an idea in mind for my own gown," Mrs. Danby began as she took her seat. "But, of course, I want the design to be yours. After all, your work is the talk of the town."

Catherine pushed aside the sketch she'd worked on for Winifred, but Mrs. Danby picked it up. "Is this what you had in mind for my daughter?"

"Yes. I believe it will complement her . . . assets . . . as you put it."

Mrs. Danby looked at the sketch for several moments before putting it down. "I believe it will."

Catherine hadn't expected the older woman's acceptance of her design, but she didn't really have a chance to say anything as Mrs. Danby launched into a tirade of ball gowns from the past that were most displeasing. After nearly five minutes, Catherine stopped her.

"I am afraid my time is limited today. Perhaps you could tell me what you *do* like."

Mrs. Danby looked at her for a moment before suddenly declaring, "Flounces. I like flounces."

Catherine nodded and began to sketch out a skirt with three tiers of lace flouncing. "Perhaps lace over silk?"

The older woman thought for a moment. "Yes. Yes, that sounds quite regal. I hear from your speech that you are English. I would like a gown that would be suitable for court. I want the finest gown of any other woman in this town. I am willing, also, to make it quite worth your time and trouble to make the other gowns less . . . less . . . exotic."

"Less exotic?" Catherine questioned.

"Yes. I want to stand out at the party. I want every other woman there to die of envy when they see my gown."

Catherine tried to imagine a ballroom with Mrs. Danby sweeping through, ladies dropping to the floor in death as she passed by. Did people never listen to the words they spoke?

"And what of the bodice?" Catherine questioned, moving on quickly.

"I want it low. I want my husband to take note," she said rather smugly. "I still have a good figure, and I mean for him to remember that fact."

Catherine looked at the woman momentarily. She had to be at least sixty years of age, but it was true that her petite frame was rather well filled out. "Perhaps this," Catherine said as she quickly sketched a bodice. "We call this style *corsage à la Grecque.* You can see that it is low and off the shoulder. The bodice is comprised of vertical pleats that accentuate the bosom."

"Oh, I do like that."

"It was more popular in the forties, but we can recreate it and give it a completely refreshed look. And I happen to know something similar was recently recreated for Her Majesty Queen Victoria."

"Oh, that's simply divine. Yes, that's the style I would want for my gown."

Catherine nodded. "And may I suggest the sleeve short and tight at first, then trailing down with lace that would imitate the flounces, like this." Catherine drew three tiers of material that came to the elbow.

"That is perfect. Oh, but I can scarcely imagine how I will ever wait for the gown to be created."

Catherine looked up and could see from the woman's expression that she was already imagining herself and the response she'd create. "What colors do you have in mind?"

Mrs. Danby looked at Catherine only a moment before opening her mouth. "I want whatever will make it look the richest. Perhaps a gold?" She looked at Catherine as though awaiting her approval.

"Let me look at what is available and give you several ideas from which to choose. We will have new materials in from France any day now. I am sure we will find something suitable in that selection."

"Of course. How exciting!" Mrs. Danby nodded in great satisfaction before adding, "But there must not be another gown made with the material you use for my creation. Upon this I insist."

"You may discuss that matter with Mrs. Clarkson. I have little say over such affairs."

Winifred reemerged at this time. She looked at her mother and then to Catherine before lowering her gaze to the floor. With her quiet, sweet demeanor, Catherine imagined that in another time and place, they might have been good friends.

"I will collect a variety of samples. I would like to suggest a delicate pink or perhaps rose color for your daughter's gown. It will make a good show against her creamy complexion. We can trim it out with a choice of colors, but I would also consider some real roses on the neckline."

"Oh! Oh! That sounds so marvelous," Mrs. Danby said, clapping her gloved hands together. "Oh, but I wish I were twenty again. I would show them all a thing or two."

Catherine had no doubt the woman would create quite a show at that. "I will also have a more detailed sketch for you in a day or two."

Mrs. Danby took hold of her daughter. "Come, Winifred, we must allow Miss Shay to get on with her other customers. I am so excited. I know I shan't sleep a wink until I have that gown in my possession."

"I will send word when the materials have arrived," Catherine promised as she got to her feet. "When the materials are available, we can also discuss the laces and trims."

"Of course, Miss Shay. Thank you so much. We shall look forward to our next meeting."

❦

"You look very lonely in this room."

Carter looked up to find an attractive young woman standing by the door. She wasn't the same girl who had come to serve him tea and cakes earlier. That girl was hardly more than a child. No, this young lady was a woman full grown, and it appeared she had learned the art of enticing men with her looks.

"I am Felicia. I work as the Second Hand. That's a position just under the foreman. I have a great deal of experience," she said suggestively.

Carter found her completely wanton and looked back to the book he'd been glancing through.

"Are you so very shy you will not speak to me?" The words fairly purred from her lips as she sauntered across the floor. "I'm quite entertaining."

Carter looked up. She was a pretty blond thing with a figure that demanded notice, even from behind the heavy cotton apron. "I am certain you speak the truth."

Felicia grinned. "You have me at a disadvantage, sir. I have given you my name and even more."

"Felicia, what are you doing out here?" Mrs. Clarkson demanded as she came into the room. "You have more than enough work to keep you busy. Not only that, but Lydia is asking after you. Go see what the child needs." She turned, dismissing the young woman. "Mr. Danby, may I offer you more tea?"

Carter watched Felicia leave. She was not happy about it, but it was clear she'd heard his name and was probably even now committing it to memory.

"I am fine, thank you, Mrs. Clarkson. I do not require anything else." He thought of the young woman he'd met earlier. Miss Shay had an odd sense of familiarity about her. He would have sworn he knew her. Yet how many dressmakers had he been introduced to? She must be, he acknowledged, his first.

"Very well. I am certain your mother and sister will soon join you. I have, even now, Miss Shay's next customers waiting."

"Speaking of Miss Shay," Carter said, putting aside the book and getting to his feet, "I wonder if you might tell me more about her. My mother says she is much sought after for her creations."

"Oh yes. She is quite talented. When in France this summer I showed several of her drawings to my friends in fashion. They were quite impressed. I would not find it unusual at all to see her name mentioned with the likes of—"

"Oh, there you are," Carter's mother declared as she came into the room. "Come, we must get home. I have so many things to accomplish yet today."

Carter felt a brief sense of disappointment that he couldn't further question Mrs. Clarkson about Miss Shay. He was even more displeased to realize that Miss Shay had not come to see them off.

"Were you pleased with the ideas Miss Shay created?" he asked as he extended his arm to assist his mother out the door.

"Oh, goodness yes. The woman is so very talented. I shall be quite pleased to utilize her services over and over. She understands me completely."

"And what of you, Winifred?" Carter asked, looking back over his shoulder as they descended the outside stairs.

"I liked her very much. I felt she completely understood me, and I her. It was as if we had known each other for many years."

Carter nodded but said nothing. It was strange, he thought, but he had the same sensation.

CHAPTER 4

*C*atherine rose early the next day, hoping to talk to Selma and Dugan privately before the household was awake to overhear. In the kitchen, Selma was already at work frying up sausages and potatoes. The girls ate a hearty breakfast together at five-thirty every morning and started their day's work at six, a routine with which they were all quite familiar.

Explaining the situation from the previous day, Catherine waited for Selma's comment. The older woman considered the matter solemnly for several minutes while she turned the sausages.

"I believe there is little to worry over. You are much changed in the five years since Mr. Danby last saw you," Selma began.

"You hardly look the same. Then you were but a girl of ten and seven. You wore your hair in ringlets and had not yet acquired a woman's figure. He only met you for a short time amidst his busy travels. Not only that, but you go by a different name—there is not even that fact to associate you with his memories."

"I thought of all this myself," Catherine whispered, "but his expression suggested that he found something familiar in me."

"Perhaps, but again, what if he does remember you? He is an American and not at all associated with your father or his business. He most likely has no knowledge of what happened to your father. If he should remember you, it would hardly be a lie to tell him your family fell on hard times and you moved to America with us to better your fortunes. I'll speak to Dugan on this matter, but I would not let it worry you. Mr. Danby is most likely no threat to us."

Catherine wanted to believe this. She prayed it might be so. In fact, she'd wrestled in thought and prayer throughout the night, wondering if God had suddenly overlooked her protection.

Later in the day, after the last of the afternoon appointments was concluded, Catherine sat down to work with the newest of the sewing staff. Beatrix was only fourteen and had not yet come to live at Mrs. Clarkson's house. She was new to her training but very talented. The girl was the eldest of a large Irish family, with three brothers and three sisters her junior. Spirited and bright, Catherine found Beatrix a joy to work with and teach.

"See here," Catherine said as she took hold of the pattern, "we can increase the bust in this fashion." She took a pencil and drew along particular lines as Beatrix nodded.

"I've had to do that for me mum."

"Good, then you're already familiar." Catherine stood back and handed the pencil to Beatrix. "Now show me how you would best expand the waist for a thicker woman."

Beatrix studied the pattern for a moment. "I would be cuttin' a fuller side seam to begin with." She traced it out and then straightened. "I would maybe be takin' a smaller dart in the front and maybe eliminate the darts altogether in the back."

"That could cause the garment to drape awkwardly," Catherine stated. "See on this piece?" She drew Beatrix to another table and showed her a blouse bodice that had been cut but not put together. "Maintaining the darts will allow for some semblance of narrowing at the waist, even if the dart is very small."

"Aye, I can be seein' that now."

"Catherine!" a young woman declared, entering the room as though she owned the place.

Catherine looked up to find fifteen-year-old Lydia demanding her attention. The girl had a way about her that always demanded something. "What is it, Lydia?"

"I need you to approve this bodice. I've basted it together, and Felicia says it's perfect."

Used to Felicia's interference, Catherine sighed inwardly but was careful to show no emotion. "Sit down, Lydia." She turned to Beatrix. "Go back to the pattern and show me how you would increase the sleeves for a woman with heavy arms." The girl went immediately to the task.

Catherine took up Lydia's bodice and began to look it over for problems. "This gap will not do," she told the girl. "Do you see here how the pieces of the bodice must fold in to each other?"

Lydia looked at the lines of the garment. "I did it the way Felicia told me to, and she said it was fine."

"But Felicia is not the one who has to approve your work, Lydia."

Toying with her braid, Lydia's expression was haughty rather than contrite. Catherine put the piece down and looked at the girl. "Do you not like working here, Lydia?"

The girl seemed to immediately understand the implication. Catherine continued, "I cannot move you up to the position of Improver if you cannot learn to properly drape material and fit patterns. I know you are having difficulty adjusting to living here at the sewing house, but that cannot be an excuse for slothful work and insolent behavior."

Shadows played on the girl's face as the light of day faded and gave way to twilight. They were fortunate to have gas lighting in the first floor of the house, but it was often not enough to work by, and Catherine felt the need to light an additional lamp while Lydia considered her words.

"You show talent, Lydia. Do not be discouraged by correction; rather, let it be the guide to refining your skills."

"But Felicia said—"

"Lydia, Felicia is not in charge here. Perhaps we should call upon Mrs. Clarkson to resolve this matter. If you will not take direction and correction from me, I will have no other choice. Is that what you wish?"

Lydia hung her head. "No, ma'am."

"Very well. Take this bodice back and tear out the basting. Refit the seams and rework the piece until there are no gaps. Then bring it back to me to check. I'll expect to see it yet tonight."

Getting up in a huff, Lydia snatched up the piece and stormed out of the room. Even Beatrix was stunned by her behavior.

"Me mum would have her hand across me backside for such manners," Beatrix couldn't help but declare.

Catherine wanted no part of encouraging the girls to be set against each other. She looked at the feisty redhead and pointed to the pattern. "Focus on your own work, Beatrix. No one likes to receive correction. Pride is a fierce enemy, and we must remember that fact if no other."

"Aye, but she had no right to be so angry," Beatrix said as she turned back to her work. "We are here to learn."

"That is true enough, but Lydia also misses her family. She is homesick and it is sometimes hard for her here. She comes from a large family like yours, but her heritage is German. They were all very close but very much in need of Lydia's learning a trade, and so they sent her to Mrs. Clarkson. She apprenticed here for a year, like you're doing, before she came here to live."

"I can hardly wait to move here. Our house is very small and there is no quiet once the sun comes up," Beatrix said as she put down the pencil. "There's never enough food for everyone. If I didn't eat lunch here, I might not be gettin' anything at all," she said with a laugh, but Catherine knew the truth of it in her voice.

"That reminds me. I'm going to be increasing your training and need you here first thing in the morning," Catherine said, knowing that Mrs. Clarkson wouldn't mind. "I would like you to join us for breakfast at five-thirty every day but Sunday. That way if there should be any important discussions prior to the workday, you will already be there to hear it. Will that work for you?"

Beatrix's face lit up. "I'm thinkin' it will suit me just fine."

"Well, it's the least we can do. I realize you get no pay at this point in your training, but you work very hard and need nourishment. Eventually, we'll have you stay into the evening hours and then you will also join us for supper."

"I'll be lookin' forward to that." She shook her head, and her red braids danced around her shoulders. "I am countin' me blessin's."

The idea of living in a small tenement with nine people was beyond Catherine's comprehension. Even the sewing house, with its four floors, offered the eight people who lived there on a regular basis far more room than the three-room home Beatrix described.

Catherine wondered if they might bring Beatrix into the house sooner. There was room for her to stay with Dolley and Martha. A thought began to stir in her mind. She would speak to Mrs. Clarkson about it later that night. Even if she needed to offer Beatrix space in her private room, it would be worth the effort.

"Well, it looks as though your day is done," Catherine said, examining the pattern enlargements Beatrix had drawn. "These are quite perfect." She looked up and found Beatrix beaming her a smile, and though Catherine had long ago lost the ability to claim such simple joy, she offered the girl a brief smile in return. "I will see you here at five-thirty tomorrow morning."

"Yes, ma'am," Beatrix said and curtsied. "I'll be lookin' forward to it."

❦

Catherine awoke early the next morning and immediately sought out Mrs. Clarkson. The woman was struggling with her hair and was happy to admit Catherine when she offered to help.

"I wondered if we might talk about one of the girls," Catherine said as she combed the woman's brown curls into order.

"But of course. Is there a problem?"

"No. Not exactly," Catherine said. She wound the thick mass into a bun, as was Mrs. Clarkson's manner. "I learned yesterday that Beatrix's only meal of the day was the luncheon she shared with us here."

"Oh dear. That will never do."

"I thought not as well. I asked her to start joining us for breakfast and to put in more hours. She's very talented. More so than any young woman we've yet employed."

"I doubt that she's more talented than you, my dear."

Catherine felt her cheeks grow hot as she secured Mrs. Clarkson's hair. "I would not venture to say, ma'am. However, I would like to suggest something in Beatrix's regard."

Catherine stepped back as Mrs. Clarkson secured a mobcap over her head. Although fewer women favored such adornment, Mrs. Clarkson preferred it over other alternatives. "What is your proposal?" her employer questioned.

"I would like to suggest Beatrix move into the house. She hasn't the same disdain or fears that Lydia has. In fact, she actually counts the days until she can come here to live. Her family, as you know, shares a three-room apartment. There are nine of them and all of the children share one room. We have plenty of room. There is still the empty bed in Martha and Dolley's room."

"I think the idea of her living here is perfectly acceptable. I don't know why I didn't think of it. I suppose given Lydia's unhappiness here, I was just as glad to have Beatrix remain at home. However, if she would not mind living here, then it would benefit us all. We will announce it this morning at breakfast. How delightful. I'm sure she will be very happy."

"I'm quite sure she will be as well," Catherine replied. She started to leave, but Mrs. Clarkson stopped her.

"I must say, Mrs. Danby seemed quite pleased with your designs. She has offered to pay a great sum for the gowns."

"She also hopes that you will not allow any other gown to be made from the same fabric," Catherine said, remembering the woman's request.

"For that price, I am certain we can oblige. I did want to make certain you weren't feeling overwhelmed with the work. Have you taken on too many designs?"

Catherine considered the matter for a moment. "No, though I believe we will have more than enough work for everyone. We might want to consider hiring outside workers to do some of the base work and free up the ladies here to do the detail and trimming."

"I am sure you are right about needing additional help. With the growing number of gowns we must create by early December, it would behoove me to take this matter quite seriously." The clock on her mantel chimed half past five. "Oh dear, we are late."

They made their way down the stairs and took their places at the already full table. Beatrix sat between Lydia and Martha and chatted amiably with each girl as they waited for Mrs. Clarkson to bless the food.

Catherine sat down between Felicia and Martha, the aroma of cinnamon apples causing her to realize her hunger. A quick prayer of thanks was offered and then Selma came in with a large bowl of gravy, while Dugan followed with an equally large platter of biscuits.

"Ladies, I have an announcement to make," Mrs. Clarkson declared as the girls began reaching for the items already on the table. "I have decided to ask our Beatrix to join us here at the sewing house." Beatrix looked up at the woman in stunned silence. Mrs. Clarkson continued. "I know it is not often that we bring in someone so young or with so little training; however, Beatrix is proving herself quite capable, and Catherine assures me she will continue to benefit us all. With the Christmas orders already pouring in, we will need every pair of hands working day and night. Do you think your parents will approve this, Beatrix?"

Everyone turned in unison to look at the redhead. She slowly smiled and nodded. "I'm thinkin' me mum will be quite happy with the news."

"Wonderful. I will call upon her later today and you will accompany me. If she is agreeable, we will bring your things back with us. You may, of course, visit your family on Sundays."

Catherine knew a sense of peace about the entire matter. Beatrix would be much better off here. She would get decent meals and a bed to herself. And while the work was long and tedious, she had a flair for it and would no doubt thrive.

Thoughts of Carter Danby came back to haunt Catherine as she picked at her breakfast. She was determined to never see him again. There was always the possibility that he would accompany his mother or sister to Clarkson's, but if that happened Catherine would simply have to find a way to make herself scarce. She could not risk his learning her true identity.

If he remembers who I am, it will ruin everything. My father's imprisonment will become public knowledge, and the scandal may force us to move. If that happens, I will end up using all of the money intended for Father.

She sighed and glanced up to find Felicia watching her oddly. "Are you quite well, Catherine?" Her words dripped sweetness, but there was no sincerity of concern.

"Quite," Catherine replied, although she knew nothing could be further from the truth.

CHAPTER 5

*C*arter looked at the older man as he studied the designs for his new palatial home. Charles Montgomery was highly esteemed in Philadelphia's financial circles but less respected by the area architects. As Carter had heard it, Montgomery had browbeat or badgered most every other prominent architect until no one wanted to work with him, no matter the benefit to their career or purse. Still, Carter felt quite honored to have his designs accepted. Montgomery was at least a man who knew his own mind, and that helped considerably in deciding what worked and what didn't. Carter would much prefer making changes now instead of later, when the building was being erected.

"I must admit, Danby, I do like what you've done here by adding the cupola. It's almost as if you've combined the Greek with the Italianate designs. I like it very much."

Carter looked at the plan and then met Mr. Montgomery's satisfied gaze. "I believe it will blend quite easily into the design. By putting the rounded turret to cap the cupola, it brings the focus back to the Greek Revival style. Also, we can put windows all around, and that will in turn bring light down into the darkest center of the house."

"Yes. It's a fine idea. I believe Mrs. Montgomery will be quite pleased."

"I'm glad to hear it," Carter said, returning his attention to the design. "Are there any other changes you'd like to see made?"

"The pillars on the front porch. What style did you call that?"

"It's Doric. It is a very simple and unadorned style. However, if you prefer something with additional decoration, there is the Ionic style." Carter took up a separate piece of paper and sketched out a pillar with a scrolled design at the top. "These are volutes."

"Hmmm, well, I don't know. Mrs. Montgomery wanted something more ornate."

"Then perhaps the Corinthian style is in order. It's not as often utilized due to the expense of creating the artwork." Carter attempted to sketch out the design and held it up. "These are called acanthus leaves. Note that the fluted pillar narrows slightly at the top, is banded, and then the ornamentation flares the pillar out again, giving it a crown effect."

"Yes. Yes. This is more to her liking, I am sure. Can this design be repeated?"

"It's costly, but the workmen can add similar detail to the window crowns and elsewhere."

"Good. Then let us proceed with that design. I am quite certain my wife will be pleased."

Carter wrote several notes on the side of the design. "And have you decided about the kitchens?"

"Yes. Mrs. Montgomery said to place the summer kitchen as a detached room connected by the walkway, as you suggested. She has never cared for the summer kitchen to be attached to the house even in part. It defeats the purpose of keeping the heat from the living quarters. Not that we are here for long in summer. I cannot abide summer in Philadelphia. Although I am told this new country acreage may well prove cooler and less difficult."

"Perhaps that will be true," Carter said, adding yet another note on the paper. "Very well, unless you can think of anything else, I believe I have all the details needed."

"And you can arrange for the workmen? I would, of course, wish to interview them and discuss their prices."

"Of course." Carter straightened and followed Mr. Montgomery, who was already moving toward the door. "I will arrange a meeting. Would you prefer that we come to your home, or should I arrange to hold it here?"

"My house will be acceptable. See if you cannot arrange something prior to the twentieth, however."

"Today is the seventeenth. I see no reason why I cannot get at least a few of the men together in short order. Why don't we say the nineteenth at your house, two o'clock?"

"Very good. I shall look forward to it."

Carter showed Mr. Montgomery to the foyer and waited until the butler arrived with the man's hat, gloves, and coat. Once

Montgomery was on his way, Carter headed back to his office. Winifred waited for him, small and delicate against the dark wood of the large desk and bookcases. In fact, the darker greens and browns Carter had chosen for the office appeared only to make Winifred seem even smaller.

"I'm so sorry to interrupt. Are you terribly busy?" she asked.

Carter came to her and planted a kiss on her forehead. "I always have time for you. Sit and tell me why you've come."

"I need to ask a favor," she said, taking a seat as instructed. "I need to go to the dressmaker's and pick materials for my gown. Mama has already chosen hers, but Miss Shay has some additional fabrics coming in that I wish to see. Surprisingly enough, Mama agreed to let me choose for myself."

"That is amazing," Carter said with a grin. "She must be overly concerned with planning for the ball itself."

Winifred smiled and her dark eyes seemed to twinkle. "I thought perhaps that might be the case. Either way, I didn't wish to forgo the opportunity."

Carter picked up the plans for the Montgomery house and rolled them. "I find myself quite free this afternoon and would be happy to escort you to Mrs. Clarkson's. I shall have Joseph bring the carriage around. How soon would you like to go?"

"I can be ready immediately. I have only to go retrieve my things," Winifred said, getting to her feet. "I shan't be but a moment."

Carter secured the plans in a tall bookcase with glass-paneled doors. He liked his office in order, but even more so, he liked having his affairs away from the prying eyes of his father and brother. More than once he'd found his brother, Robin, snooping about. Locking the doors to the case, Carter couldn't help but be reminded that this was yet another reason he should consider moving to a house of his own. Perhaps with another job or two—maybe a large government project—he would feel secure enough to do just that. Of course, there was always the possibility of partnering with someone. His old mentor, Hollis Fulbright, came to mind. The flamboyant man had shown great appreciation and affection for Carter during the days he apprenticed with him. Carter could easily see himself working with someone like Hollis Fulbright.

Carter and the carriage were ready and waiting when Winifred reappeared. She had positioned a green bonnet on her head and allowed Wilson, the butler, to help her into a trim little black coat. She seemed so happy. Carter wished he could find a good husband for her. If his father pushed forward with his own plans, Winifred would no doubt be married off to a wealthy man twice her age, never to know true love.

Once they were in the carriage, Carter couldn't help but comment on Winifred's spirits. "You seem quite content today. I don't believe I've seen you smile this much in ages."

"I am happy. I truly like visiting with Miss Shay. She cares about what I have to say and offers good suggestions when I ask for advice."

"And what kind of advice do you seek?" Carter asked in a teasing voice.

Winifred smoothed out the material of her green skirts and folded her black-gloved hands in her lap. "I ask her about clothing mostly. She knows a great deal about fashion. I like hearing about England, too. While we waited for Mama the other day, Catherine told me about London. I think I would very much like to see it. I think you would enjoy talking with her too. She is very well-read on other topics and seems quite accomplished."

"Indeed? That is rather an oddity for a seamstress, is it not?"

Winifred shrugged. "She does not have much free time. She told me they work some fifteen to twenty hours a day during the social seasons. They even work on Saturday." She shook her head. "I cannot imagine having to work for my keep."

"Nor shall you ever have to worry about it," Carter replied. "Not so long as I have breath."

"I wish it could be so for every young woman. It seems quite unfair that some women may merely run a house and direct servants, while others must slave for their very existence."

Carter was rather surprised by his sister's comments. He had never heard her talk quite like this. "There are a great many unfair situations in this world," he admitted. "I suppose we must change what we can and help those less fortunate to endure as best they are able."

"I suppose you are right," Winifred said, looking to the world outside the carriage. "Do you have plans for Sunday? There is a lecture being given by the antislavery people."

"I already have arrangements," Carter answered. "Lee and I plan to go riding."

"Oh, that sounds quite delightful."

There was something in her voice that drew Carter's attention. She sounded so wistful that he thought perhaps Winifred had been too long neglected. "You would be welcome to join us. I know that Lee would not care."

"Mr. Arlington is a very ... good ... friend," Winifred said, seeming to pick her words carefully.

Carter checked his watch. "He is indeed. I cannot imagine a better friend in all the world."

"I wish I had a friend like that. Unfortunately, it is unseemly for a woman to share a man's company to any degree of intimacy—unless, of course, they are courting or related. And the young ladies I grew up with are far more concerned with their social standing and the next party or gown. I find myself quite weary of their company, yet I always end up going back to their affairs simply out of desperation to have someone with whom to talk."

"I am sorry for that." Carter looked at her as if seeing her for the first time. "I did not realize how miserable you'd become."

Winifred reached out a gloved hand and patted his arm. "Do not fret over it. Mother says it's my own doing. My shyness makes people uncomfortable. However, I would never have become so shy had my peers been less opinionated and harsh. I have no desire to spend my evenings gossiping about a friend who had, until that moment, been perfectly admired. Women, Carter dear, can be so very nonsensical."

Carter laughed out loud at this. "You are wise beyond your years, little sister. So may I plan on your accompanying us Sunday after church?"

"Where will you ride? I am certain I cannot keep a saddle for as long as you and Mr. Arlington, but I would like to come." There was an excitement in her voice that Carter had not anticipated.

"Then we will plan on it. We'll set out after dinner, so long as the weather is good, and keep to the park."

The carriage slowed and then drew to a stop. Carter glanced out to see the sign announcing Mrs. Clarkson's.

"It would appear we have arrived."

Carter helped Winifred from the carriage and followed her to the sewing house. He found himself feeling rather excited to once again meet the beautiful Miss Shay. He'd thought more about her in the last week than he'd thought of any other woman. Hearing Winifred talk so highly of Catherine only intrigued him more.

A very young redheaded girl greeted them as she opened the door. "G'day to ya both." She curtsied and stepped aside.

"We're here to see Miss Shay," Winifred announced. "I am Miss Danby."

"I'll be lettin' Miss Shay know yar here." She showed them to the same sitting room Carter had occupied on his first occasion to Mrs. Clarkson's. He could only hope that the wanton Felicia would be occupied elsewhere.

"Would ya be wantin' some refreshments?"

"No. I believe our stay will be quite short," Winifred replied, looking to Carter to make certain her response was acceptable.

"I am fine," he assured.

The girl curtsied again and went about her duties. Carter thought of the fluid and graceful movements he'd noted of Catherine Shay compared to this awkward little girl, then considered his sister's comments about Miss Shay's intelligence. She clearly wasn't like the others in the house. There was an air of refinement to her manners and speech. Of course, she was English, and that alone could account for a great deal. She might well have been part of a noble family. Many had fallen on bad times, and it wasn't, as he understood, that unusual for them to come to America to seek to better their situations. Perhaps that was the mystery behind the beautiful Catherine Shay.

Carter smiled to himself. *I have a great imagination.*

"What are you smiling about?"

He met his sister's gaze and his grin only broadened. "I was just thinking that with very little trouble I easily allow my imagination to run wild. I suppose it bodes well to have a creative nature, since my passion is architecture. However, I sometimes find my thoughts getting the best of me."

"And in what way do they get the best of you, brother?"

Carter shrugged. "In ways that might well serve to get me into more trouble than expected." He grinned. "But never fear. I have a tight rein on my thoughts. They shall not be my ruin today."

The door opened suddenly, and there she was. Carter forgot what he was saying and simply stared at the vision before him. Hang his imagination; this woman was far more intriguing in the flesh.

"I have some things here that I believe ..." Catherine began, but her words faded as she found herself face-to-face with Carter.

He smiled broadly and gave a bow. "Good afternoon, Miss Shay."

"Sir." The reply slowly spilled from her reluctant lips.

Catherine found she couldn't look away. He was so very handsome. His face had a rather rugged look, perhaps more so than she'd noticed five years ago. Of course, if she had changed, he certainly could as well. She thought he looked wiser and, ultimately, more at ease with himself. How strange that he'd never married. Of course, a man of means had no need to rush into an arrangement that he might find drained his riches rather than added to them.

"So, my sister tells me you are quite accomplished at designing ball gowns."

"I told him I'd never seen anyone quite like you. Most seamstresses create gowns based solely on patterns that have already been established—or at least gowns that are available to copy," Winifred said with such sincerity that Catherine momentarily forgot her fears.

"You are very kind to say so. I enjoy what I do."

"I believe that helps one to do an exceptional job," Carter offered.

"My brother is also a designer," Winifred said with a smile.

"Yes, I know." Catherine headed to the table and put down her things. "He's an architect."

"How did you know?" Winifred asked in surprise.

Catherine felt her breath catch. "Ah, well, I believe your mother must have mentioned it." She caught Carter's look of surprise, then watched his expression relax.

"Of course. Mother has a way of mentioning a great many things."

Winifred giggled, and Catherine chose that moment to refocus the discussion. "These are the fabrics I found, as well as some of the trims I had in mind."

Winifred took her seat and began to review the pieces. "This is perfect. I love the shade. Oh, Catherine, I am so excited about this gown. Perhaps for the first time in my life."

Catherine saw the exchange of looks between brother and sister. Carter seemed very happy for his sister, and his joy at her pleasure touched Catherine deeply.

"You'll impress many a potential suitor in this gown, to be sure," Carter teased.

Winifred blushed. "I don't care about impressing many suitors. I would be happy just to have one—one who would meet my needs."

Carter laughed, surprising Catherine. "And what would those needs be?"

"He must love me, silly. I won't marry for any other reason, despite Father's ranting." She looked up suddenly, as if she'd said too much.

Catherine pretended to be busy checking something on the sketch. "I have some burgundy cording that I think will work well for the trim on the waist of the bodice." She looked for the piece among her swatches.

"Do you have a suitor, Catherine?"

Catherine's head shot up at Winifred's question. She blinked blankly several times. "Ah . . . no. My work here . . . well . . . it keeps me very busy."

"I can hardly believe someone so beautiful would not have many suitors," Winifred replied. "Wouldn't you agree, Carter?"

"I do find it very surprising. Either the men in Philadelphia are blind, or perhaps they simply do not frequent women's dressmaker shops. I shall have to put the word out that there are lovely young ladies being overlooked."

Catherine knew her composure was quickly slipping away. When the clock chimed three, she nearly jumped a foot. "I'm sorry," she said at Carter's and Winifred's startled expressions.

"I have so many appointments and I didn't realize the time had passed so quickly. If you approve of the materials and design, then I will get the girls to create a pattern of the bodice." Catherine quickly gathered the swatches as she spoke.

Just calm down, she told herself. *You'll give yourself away for sure if you don't appear at ease.* She forced herself to stand still and look at the siblings as if bored.

"Do you have any questions?"

Winifred got to her feet. "No, everything looks perfect. I'm glad we waited for this fabric. I very much like the silk, and the trims and laces are lovely. I will wait to hear from you."

Catherine could hardly draw breath until they'd stepped out of the house. She hurried to put her things away and nearly collided with Lydia.

"I'm sorry, Catherine."

"No harm done. My mind was elsewhere."

Lydia looked at her as if considering something uncomfortable. "I . . . well . . . I'm glad you had me reset the basting in the bodice. It looks much better."

"We all have to learn, Lydia. You wouldn't be here if you didn't show talent. I simply didn't want you to settle for a job only done in part."

Lydia nodded. "I want to do a good job."

"And you do," Felicia said as she came into the room behind Catherine. She looked at Catherine as if daring her to argue. "You mustn't allow anyone to tell you otherwise."

"Lydia is a very talented young woman," Catherine said, stepping aside to put her things away. "But even talented people need guidance and direction."

"Are you about to preach a sermon?"

Felicia's smug expression helped Catherine to recover from her earlier bout of nerves. "I will leave that to the theologians," she replied. "Now, if you are both in need of work . . ." Catherine let the words trail off as she observed each young woman.

"I have a job," Lydia said quickly. "I just wanted to thank you for helping me." Lydia quickly hurried from the room.

Catherine lost no time in turning to face Felicia. "You would do well to remember your place in this house. I won't have you undermining my authority with the girls. Nor will I have you discredit a young woman putting aside her pride to accept direction. I hope that I will not find it necessary to take this matter to Mrs. Clarkson."

Felicia's eyes narrowed. "One day you'll be sorry you've made an enemy of me."

"I have never tried to make an enemy of you, Felicia, but I do require respect for my position." Catherine put away her scissors and closed the drawer. "Now if you'll excuse me."

She headed out of the pattern room and went to check on the progress being made by some of the other girls. She wasn't sure, but she thought Felicia muttered something about getting her due.

Catherine sighed. Between having to worry about what Felicia might do and whether or not Carter Danby would remember her true identity, Catherine felt her energy drain away. Unfortunately, there were still many hours of work to complete. She whispered a prayer and knew that no matter the trials that came her way, she had to keep going for her father. Every dollar she saved meant a chance for him to be freed. No one was giving him any help. No one was worried about how tired or worried he might be—no one, except Catherine.

CHAPTER 6

A few days later, Mrs. Clarkson addressed everyone at breakfast. Although she often gave news at the morning meal, today was different. The sense of anticipation was even greater due to her including Selma and Dugan.

"It is nearly October and we have a large order—the largest ever, in fact—of gowns to complete for the Christmas season, with some additional costumes requested for the New Year's Eve parties. It will require a great deal of dedication and work on our part. I am, however, prepared to offer large bonuses to compensate for the extra work. These bonuses will extend even to the girls who are not yet making a regular salary."

Catherine noticed the exchange of smiles between Lydia and Beatrix, the only two who weren't being paid. The news would no doubt be very well received by their families.

Picking at her eggs, Catherine continued to listen, knowing that the days to come would be quite taxing. Last year she had worked eighteen hours a day, without proper meals, for over six weeks. There were even a few days when she had no more than four hours of sleep. The memory of her aching shoulders and tired eyes made her wish the season were already behind them.

"And of course we must complete all the work orders, even if it requires getting additional help. Which, I'm happy to say, I have already arranged for. Most will help with the bulk work. They can easily hand-stitch undergarments, skirts, and the like. Selma will continue with cooking and cleaning; however, we might allow the deeper cleaning to go for the time, allowing her to help us with bastings and fittings. She is quite good at this, as those of you who were with us last year will remember."

"But if you're hiring all this extra help," Felicia said with a pout, "that will mean less opportunity for us to earn extra money."

"Not at all," Mrs. Clarkson assured. "We have taken double the number of gowns as we had last year. And while we have two more girls on staff, they are not yet able to do much of the finish work. There will be plenty of chances to earn bonus money, I assure you."

Mrs. Clarkson looked down at a piece of paper she held. "I want also to announce that Lydia is being moved into the position of Improver. She will now work with Felicia. Felicia, I will periodically check the garments Lydia sews and approve or reject the work. My review of your work will be judged not only on the garments you sew but the ones Lydia helps with as well."

"So if she does a poor job, I will be held responsible? That hardly seems fair."

Catherine held her tongue, despite wanting very much to give her a piece of her mind. Mrs. Clarkson would handle the matter.

"Yes, that's exactly how it will be. A supervisor is no better than the subordinates she oversees. If she cannot get the proper job out of her worker, it is a reflection on her abilities to lead, instruct, and train. Lydia's work will be a reflection of your teaching."

"I'll do a good job, I promise," Lydia interjected.

Felicia looked at her rather sourly for a moment, then smiled. "I know you'll do exactly as I say."

Catherine felt sorry for Lydia. The tone of Felicia's voice made it clear that she would treat the girl like a slave. Picking up her nearly empty cup of tea, Catherine drank the last of it as Mrs. Clarkson continued.

"Dolley, you will work as a team with Catherine and Beatrix."

Orphaned at fourteen, Dolley had worked in Mrs. Clarkson's house ever since. She had proven herself quite industrious and, despite her rather plump figure, was probably the most energetic of all the workers. Pushing back strands of dull blond hair, Dolley threw Catherine a smile. They worked well together, and as an Assistant with over a year's experience, Catherine knew Dolley could sew even the most intricate garment.

"Martha will work with me," Mrs. Clarkson continued. "As will Selma when time permits. Our projects are divided into these three groups. I will post the assignment of customers so that there are no questions over what group is responsible for each project. Does everyone understand?"

"I only have myself and Lydia," Felicia said, shaking her head. "That hardly seems fair. How can I hope to get as many pieces of work completed?"

Mrs. Clarkson nodded. "Catherine will oversee the designs and create new pieces as needed. So you see, her team will mostly rely upon Dolley and Beatrix to accomplish the work. Even so, I have already accounted for your needs. Extra help will be available to you to sew some of the bulk work, as mentioned. And because Lydia is still quite new in her training, I have assigned you gowns where the patterns have already been created. You won't need to worry about remaking the patterns or designing any part of the gown."

Felicia knew better than to comment further. She was getting the easier end of the work load and knew it very well. She sat back and folded her arms against her chest but said nothing more.

"Now, does everyone understand their position and station here?" The girls all nodded and Mrs. Clarkson smiled. "Good. Catherine, do you have anything else to add?"

Catherine considered the situation for a moment. "Everyone must feel free to come to me if you have any questions on the designs. I tried to work intimately with each customer, paying close attention to her form. Some of the details we've included on the pattern might not make sense, but rather than overlook them or change them, I would ask that you consult with me first."

"Yes," Mrs. Clarkson said, nodding quite soberly. "This is critical. Catherine's designs are the reason the women have flocked to us in great number. You must put aside any petty jealousy or conflict with this thought and do a job worthy of the customer's faith. They enjoy Catherine's creativity, but Catherine herself knows that the entire sewing house is needed in order to bring a design to life. We are a team, and we need each person to do what they do best. There is no room for squabbles or animosity, and should such attitudes surface, they will be dealt with swiftly. If they are unable to be resolved, it might well result in my having to dismiss you. Understood?"

The girls nodded in unison, except for Felicia. She eyed Catherine with a look that suggested she thought otherwise, but then quickly looked to Mrs. Clarkson and replied, "I understand completely."

Catherine was certain the anger Felicia held for her would result in no good. The girl had been jealous of Catherine for as long as they had worked here. They had come to Mrs. Clarkson's at nearly the same time, but Catherine's skills had already been in place. Not only that, but her artistic abilities and intimate knowledge of gowns that would please the wealthy did nothing to endear her to Felicia—yet everything to promote Catherine's position with Mrs. Clarkson. Felicia had caused Catherine grief ever since.

Catherine sighed and pushed back her plate. It looked to be a long season.

❦

Carter rechecked his notes from the previous day's meeting at Mr. Montgomery's house. The carpenters were all to his liking, and the initial estimates for the various labors involved were also approved. If the weather held mild, they could actually begin some of the initial work—clearing ground and hauling materials in preparation for the start of construction.

Analyzing the size and detail of the project, Carter was certain the building would take at least three years to complete. Montgomery wanted it sooner, but Carter had stressed that it was imperative to do it right, lest the entire thing come crashing down. He would not encourage the men to rush a job just to meet an unreasonable timetable. If Montgomery insisted on that, he had the wrong man.

The front door crashed with the impact of someone slamming it shut. Carter got up from his desk to see who had come, but he felt fairly certain he would find his brother, Robin, as the only other person to enter in such a manner was their father, and he was tied up in Baltimore at meetings.

"Father!" Robin called out from the foyer. "Father!"

"Sir, your father has gone to Baltimore on business," Wilson announced as Carter made his way to the scene.

Robin let loose a stream of obscenities. "Why is he never here when I need to talk to him?" He looked at Carter, as if trying to ascertain whether he could be of any help, then threw off his coat and tossed his hat and gloves at Wilson. Storming past Carter, he demanded, "Come with me."

Carter rolled his gaze heavenward and shook his head at Wilson. The butler seemed to completely understand but offered no other word on the matter. Carter knew he would never speak his thoughts on the matter, but there were times when he would have loved to have had a long conversation with Wilson regarding the Danby men.

With a sigh, Carter followed Robin down the hall. He wasn't surprised when his brother waltzed into Carter's office as though he owned the place. Without asking, Robin threw himself into a large leather chair and began to rant.

"What, pray tell, is Father about in Baltimore?"

Carter went to his desk and took a seat. It looked as if this tirade might take some time. "I believe there were to be meetings about a cotton contract."

"Oh, that's right. I remember him talking about it. He wanted me to go, but I was already committed to a deal in Kentucky. That, however, was canceled last week. I'm surprised he didn't insist I go to Baltimore in his place." His brother got up and crossed to the butler's cord. Pulling it, he shook his head. "Why do you not have any liquor in this room?"

"I suppose because I'm not given to drink it," Carter replied and leaned back in the chair.

Robin cursed again and paced the room nervously. He was not all that different in appearance from Carter. Both men had dark brown-black hair and dark eyes. Both stood about the same height and had managed to refrain from overindulging in food. Yet there was a darkness, a sense of arrogance and self-serving, that shadowed Robin. He was used to having things his way, and apparently today that record had gone otherwise against him.

Wilson appeared and looked to Carter. "Yes, sir?"

"He didn't call you, I did," Robin answered before Carter could. "Bring me a drink. Bring a whole bottle. Make it brandy. The good stuff."

"Yes, sir." Wilson looked to Carter. "Will that be all, sir?"

"You might as well have Mrs. Colfax bring me coffee. What of something to eat, Robin? Would you like something?"

"No! Just the brandy. And I want it now."

Carter nodded. "Just coffee and brandy, Wilson. Thank you."

Without another word, the butler exited. Carter looked at Robin and could tell his brother was more than angry; he seemed almost distressed. Carter squared his shoulders and met the matter head-on.

"You appear to be in quite a state, Robin."

"I will speak on it after I have a brandy." Robin marched with the intent of a soldier about to take on the enemy as he made his way to one of the windows. Pushing back the heavy green draperies, he threw open the window and drew several deep breaths. Closing it just as quickly as he'd opened it, Robin turned and stared at the door. "What in the world is taking that imbecile so long?"

As if on cue, Wilson returned. Carter waved the man off after he put the tray of coffee and brandy on a small table in the center of the room. "Thank you, Wilson. We can serve ourselves."

The butler nodded and left the room, careful to close the door silently behind him. Carter poured himself a cup of strong black coffee and took it back to his desk. Robin just as quickly poured himself a brandy, downed it, then poured another before retaking his seat.

"Will you tell me now what has you so distressed?" Carter asked again and waited for Robin to speak.

"You know, of course, about Elsa," Robin began, then held up his hand. "I don't wish to hear any of your condemnation about my having a mistress."

"I wasn't going to offer any," Carter replied. "You already know full well how I feel about your mistress as well as Father's. What is the problem with Elsa?"

"She's allowed herself to become pregnant."

"She didn't do this alone, I assure you," Carter said pointedly.

Robin pounded his fist on Carter's desk. "She could have prevented it. She has before."

Carter tried to control his anger. His brother's and father's casual attitude toward such matters was more than irritating; it was downright alarming. Of course, they weren't the first men of means to conduct themselves in such a way, but Carter had little sympathy for either one or the ordeals they faced with their mistresses.

"Again, I'm rather confused as to why you are here. Your mistress is pregnant and your wife is sure to find out. There is hardly anything Father can do about it."

"I believe he knows someone who can take care of such matters," Robin said, gulping down the remaining brandy in his glass.

"You mean, do away with the child?"

"Of course. I do not need an illegitimate brat running about town."

"Shouldn't you have thought of that before dallying in an adulterous affair?"

"It's not adultery. Elsa was quite consenting and knew that I would never leave Anne. It's hardly the same. No promises were made or broken."

"It is the same. It is adultery. You were married in the sight of God and man to one woman. To take another to your bed is most assuredly adultery."

Robin sneered as he got up to pour himself another drink. "So you would call our father an adulterous man as well?"

"I would and have," Carter replied. "Sin is sin. It matters not who takes a hand in it. I will not lie to comfort you."

"You are ever so pious and good, Carter. We can none of us hope to live up to your standards, I'm sure."

"They are hardly my standards, and I am neither pious nor good. I am simply a man trying to live by the Word of God."

"Don't play that card with me," Robin replied, slamming down the brandy decanter. "I pay my tithe and take my seat in church on Sunday, just as you do. Choose your way, but do not choose mine."

"So you would have an innocent child killed in order to save yourself misery?"

"It is hardly a child at this point. It is an unborn, unwanted mistake, and I mean to set the matter right as soon as I can."

"And what does Elsa have to say about this?" Carter pushed aside his coffee. Robin's news had soured his stomach.

"She has no say in this matter. She lives by my generosity and good graces. I will not concern myself with her thoughts or feelings on the matter. She's hardly old enough to know her own mind anyway."

"Yes, eighteen is a tender age. Much too tender to have been forced into such a life."

"Watch your tongue, brother. I do well enough by that young chit. She would be slaving away, losing a little of her youth and life every day in the mill, had I not taken a liking to her. I buy her nice things and have set her up quite well in a very cozy little apartment. She eats regular meals and lives to do nothing but my bidding. Life could be so very much worse."

"And if you have your way, it sounds as though it will be," Carter answered, getting to his feet. "I think it is time for you to go, Robin. I can barely stomach your presence, and should you open your mouth to further denigrate that woman or the child she carries, I might very well find myself obliged to punch you in the mouth."

Robin looked rather aghast at this. He might be Carter's senior by six years but was less endowed where muscles or courage were concerned. Carter had bested him in many a squabble when they'd been younger, and by the look of it, Robin had not forgotten this fact.

"Very well." Robin got to his feet and slammed back the last of his drink. He left his glass on Carter's desk and headed for the door. "When is Father to return?"

"Tomorrow. It should be soon enough for you to plot the death of your unborn child."

Carter didn't even bother to see Robin out. As soon as he had crossed into the hallway, Carter slammed the door closed behind him and made a very loud show of locking the door.

He couldn't understand how his father and brother could so easily abuse another human being. Worse still was the thought that his father had arranged the death of other Danby children simply to keep himself from being inconvenienced. How many brothers and sisters might Carter have known had his father been a man of conscience?

"Of course, were he a man of conscience, he would not take a mistress," Carter said in disgust.

CHAPTER 7

You've touched my work and ruined it!" Lydia declared, pushing Beatrix back against the wall.

"I wouldn't be havin' any need to touch yar work," Beatrix replied in a raised tone. "I have me own work."

Catherine watched from the doorway as Beatrix went back to the cupboard to get more pattern paper.

"I didn't put this smudge on the sleeve," Lydia countered. "I'm always very careful to wash my hands before working on any of these pieces. You must have touched it after you put coal in the stove."

"But it wasn't me what put coal in the stove," Beatrix said, forcing her way past Lydia. "I've been workin' in the other room to help Catherine make patterns."

"Felicia stoked the fire," Catherine stated matter-of-factly.

Felicia crossed her arms and looked bored with the entire matter. "Are you implying that I smudged the dress?"

"You are the one who works with Lydia now—the one who handles her pieces. You were also the one to stoke the fire after complaining quite loudly about the chill in the room. My suggestion is that you help Lydia get the smudge off the material and get back to work. None of us have time for such petty arguments."

"But it's white satin!" Lydia said, her tone suggesting she might very well cry.

"Mrs. Clarkson has a list of remedies. For white satin you need some old bread crumbs and cornstarch. Mix it together, rub the stain. Be sure you wear gloves when you do this. The smudge should come right out. You have only to use a soft cloth on it to buff the sheen."

"You always have the solution, don't you, Catherine?" Felicia's tone was more than a little sarcastic.

Beatrix picked up the pattern paper she'd come for and headed out of the room, while Catherine finished dealing with the matter. "Stop fretting, Lydia. No one here wants to be the ruin of anyone else. We all have our jobs to do." Catherine looked hard at Felicia. "I'd like to speak with you privately."

Felicia motioned to Lydia. "Go take care of the smudge, then find the black jet we need for Mrs. Wyman's gown." Lydia nodded and hurried from the room, apparently grateful to escape.

"What do you have to say, Catherine?" Felicia asked, arrogance in her expression.

"I know you are the one who smudged Lydia's material. I can see the coal dust on the sides of your apron where you thought you'd eliminated the problem. Your sloppiness may well cost you if the mark cannot be removed from the material."

The younger woman's expression changed to one of anger. "I will not pay for something I didn't do. If you see coal dust on my apron, that is no reason to believe it would also be on the material. Lydia was no doubt careless, or Beatrix is more deceitful than you realize."

To Felicia's obvious surprise, Catherine reached out in a flash and grabbed hold of her arm. Holding up the younger woman's hand, Catherine revealed that there was still residue from the coal on Felicia's fingers.

"I would say maybe the deceit runs in a different direction."

She dropped her hold on Felicia and headed toward the door just as Dolley came in to retrieve something.

"It's a terrible time of year to be in want," Catherine said without emotion. "I would hate to see anyone lose their place here because they were unwilling to work together."

She didn't wait for Felicia to comment but quietly left.

Dolley was gone when Lydia returned. "I can't find the cornstarch."

"Oh, how I hate that woman," Felicia said, throwing a spool of thread at the now-closed door. "She thinks herself so high-and-mighty."

Lydia seemed uncertain of whether she should speak or remain silent. Felicia was just as glad that the girl was quiet. Something needed to be done to put Catherine Shay in her place, and Felicia needed time to think about what she might do to accomplish such a thing.

"Did you hear what I said? I can't find the cornstarch."

"Oh, hang the cornstarch." Felicia stormed to the far side of the room and washed her hands in a basin of water. As she dried her hands, an idea came to mind. Catherine's parents lived on the fourth floor. If they could be discredited or if something could be found that might put Catherine herself in a bad light, it would be found in their quarters.

"So long as Catherine Shay is here," Felicia said in hushed tone, "we neither one will know any peace or advancement. She has become Mrs. Clarkson's golden goose, and no doubt the old lady will take Catherine's side over ours."

"I can't be fired. I need this work. I hate being away from my family, but they would disown me if I were to leave here now," Lydia said, sounding close to hysterics.

"Oh, stop being a ninny." Felicia didn't try to disguise her disgust at the girl's fearful outburst. "No one is going to fire you. But I have in mind something that just might see Miss Shay dismissed."

Lydia shook her head. "She brings in too many customers. Mrs. Clarkson will never let her go."

"She'll let her go if there is a scandal that causes the customers to stay away," Felicia mused.

"But what kind of scandal? Catherine never goes anywhere but church and the park. And now with the season upon us, she rarely goes out but to church on Sunday."

"I'm sure we can find something, but it will mean spending time in search of that something. I will need your help, Lydia."

The girl fingered her coiled braid and bobbed back and forth on one foot, then the other. She often did this when nervous, and Felicia had come to detest it. "Oh, for pity's sake, stand still. You bounce about like Mrs. Davidson's stupid dog."

"I can't help it. I don't want to get in trouble."

"And you won't—if you do exactly as I say." Felicia's voice took on a tone of confidence. "I have some ideas and feel certain we can have matters under control—if not by Christmas, then shortly thereafter."

Felicia went to her table and surveyed the gown she'd been working on for the last week. "Come and sit here. I'll show you how to properly create bouillons. They can be quite tricky." She held up one of the puffed-out pieces of tulle and smiled. "And we can discuss my plan without being overheard."

Lydia looked at the closed door and moved away quickly as if their conversation had already been revealed. She sat down beside Felicia and twisted her hands together. "Are you sure we should do anything at all? I mean, well, Catherine is usually very nice. I know she's in charge and sometimes makes me redo my work, but it's only because I've done it poorly to begin with."

"Bah. She likes her authority too much. She loves to pick apart perfectly good pieces and make you rework them, because it makes her feel that she has control over you—over all of us. She may act one way and fool you into believing her considerate, but believe me, I know better. She has threatened me more times than I care to remember."

Lydia's brown eyes widened in surprise. "She threatened you?"

"Yes," Felicia said, trying to sound as ominous as possible. "And she'll threaten you as soon as she sees how good you are at this job. Anyone who shows skills to match her own constitutes a problem for Catherine Shay. She's afraid we'll remove her from her throne."

"But Mrs. Clarkson said we should all strive to do a job of which we might be proud. She says that one day we'll all be so accomplished that every one of us will be a Second Hand and—"

"And you can hardly believe that," Felicia said, jerking an unworked piece of tulle to the table. "How can everyone be a Second Hand? It's a position of authority. We can't all be in charge."

"Well, I know that, but Mrs. Clarkson said that she'd like to have a house with several people who are able to work at the Second Hand level and then have additional girls hired under them. She wants to create the largest, most popular sewing house in the city."

"Lofty dreams, to be sure, but they aren't realistic. She also said she'd like to see each of us master our skills and start our own sewing houses in other cities. I don't think Mrs. Clarkson truly knows what she wants. But I do. I want Catherine Shay gone from this place before she can hurt anyone else I care about."

Lydia's brows drew together. "She hurt someone you cared about?"

Felicia did her best to put on a face of grave sorrow. "Yes. I don't like to talk about it."

Pushing the tulle away from her, Lydia leaned forward on the smooth wooden table. "Can you not tell me?"

"I'm not certain I can. It's very painful." Felicia put aside the material and looked past Lydia to the window. She hoped her faraway expression would stir deep sympathy from the young girl. "I had a friend here. An older friend. When I first started with Mrs. Clarkson, Betsy was the Second Hand. She was so considerate and . . . well . . . she had to leave. And all because of Catherine."

"But why? What did Catherine do?"

"She stole something and blamed it on Betsy. It was so sad and no one would believe Betsy, except for me. Catherine had staged it all too well, and even Mrs. Clarkson was certain that her version of the story was true."

"That's awful. What did she steal?" Lydia asked, engrossed in the story.

Felicia shook her head. "It was a necklace. Betsy and Catherine went shopping together and while they were at the store, Catherine slipped the necklace into Betsy's reticule. The necklace was quite valuable. It was, in fact, at the store to be repaired and belonged to a wealthy woman in town. Anyway, Betsy came home and found it in her bag and was so upset. She had no idea how it had gotten into her purse, you understand." Lydia nodded, as wide-eyed as ever.

"Well, apparently someone at the store recalled Betsy and Catherine being near the necklace, and the police came to investigate its disappearance. Betsy, being a poor girl, had decided to try the necklace on before returning it. I know this to be so, because I was with her when she found it. She had just tried it on when Mrs. Clarkson entered the room to ask Betsy to come speak to the police. It was so horrible."

"Did they take her to jail?"

Felicia pretended to dab at a tear. "Yes. They wouldn't even listen to her try to explain her side of it. They condemned her before she even had a chance to clear her name. It was all Catherine's fault."

"How can you be sure?" Lydia asked in a whisper.

"Because Betsy and I were good friends. The best of friends. Besides, I overheard Catherine admit to the deed."

"Oh my." Lydia was obviously considering the entire story, just as Felicia had planned.

"You see, my dear, some people aren't at all what they appear to be. You must be on your guard at all times. And sometimes you must bend the rules in order to protect the better good of all. That's why we must gather information that will see Catherine either arrested or at least forced to leave."

"But what if she's done nothing to be arrested for?" Lydia questioned.

"Of course she has. She's broken the law on many occasions," Felicia replied. "She's just managed to get away with it. We're going to see that she gets caught."

"How?"

Felicia took up the tulle again and began to smooth it out. "We're going to go through her things—maybe go to the fourth floor and go through her parents' things as well."

"We'll get caught." Lydia pulled back as if already facing apprehension. "You know about Mrs. Clarkson's rules regarding other people's rooms. We're never to go in uninvited. If she catches us—"

"She won't. We'll wait until an opportunity reveals itself. Maybe we'll feign sickness on Sunday. Then while everyone is out to church, we can snoop about."

"I don't know," Lydia said, sounding more than a little troubled about the matter.

"You'll do as I say," Felicia said sternly. "If you don't, you'll have to leave Mrs. Clarkson's. I could never work with or approve the work of someone who could not be trustworthy and obedient."

"Oh, please don't say such things. I'll help you however I can. I have to work and now that I'm an Improver, I can actually make money and help my family. If I lose this job, I'll have no references and no hope of securing another position."

"Then you must do everything I tell you and all will be well." Felicia smiled. "I'll have no reason to speak against you if you do whatever I say."

CHAPTER 8

Sundays, Mrs. Clarkson had ordered, were to be days of rest. No matter how many gowns were yet to be made or customers clamoring to be satisfied, the Lord called them to remember the Sabbath, and they would. Catherine was quite grateful for the rule. She cherished her time away from the sewing house. Going to church with Selma and Dugan reminded her of the life she'd once known. Closing her eyes, she could almost believe her father was beside her, safe and happy. Sundays always managed to restore Catherine's sense of peace and hope. This Sunday was no exception.

The service had been quite gratifying, and Catherine had put Felicia's angry words behind her. Strangely enough, both Felicia and Lydia had fallen ill that morning and remained behind at the sewing house. Worried that her girls had contracted something serious, Mrs. Clarkson had also stayed behind.

Catherine didn't believe them to be all that sick. They had been well enough the night before, but then again, she knew illness could come on quickly. She prayed for them, despite her frustrations with Felicia.

"A good Christian woman," her mother had once said, *"puts aside the wrongs done her and prays for her enemies."*

So Catherine prayed for Felicia's recovery and that her attitude might be sweetened. She prayed, too, for Lydia and hoped that Felicia's bad habits would not overcome the girl's gentle nature.

Catherine put both young women out of her mind, however, as she climbed the stairs to her room. She had done her duty to pray for both and now the day was her own on which to dream. She had already decided to change her clothes and go out for a walk in the park. Selma had promised to pack her a little picnic to take along, and Catherine looked forward to the peace and quiet she might enjoy.

Finding her door slightly ajar, Catherine wondered at it but gave it no deep thought. It was possible Mrs. Clarkson had needed something or that Catherine herself had not secured it when she'd left for church. She focused instead on undressing.

The three-flounced green silk gown she wore was something Catherine had found at a secondhand store. The hem had been quite ragged, but it wasn't of concern to Catherine, as she was shorter than the former owner. She had purchased the quality piece for very little money and had remade it. It suited her Sunday needs quite well. Amazingly, Catherine found that she didn't miss the large wardrobe she'd once owned. She had new appreciation for the things she possessed, as well as the servants who had once waited on her.

Grateful that the style buttoned down the front, Catherine was able to undress without seeking out Beatrix's help. The girl had gone home the night before to help her mother prepare the family for church and to take home her first bits of pay.

Catherine smiled, knowing that it would mean a great deal to the large family. She liked Beatrix very much and was happy to find the girl quite talented and quick to learn. It wouldn't be long before she surpassed Lydia and maybe even Dolley.

Shrugging out of the gown, Catherine then carefully hung it in her wardrobe and took out a walking-out gown of dark blue. The dress was quite simple in its lines, and the little fitted jacket that accompanied it reminded Catherine of riding habits she'd once owned.

She thought of England and her father. Funny how little things triggered her memories. One day she'd been at the market, and the overwhelming aroma of lavender had assaulted her senses to send her back in time. Her mother had loved lavender soap and she always carried the faint scent with her after a bath.

Life had been so different when they'd all been together—her mother and father and brothers. Influenza had robbed her of so much, taking even her beloved Nanny Bryce, the woman who had tucked her into bed each night . . . who had taught her intricate skills with a needle and thread. Her thoughts went back to their last Christmas.

"I hope Father remembers that I want some toy soldiers to play with," her brother Nelson announced. Named for their father, the boy was his spitting image, and he stood watching at the window in hopes he would glimpse their father's arrival from London.

"Toys are for babies," her thirteen-year-old brother, John, declared.

"They are not," Nelson protested, turning from the window. At ten years of age he wavered between childhood and the grander responsibilities of becoming an adult. "Father said they are good to teach strategy and technique. Isn't that so, Cat?"

Catherine smiled at her little brother. The nickname only served to endear him to her. "It's true, Nelson. John, you know very well that Nelson hopes to join the navy one day. He must learn all about such strategies."

"He could read about it in books."

"And what did you ask Father to bring you for Christmas?" Catherine asked John. She hoped if she turned the focus to him, he might be less inclined to belittle Nelson's choice.

"I want the materials to make a sailing ship. Father is going to show me how to create one of wood. He said I must understand ship construction so that I might one day take over the business."

Catherine's thoughts returned to the present, leaving an ache in her heart that could not be filled.

"They're all gone now," she whispered as she secured the buttons of the jacket. "All but you, Father, and I cannot seem to find any way to help." The thought of him wasting away in some dark, damp prison often brought nightmares and left her with a dread she couldn't shake.

"This kind of thinking will do me no good, and it certainly cannot help Father," she admonished aloud. "I must be strong for us both. I must trust that God has not forsaken us."

Catherine hurried downstairs to find the little cloth bundle Selma had prepared for her. She couldn't and wouldn't allow the past to overshadow her thoughts. If she did, she might well lose hope. The reverend had said just that morning that hope was necessary in the face of adversity.

"There you are," Selma said as she came in from the pantry. "I packed you some cheese and bread and an apple."

Catherine smiled. "It sounds perfect."

"Are you sure you wouldn't like to have lunch with Dugan and me? You could still go for your walk later."

"No. I need to be alone for a while. I hope you understand."

Selma came and gently patted her arm. "Of course I do, deary. You needn't fret about that. You go along now. Enjoy your day. The sun is shining and the weather is quite mild. It's perfect for dreaming."

Catherine shook her head. "I doubt that I will allow myself a dream. Unless, of course, it's a dream of . . ." she lowered her voice, "how to help Father."

"I know. I pray for that daily. God will answer in His time. You can be sure of it."

"I want to believe that," Catherine said, "but I find it hard sometimes. Five years it's been! I'm trying my best not to fret, but there are days when the hours seem so long, and I fear I might never see him again." Catherine took up the bundle and squared her shoulders. "I should go or I'll soon be in tears."

"Have a pleasant time, and try not to dwell on your father. Find yourself a distraction."

Catherine thought of Selma's words as she made her way down the street. It was a beautiful day with just a hint of the changing seasons in the air. Philadelphia was nothing like Bath, and it was easy to get caught up in the differences. Bath was all pale stone and misty meadows, with gentle reminders of centuries gone by. Philadelphia seemed entirely too new—too American. The brick and stone used here colored the town in a festive manner, compared to Bath's pale blond stone.

The park was surprisingly empty when Catherine arrived. No doubt it would fill soon enough. She enjoyed watching the people as they strolled or rode by. There was a little pond where ducks swam and children often sailed boats. Catherine always felt a sort of aching deep inside as she watched the children. Perhaps a part of her longed for a child of her own, but there was also another part that mourned the past and the childhood innocence she'd lost in the wake of life's trials.

Settling under a large oak, Catherine unfolded her bundled lunch and began to eat. The apple was sweet and cold, and set against the flavor of the cheese, Catherine thought it a most refreshing meal.

Father would like it here, she thought as she had on previous occasions. *He would like Philadelphia. He would no doubt say it was full of interesting people who had little to hide and much to share.* She smiled at the thought. Her father had never known a stranger. He loved people and was generous to a fault. Even his partnership with Finley Baker had been borne out of a sense of obligation to a family friend. Baker was the son of one of her father's friends. When Baker's father had died without a pence to his name, it was Nelson Newbury who took pity on Finley and gave him a proper job.

Catherine tried not to hate Finley Baker, but it was almost impossible. She had no desire to think kindly of the man or to wish him well. And despite her mother's admonitions to pray for her enemies, Catherine found it impossible to pray for Finley Baker unless the prayer was in regard to his being caught. His actions and deception had put her father behind bars.

I cannot let my thoughts run away with anger toward Mr. Baker, she thought. *It will serve no purpose and only ruin my outing.*

She picked at the bread and watched as a couple passed by. The woman was overdressed for a Sunday walk. Her satin gown and lace shawl would have been more befitting a party. The gentleman, too, was quite nicely attired, so in all likelihood they were on their way to a festivity that required such dress. They clearly enjoyed each other's company.

Catherine watched as they paused for a moment not far from the little bridge that crossed a stream of water. The man gently touched the woman's face with his gloved hand. She blushed and cast an adoring gaze into his eyes. He took her face in his hands and kissed her. Then, as if they were both embarrassed by the unexpected display of affection, they hurried on their way.

Longing for such a love affair of her own, Catherine closed her eyes and tried to still the ache in her heart. She had once dreamed of the man who would sweep her off her feet. A man whom she would know at a single glance was to be her husband—her life.

"Why, Miss Shay, is that you?"

Her eyes shot open at the sound of a voice she clearly recognized. Carter Danby sat atop a fine sorrel gelding. Mr. Danby smiled and tipped his hat. His buff-colored trousers and dark blue coat fit him to perfection. Beside him on a smaller black mare rode his sister, Winifred, and on her left was another male rider.

"Good afternoon, Mr. Danby. Miss Danby."

Mr. Danby was already getting off of his horse, much to Catherine's horror. "Come, let us visit with Miss Shay for a time," he told the others. He took hold of Winifred's mare while the other man quickly dismounted and went to help her down.

They dropped the reins, much to her surprise, and allowed the horses to graze in a patch of grass to Catherine's right.

"Will they not wander off?" she asked as Carter came to join her.

"No. They've been trained in this way. When the reins are dropped to the ground, they believe themselves tied."

"How is this so?" Catherine had never seen such a thing.

"When they were in training, we would drop the reins but secure them with a peg to the ground. The horses would pull away but quickly found that they were secured. After a time, it was no longer necessary to use the peg. Whenever the reins were dropped, they believed themselves staked to the ground."

"I'm very glad to see you," Winifred said, taking a seat on the grass beside Catherine. She seemed rather nervous, and Catherine couldn't help but wonder if the cause was the dashing young man who had joined them on their outing.

"Miss Shay, may I introduce Mr. Leander Arlington. Lee has been my close friend for many years."

"Mr. Arlington," Catherine said with a nod.

"Ah, I hear from your voice you are English. I must say I'm quite fond of England. I have family there on my mother's side. Are you familiar with Plymouth?"

"A little," Catherine said, feeling her chest tighten. She longed to leave before too many questions were asked. "I'm sorry, but I should be going. I'm expected home." It was true, she was expected sometime, she just hadn't said when.

"No, please stay," Winifred said, pulling at her sleeve. "I have so wanted to know you better."

"It's hardly proper," Catherine said, clutching the remains of her lunch.

"And why is that?" Carter asked, his dark eyes searching her face as if he might find the answer written there.

"I am not of your social class," Catherine said. "I am a common worker."

"Classes here do not hold the same interest as in your homeland, Miss Shay," Mr. Arlington declared. "Part of our decision for liberty was based in the desire to break free of such chains. Although we have our families who still hold to such tradition, you will find that much of America is happy to intermingle."

"I doubt that seriously, sir. Granted, I do not know this country as well as one born here, yet I see how the classes are divided and how people know their stations."

"Perhaps people choose to maintain the separation because they are afraid of breaking down those barriers," Mr. Danby said softly.

"I think you make a good point, Carter," Mr. Arlington replied. "And I believe there are those who belittle others in order to feel more comfortable about themselves."

Winifred cast a sidewise glance at the man. She seemed to hang on his every word, and Catherine became quite certain that she fancied the man as a suitor. Perhaps that was what this outing was all about. The man wanted to court Miss Danby, and Carter was acting as escort.

"Well, I should go now," Catherine said, trying again to get to her feet.

"Please don't go, Catherine. I very much enjoy your company," Winifred said with great pleading in her tone.

"As do I," Carter said with a grin.

"You can count me among your numbers," Mr. Arlington added with a sweeping bow. "I find you quite well-spoken."

"You hardly know me and have definitely not heard enough to know whether I am well-spoken or not," Catherine stated in a guarded manner.

"Then you must stay so that we might ascertain this matter firsthand," Mr. Danby said, his tone teasing.

"Have you seen the flower beds?" Winifred asked Catherine. "There are some very beautiful arrangements. There are roses that defy description. I saw them briefly the other day from the carriage and want to examine them more closely."

"Leander, why don't you escort Winifred to the roses. I would like to talk privately with Miss Shay for just a moment before she leaves."

"Of course." Mr. Arlington reached down to offer Winifred help in getting to her feet.

The girl blushed profusely but kept her head bent so that he might not see her reaction. Catherine thought it quite sweet and innocent and might have enjoyed the scene had it not been for the unnerving thought that Carter might expose her secrets.

As Winifred got to her feet, Catherine quickly scrambled to hers as well. To her surprise, Carter stood even more quickly and took hold of her arm to steady her as she tried to arrange her skirts.

Winifred paused and offered a sweet smile. "Catherine, I very much enjoyed seeing you. I wish you didn't have to leave. I hope we'll get another chance to talk soon."

Winifred's words were so sincerely delivered that Catherine had no doubt the young woman had come to like her. Catherine nodded and tried to seem cordial as she pulled away from Carter's touch.

"I hope so too, Miss Danby."

"You promised to call me Winifred," she reminded.

"Winifred. I am sure we will visit very soon. I will need, after all, to have you in for a fitting."

"I'll look forward to seeing you then." Winifred turned and allowed herself to take hold of Leander's arm.

As they walked away, Catherine couldn't help but think they made a nice couple. She hoped Winifred might find true love. If not with Mr. Arlington, then with someone who would cherish and respect her.

"Do you really need to go, or are you simply afraid of talking to me?" Carter asked matter-of-factly.

Catherine frowned. "I am expected, just as I said. I have no need to lie to you or anyone else."

"But you remain a woman of mystery, Miss Shaw. I feel there is something you want to remain hidden from me."

She met his gaze and instantly wished she had not. He had intrigued her five years ago, but now . . . now Catherine couldn't deny the attraction she felt toward him.

He moved closer and smiled. "Why should you fear my knowing you? To be honest, I am certain I've already made your acquaintance, and if that is true, then you must remember it too. Why should you not take pity on me and remind me of that place and time?"

"Had we met, as you say, it could hardly have been all that memorable, since you cannot bring it to mind," Catherine replied coolly. She fought to compose her emotions, but Carter moved closer and took hold of her gloved hand.

"What does come to mind," he said in a hushed tone, "is that you are not all that you pretend to be. Or perhaps it is that you are much more than you pretend to be. Is that it?"

Catherine tried to pull her hand away, but he only grinned. "Release me, sir."

"Not until you tell me the truth."

"And what truth is that?" She felt her heart pounding so hard she was certain he could hear.

"The truth, my dear Miss Shay, that we have met before."

Catherine considered his comment and nodded. "Then I can in truth reply that we have met before."

"Ha! I knew it." He dropped his hold and slapped his thigh. "Now you must remind me of all the details."

Catherine turned to walk away. "The details are very few. I met you when you accompanied your mother and sister to Mrs. Clarkson's, and then again when Winifred came to pick out her fabrics."

He came after her. "That's not fair. That isn't what I meant, and you know it."

"I know very little about what you might mean or not mean, Mr. Danby, for I simply do not know you."

With surprising speed, Carter Danby turned her in his arms, and for a moment Catherine thought he might pull her tight. She froze in place.

"Then I mean to change that, Miss Shay, for I find you fascinating and quite beautiful." He winked and released her. "I mean to change it very, very soon."

CHAPTER 9

$\mathcal{T}$he very next day, Carter sat in Lee's office and set his plan in motion. "Lee, I want to hire you to learn what you can about Miss Shay."

Lee leaned back in his chair and smiled. "I cannot imagine why you should want to know anything about her. She is, as she said, but a common worker. A seamstress." He chuckled. "A seamstress who, as I hear it, designs gowns that every woman in Philadelphia wants to have. I thought her fascinating and can see why you do too."

"She is very talented and fascinating, but that aside, she is also—"

"Very beautiful," Leander interjected.

Carter grinned. "That she is."

"Are you losing your heart at last?"

Carter shrugged. "I might be. I know I find myself thinking of her at the strangest moments. Like the other day as I was looking over a house design, I found myself wondering if Catherine Shay might like such a place. She is, I believe, something more than she lets on. I feel confident we've met before, but I simply cannot remember the time or place."

"So what do we know of her?" Lee asked, taking up his pen.

"She lives at Mrs. Clarkson's sewing house. I believe her parents live there as well, although I'm not certain. When my mother and sister first went there, Winifred recalls something being said about the cook being Mrs. Shay."

Leander jotted down the information. "And she is obviously from England."

"Yes, but I have not yet heard her say which part of England she called home," Carter admitted.

"What else do we know?"

"Very little," Carter said, folding his arms. "Winifred adores her. She says Catherine Shay is the kind of woman she'd like to have for a friend. You know how much Winifred has been hurt in the past by some of her so-called friends. I think she sees Miss Shay as being cut from a different cloth—of having less pretense due to her station in life."

"Perhaps Winifred can learn more about her. They will, if I remember right, be spending some time together regarding a gown."

"That's true. Winifred has already told me there will be several fittings before the gown is complete. Maybe I can even coax Mrs. Clarkson into allowing Catherine to have some time away from the shop in order to be a companion of sorts to Winifred. I know there are occasions Winifred would love to have her company. And maybe some of those times can include me as well," he said with a grin.

"In the meanwhile, I'll do what I can to get information," Leander promised. He put down the pen. "Is there anything else?"

Carter laughed. "As a matter of fact, there is. Remember our discussion about finding a good wife?"

"Of course. My mother reminds me of such a quest as a matter of daily conversation. Why?"

"Winifred." Carter watched Lee's face for any sign that might reveal his heart one way or the other. Instead, the poor man simply looked confused.

"Winifred?"

"My sister has come to greatly admire you, in case you haven't noticed. Well, the fact is, I believe she has always admired you. I would dare to say those feelings are even stronger than mere admiration."

"But I'm ten years her senior. She's but twenty years old."

"Is that your only concern?"

Lee seemed to consider the question for a moment. "I suppose it is. I very much enjoyed our outing yesterday. Your sister is charming, albeit shy. She has a sense of grace and gentleness about her that I find . . . very appealing." He paused and shrugged. "To be honest, I've grown to care deeply about her because she is your sister. But . . ." His voice fell silent.

"But what?" Carter asked.

"Lately I've begun to feel something entirely different for her. But knowing I'm much older, I put it aside."

"Age should not matter," Carter stated matter-of-factly.

"And that is all you have to say about it?"

Carter laughed. "I don't know why I'd not considered it before now. Winifred adores you, and if you find yourself capable of the same feelings, I cannot imagine a better match. I know you to be an honorable man who will not act as my brother and father, which would in turn break my sister's heart."

"I should say not. I am quite fond of your sister and would never seek to hurt her. I suppose I always considered myself too old to be of interest to her."

"Yes, no doubt we shall very soon need canes and milk toast," Carter said as he got to his feet. "I will do what I can to put the two of you together."

"What of your father?"

"My father's desire to force Winifred into a financially advantageous marriage is of concern. However, we can make arrangements to do things as a trio. This will give you time to explore your feelings and know my sister a little better."

"I suppose it would be to everyone's benefit. But seriously, Carter, if we desire to marry, what then? Your father's plan to sell her off to the highest bidder is hardly going to put me in his regard. I'm not a wealthy man, nor is my family wealthy."

"They have riches enough, and more important, you are socially accepted in every circle. But even so, we can worry about that another day. I need to get home. Don't forget to check into Miss Shay's background. I will pay you whatever you ask."

"Hmmm, maybe I will become a wealthy man after all," Lee teased.

Carter pulled on his hat. "Perhaps you shall."

Catherine's image remained in Carter's mind all the way home. He thought of her kindness to Winifred, her lack of pretense despite her awareness of his mother's control over his sister. And, as Leander pointed out, she was beautiful. Her chocolate brown hair begged his touch, and her face was that of an angel.

Joseph was there to meet him when Carter brought the carriage to a stop at the back of the house. The man said nothing, but his gaze flashed to the house and then back to Carter.

Carter immediately understood. His mother's shrill screeching could be heard all the way to the carriage house. Carter turned the horse over to Joseph, then went into the house through the kitchen. Seeing that Cook was nowhere in sight, he snagged a couple of cookies fresh from the oven before proceeding to his office. With any luck at all, he could avoid contact with his mother and father and leave them to their argument.

But it was not to be. Just as he approached the door to his study, his father came striding down the hall.

"I will not hear any more about it, woman. My affairs are none of your concern. You have a home and all the money you could possibly want. I owe you nothing more."

"You owe me respect and love," his mother cried as she followed him.

"Oh, Carter. I'm so glad you have come. I am so distraught. I have no hope left." She held a lace-trimmed handkerchief to her mouth and sobbed.

Carter's father stopped directly in front of him. "I blame you in part for this. Were you not so adamant in your thoughts, you might persuade your mother to be less concerned about the affairs of men."

Wanting no part of the argument, Carter reached for the doorknob. "I'm certain I do not need to be included in this conversation."

"But you must be, Carter. Your father is buying a new house for that woman—his mistress. He not only shames me by flaunting his affair in taking her to the opera and other performances, but now he buys her a stylish house."

Carter turned his gaze from his mother's reddened, tear-streaked face to his father's angry stare and then back. "My thoughts on the matter will not change Father's mind or yours. You, however, look quite distraught. Perhaps a rest would help you to better deal with this."

His mother fanned herself vigorously as though she might faint from lack of air. "Yes. I think you're right. You are the only one who cares about my condition. I shall rest. Yes. That's exactly what I shall do." She hurried off in search of her maid, while Carter turned his attention back to his father.

"Do not give me any of your comments on the matter," his father said gruffly. "I do not need to be chastised by my child."

"Did I offer chastisement?" Carter felt such a deep disgust for his father that he turned and went into his office without another word. He hadn't closed the door behind him, but he was certain his father would go on about his business. He was wrong.

"I will not have you dismiss me in such a rude manner," his father declared, coming into the office.

Carter stood behind his desk and tried hard to thoroughly consider what his reply should be. He didn't have a chance to speak, however. His father's tirade continued.

"What I do with my time is my business. I have worked hard to provide a fortune for this family. I have not deprived you of anything. Your mother has always had the best furniture, the best gowns, and the finest china. She wants for nothing yet torments me for indulging in my own pleasures."

"She wants *you*," Carter replied. "You have given her everything but yourself."

"She has everything of me that is important and necessary," the older man countered. "She bears my name, which in and of itself commands respect."

"And what of love?" Carter asked, then watched his father's face contort.

"You speak as a woman might. 'And what of love?'" he mocked in a falsetto voice. "You speak as though you were an authority, yet I do not see you leaving my house to marry and set up for yourself."

"Perhaps you will soon enough."

"You? Marry? You're far too busy with your drawings."

Carter tried to control his temper. "I have no plans to marry at the moment, but I do have thoughts on setting up for myself."

"Good. I'm glad to hear it. Then perhaps your mother will not berate me day and night."

"She would not berate you if you would honor your marriage vows and remain with her alone," Carter replied. "You and my brother make no effort to hide the fact you are taking other women to your beds, then struggle to understand why your wives should be heartbroken."

"Our mistresses are none of your concern," his father retorted.

"They become my concern when my mother is devastated and left to suffer, or when my brother storms the place looking for someone to kill his unborn child. It further concerns me when I learn that you have had a hand in killing my siblings."

His father actually appeared stunned by this comment. Carter didn't care. "Has my brother not yet told you? Or are you merely surprised to learn that I know of such matters?"

"You are never to speak of such things again," his father said in a low, menacing tone.

"Why?" Carter asked sarcastically. "Will that make them not so?"

His father slammed the desk with his fists and let out a curse. "You will not speak of it. Do you hear me? I will not have my life dictated to me. I will not seek your approval for the decisions I make. You have not had the decency to assist me in any way, yet you benefit from my efforts."

"As you benefited from my mother's money." Carter drew a deep breath. "Should not the wealth she brought you endear her even a little to your heart?"

"Enough! I will hear nothing more of this. Nothing!" Elger Danby stormed across the room and paused at the door. His tone was slightly less irate, but barely. "Your mother will only suffer more if she makes this a matter of social concern. She must learn her place and stay in it. I will not change in my ways, so she must adapt. You would do well to help her see that."

"And how do you suppose I do that?"

"I honestly don't care, just see to it. If she dares to speak of this to her friends, I will make her pay."

With that he left, and Carter could only stare after him.

CHAPTER 10

The first of October brought Winifred Danby in for a bodice fitting. To Catherine's great frustration, Carter once again accompanied his sister. Catherine tried to steel her nerves against anything he might say, but what she wasn't prepared for was Winifred's pleading.

"While Carter speaks to Mrs. Clarkson, I wanted to ask you something," Winifred began. "We have plans on Sunday to attend a musical performance, and I want you to come with us."

Catherine was fitting a sleeve to the bodice when Winifred made this announcement. Undone by the comment, Catherine very nearly put a straight pin right into the younger woman. "I couldn't possibly come. Sunday is my only day off and I'll have other things to do."

"But you must," Winifred declared. "Carter has invited Leander again."

"But I thought you liked Mr. Arlington," Catherine said, trying hard to focus on the sleeve.

"I do. In fact, I . . . I believe I love him."

Catherine straightened and shrugged. "Then why would you ever need me to come along?"

"I suppose it's because . . . well . . . I've come to enjoy your company, and you put me at ease." Winifred reached out to take hold of Catherine's arm. "Please say you'll come. I know it's a sacrifice for you, and it's rather selfish of me to ask, but I would feel so much better."

"I'm certain your brother and Mr. Arlington would feel differently." Catherine went to the table to retrieve the second sleeve. "As I pointed out before, we are not of the same class. I would never have the proper clothes."

"You could borrow one of my gowns. We aren't so very different in size."

Catherine knew that to be true. In fact, she and Winifred were almost identical in their measurements. "I can't possibly do that," Catherine told her.

Hoping Winifred would forget about her invitation, Catherine tried to push the conversation back on the younger woman. "So, are you and Mr. Arlington formally courting?"

"Oh no. I'm not certain he even cares for me. He has long been Carter's friend. I fear he's coming along only to accompany my brother."

"I cannot believe that. You are a beautiful young woman, Winifred. You are also very quiet, I've noticed."

"I cannot bear conflict," Winifred explained. "I feel I can talk to you, Catherine."

"I'm glad." Catherine concentrated on her work, hoping that Winifred would continue.

"I used to have friends—at least, I thought they were my friends," Winifred continued. "Now I realize they only cared about money and their next new bauble. They were mean-spirited, even cruel to one another. They would always talk about each other behind their backs. I knew without a doubt they were talking about me as well, but then one day I happened to overhear such talk. It was about my father. He has a mistress."

She grew quiet, and Catherine could well imagine the caustic comments Winifred might have chanced to overhear. Catherine had known such women in England. "I'm sorry that you had to bear such a thing."

"It wouldn't have bothered me, but I thought they were my friends. They were so insulting. So ugly about my family."

"What did you do?"

Winifred drew a deep breath. "I withdrew from social circles. I wanted nothing more to do with them, much to my father's frustration."

"Why should your father care, especially if they were speaking out against the family?"

"He intended to see me married to one of their wealthy brothers," Winifred said, shaking her head. "My father has always intended to arrange my marriage, just as my mother's union was arranged for her."

"And I thought we were behind our times in Bath," Catherine said without thinking. She immediately regretted the comment but knew if she drew attention to it, Winifred would find it strange. "But now you have Mr. Arlington, and you are already in love with him. Your father will no doubt be pleased."

"But Mr. Arlington isn't from one of the wealthy families. His family does well enough. His father is a judge—or rather, was—so he's highly regarded, but that will mean very little to my father."

"Perhaps you will be able to convince your father of his worth." Catherine went back to the table and picked up a piece of trim.

Winifred surprised her by jumping down from the fitting platform. "Please come with us, Catherine. I know I'm imposing on you, but it would mean so much to me."

Catherine found she couldn't resist her pleading. Winifred had been nothing but gracious and kind. "Very well. What time is the event? I can come and meet you."

"Oh no. We'll come for you in the carriage. Carter will insist."

"I'll insist on what?" Carter asked.

Catherine jumped in surprise. She was grateful to have Winifred positioned between them and could only hope he hadn't noticed.

"I've convinced Catherine to join us on Sunday for the Mozart performance."

"Splendid," Carter said, smiling. "I shall look forward to that."

Catherine could imagine after their last meeting that he would go out of his way to learn everything possible about her.

Of course, she thought, most of the outing would be in a place where conversation would be limited.

"Catherine wanted to meet us, but I told her you would insist on coming for her in the carriage."

"Indeed I will." Carter fixed his gaze on Catherine's face. "I would hardly be a gentleman if I did anything less."

Reaching for her pincushion, Catherine forced her attention elsewhere. "What time should I expect you?"

"We will plan to arrive just before two," Carter said, sounding much happier than Catherine would have liked.

"Very well." Catherine's reply sounded like a woman resolved to endure torture rather than something as pleasurable as a musical performance. In England she would have attended such affairs on a regular basis and relished the opportunity. Were it not for Carter Danby accompanying them, she might have looked forward to this outing as well.

❧

Sunday arrived and Carter found that he could hardly focus on anything until the carriage made its way to Mrs. Clarkson's.

"You're acting like a schoolboy," Leander teased in a whisper.

Carter fumbled with his gloves and cast a quick glance at Winifred to see if she'd overheard Lee's comment. She stared happily out the window, however, and didn't seem any the wiser.

When the carriage came to a stop, Carter bounded out the door before Joseph could climb down to assist him. Mrs. Clarkson's seemed quiet, without a sign of life from the windows. For a moment, Carter feared that Catherine might have changed her mind.

To his surprise it was Catherine who opened the door at his knock. She wore a beautiful gown of green silk and had secured a small bonnet atop a lovely arrangement of brown curls.

"Good afternoon, Miss Shay."

"Good afternoon, Mr. Danby."

"Have you a wrap?" he asked. "The evenings have been quite chilly."

"Oh, I'd nearly forgotten," Catherine said. She went back into the house and returned with a black shawl.

Carter offered his arm and felt a sense of great elation when Catherine took hold. "You look quite lovely, Miss Shay," he said.

"Thank you." She looked away as if embarrassed.

"You are very different from most women. You never smile. Although, I could almost swear I have seen you smile—at least, I imagine that I must have at one time."

"Then perhaps you are simply recalling from a vivid imagination," Catherine countered.

"Do you not like to smile?"

"I find my days spent in serious endeavors, Mr. Carter. I have very little to smile about."

They reached the carriage and Joseph opened the door for them. Carter leaned quite close to Catherine's ear. "Then I hope I might have a chance to change that. I'd like very much to bring a smile to your face."

He saw her blush but said nothing more as he helped Catherine into the carriage. She quickly took the seat beside Winifred and cast her gaze to her lap as the younger woman took hold of her gloved hands. Carter climbed up and joined Leander.

"Miss Shay, I'm pleased to see you again," Lee offered.

Catherine, obviously well versed in manners, raised her head to meet Leander's smile. "Thank you. It is quite nice to see you again, Mr. Arlington."

"Have you enjoyed a pleasant Sunday?" he pressed.

Her reply was simple and to the point. "Yes. It's been a lovely day."

Carter watched her and wondered again where he might have met her. He hadn't lied when he said he imagined her smiling. He had seen that smile in his deepest dreams, if not in his wakeful moments. It was clear she was much more than she admitted to being. The way Catherine walked, moved—even climbed into the carriage—proved that she'd been raised among people who'd trained her to be a lady.

So why was Catherine Shay working as a seamstress in Philadelphia?

Throughout the performance Carter watched her and continued to wonder. She seemed knowledgeable regarding music, and when Winifred asked, Catherine admitted to playing the piano after years of lessons. It was yet more evidence of her upbringing. Poor people did not have money for lessons.

During the ride home they easily conversed about the performance. Carter had noticed the stolen glances between Lee and Winifred and felt a growing confidence that they would soon be properly courting.

"I love the 'Church Sonatas,'" Winifred said. "They are some of my favorites."

"And the musicians were quite accomplished," Catherine admitted. "I've not heard better."

"Have you attended many concerts?" Leander asked.

Catherine looked out the window into the growing twilight. "I have attended whenever time permitted."

"In England?" he pressed.

Carter could see that she'd grown very uncomfortable. A part of him wanted to halt Lee's questioning and put her at ease, while another wanted answers.

"Yes, in England and in America. I've been here for five years now." She quickly turned to Winifred. "You asked me earlier whether I played the piano. What of you? Do you play?"

"I do. Mother saw to it that I had the best of teachers. Pity I wasn't the best of students."

"You play quite well, Miss Danby. I've heard you on many occasions," Lee interjected.

"Leander is right, sister of mine. You play beautifully."

Catherine patted Winifred's hand. "I should very much like to hear you play one day."

They were nearly back to Mrs. Clarkson's when Carter got an idea. "Why don't we go back to our house and have a little supper? I'm certain Cook won't mind."

"Splendid idea," Leander agreed.

"You will join us, won't you?" Winifred asked Catherine. "It is still early."

"I'm afraid not," Catherine replied. "I must rise quite early tomorrow. I have several things to accomplish before that time."

"Surely you'll need to eat during that time. Why not spend the meal with us?" Carter said. He caught Catherine's gaze and smiled. "I promise to have you back before seven."

"No. If it's an inconvenience to return me to Mrs. Clarkson's, I can walk from here." She reached for the door as if to open it and escape.

Carter stopped her hand. "We'll return you home, Miss Shay. I wouldn't allow a lady to be left unaccompanied on the streets."

"Thank you." She turned to Winifred. "My free time is quite limited. I beg you to understand."

Winifred met her gaze. "But of course. I know what an imposition our outing has been for you."

"Not at all," Catherine replied. "I enjoyed myself very much, but I need for you to understand," she looked up to meet Carter's gaze, "that I have other responsibilities."

Carter thought there was a tone of pleading in her voice. Almost as if she was desperate to keep a shroud of mystery cloaked about her. He opened his mouth to speak, then closed it again. What was it about her? Her eyes seemed to hypnotize him into submission.

They spent the remaining time in silence, and when the carriage finally halted in front of Mrs. Clarkson's, Carter moved to the door to keep Catherine from jumping out.

"Allow me," he said, dismounting. He reached up to take hold of Catherine's arm.

"Thank you for the lovely day," Catherine told Winifred and Leander. She let Carter help her down, and he couldn't resist holding her for just a moment longer than necessary.

Catherine lifted her face, and the desire to kiss her nearly overwhelmed Carter. Releasing her, he stepped to the side and offered his arm. Catherine moved slowly to accept and allowed him to take her to the door.

"Miss Shay, I must say it has been a very pleasant day for me. Thank you for accompanying us. I know it pleased Winifred, and that, among other reasons, makes it dear to me."

She released her hold on Carter and reached for the door handle. He found the loss of her touch strangely difficult to bear and longed to take hold of her again. But just as he'd resisted stealing a kiss, he held back.

"Thank you, Mr. Carter." She turned to go.

"Miss Shay."

She looked over her shoulder but refused to otherwise turn. "Yes?"

"I would very much like it if you would accompany us again. My sister has very few friends, and you have offered her great comfort and kindness."

"I'm sorry, Mr. Carter. As the weeks grow closer to Christmas, so grows my work. Your sister is very sweet, and I like her a great deal, but I cannot take time away from Mrs. Clarkson. She needs me."

"What if I need you too?" he asked softly.

This caused Catherine to turn. Her eyes widened, but only for a moment. She quickly regained her composure. "We all have needs. Good night, Mr. Danby." She hurried into the house and closed the door firmly behind her.

Carter couldn't help but smile. The expression on her face hadn't suggested distaste at his comment. There was hope for the future—their future.

Catherine had never felt this way before. Carter's attention and comments had left her breathless and her heart racing. She told herself it was because she feared being revealed, but in truth, she knew it was something more.

"So you're home," Felicia declared.

Catherine jumped and knocked a book off the corner of the table.

"You're certainly a nervous ninny." Felicia eyed her for a moment and laughed. "Were you not hiding behind so many secrets, you might not fidget so."

Catherine struggled to recompose herself. "My 'secrets,' as you call them, are none of your concern."

Felicia's smug expression left Catherine chilled, but no more so than her words. "I believe secrets are meant to be exposed, lest they be a danger to all concerned. I shall enjoy revealing your secrets."

"I have no secrets worth telling," Catherine stated, trying hard to sound nonchalant.

"Ah, but I believe otherwise." Felicia toyed with a blond curl. "England must have been a fascinating place to live. Yet you left it all behind to come here."

"Many people have done likewise. America is a wondrous country, offering opportunities that cannot be had in my homeland. The very idea of owning vast properties alone has sent many a European to your shores."

"True, but there is something more, and we both know that. This country has also served as a haven for those whose intentions have been to hide away from the past."

Catherine felt almost as if an invisible hand were clamping around her throat. Felicia seemed to know something, but she wasn't yet ready to reveal it. Catherine knew she would have to tread lightly. If she gave the young woman any sign of worry, Felicia would never let the matter rest.

Feigning a yawn, Catherine headed for the stairs. "I'm hardly old enough to have much of a past, Felicia. I wish I could offer you something more intriguing, but I'm a rather simple person with nothing more startling to offer than the news that I'm wearing secondhand shoes."

"Everyone has something in their past that haunts them," Felicia said.

Catherine refused to turn around and continued to climb the stairs. "Good evening, Felicia," she said in a measured manner. She desired only to leave the scene before her anxieties over the evening and Felicia's comments got the best of her. "We have an early morning, and I've still much to do before retiring."

She felt certain that Felicia watched her, but Catherine tried not to be flustered by the thought. There was no way of knowing for sure what Felicia was getting at. Perhaps she had overheard something Catherine said to Selma. Perhaps she was only guessing. Either way, Catherine would have to be extra careful in the future.

CHAPTER II

Carter, we're very happy to have you join us," Zilla Arlington announced. She accepted his embrace and kiss on the cheek as if he were one of her sons. "Come and tell us everything about this new house you've created. Lee tells us it's quite the estate."

She barely gave him time to discharge the servant with his hat and coat before dragging him to the family's private sitting room. "Look, Kendrick. Look who has come to call."

"Carter, my boy. Good to see you." The older man got to his feet and crossed the room. Stocky in build, Judge Kendrick Arlington was surprisingly light on his feet. He immediately took hold of Carter's hand, but rather than shake it, he merely patted it and smiled. "You have been much absent from our company."

"And don't I know that," Carter admitted. "Mrs. Arlington has grown even more beautiful in my absence."

Zilla Arlington laughed. "You do flatter in such a pleasing manner. All young men should take lessons from you."

"And all women should seek your secret," Carter countered.

"My secret?" the woman questioned in surprise. Her blue eyes sought Carter's face.

"The one regarding your youthful countenance. You must surely hold a secret to the fountain of youth, for you look just as young and lovely as when I was a boy."

She laughed in delight, and even the judge chuckled and added, "It's true, my dear. I age and age, but you remain the same."

"Oh, how you do go on. But don't I love it."

"And," Carter said, turning to the judge, "I have missed sitting here at your fire, hearing tales of your days in court."

"Well, perhaps we shall share some intriguing stories this day. I have some warm apple cider—not the hard stuff, mind you. Would you care for a mug?"

"I would," Carter said, taking a seat in a rather outdated fauteuil near the fire. The armchair was one of his favorites. "I'm chilled to the bone." Judge Arlington took the chair across from him and nodded as if in agreement to both his declaration of cold and of agreeing to drink cider.

"I'll see to it," Mrs. Arlington announced, "but only if you save your news until I return, Carter. I'll let Lee know that you're here as well. He had gone upstairs to change for supper." She paused at the door. "You will join us—won't you?"

"I had only meant to stop long enough to speak with Leander, but I would love to join you for supper," Carter admitted.

A meal with the Arlingtons was always a delight. He enjoyed the laughter and obvious love shared between husband and wife—a far cry from what he experienced in his own home.

"Wonderful. I'll tell Marta and Luppy right away. They love to cook for company. Supper won't be long; perhaps you can save your talk for the table."

Carter smiled. "I would be happy to do so."

It was only a few minutes before Lee bounded in, bearing a mug. "Mother told me to give you this. I heard you're staying for supper. You've made her quite happy."

"Your mother loves to have Carter join us. She misses the days when your brothers and sister were still at home," the judge added.

Carter took the mug and sampled the liquid. It was sweet with a hint of smoky flavor. "Thank you. This is quite good."

"Luppy made it just a week ago. I prefer it age a bit longer but found this quite acceptable. Now, if you'll excuse me," Judge Arlington announced, "I must take care of something before we break bread."

Carter stood again as the older man got to his feet. "No," the judge said, waving Carter back down. "Sit. Your words and deeds prove your respect for me more so than any chair-bobbing could." He smiled broadly and added, "I shall see you both at the table."

Once he was gone, Lee took his father's chair. "You have made their evening complete. I have never seen two more de-lighted people."

"I'm sure to be the delighted one, for the company and food will be considerably more appetizing than that which I might find at home." He leaned forward. "Your note said you had news.

I was beginning to despair. It's been weeks." He sampled the cider again and cherished the flavor and warmth.

"Yes. I couldn't get away, so I had to send my clerk. Sorry for that."

"No bother. What have you learned?"

Lee smiled. "Not as much as I would have liked, but more than we knew. Catherine lives at the sewing house with her parents, Selma and Dugan Shay. Although, I will say that through various means of reaping information, it was told to me that Catherine often refers to them by their first names, rather than call them Mother or Father. Yet their relationship seems quite close."

"Hmmm, an additional intrigue. And where are they from?"

Lee shrugged. "That I haven't yet learned. I do know that they came to the sewing house in 1851."

"Four years ago," Carter said, trying hard to place where he might have first seen her in those years. He took a long drink from the mug.

"Prior to that, they were in New York City, apparently newly arrived from England. They lived for a time at a boardinghouse owned by a man and woman named Samuelson. Other than that, I've not been able to learn anything."

"New York, eh? We could make a trip together." He grinned, seeing the approval in Leander's expression. "Perhaps the boardinghouse is still in business, and we could speak to the owners."

"I must admit I was hoping you might say as much."

"Come, boys, it's time for supper," Mrs. Arlington called from the doorway.

Carter put the mug aside and got to his feet quickly. "The aroma alone would have soon sent me in search of the kitchen, but the company shall entice me to sit civilly at the table and mind my manners."

Mrs. Arlington laughed. "You are quite a welcome addition, my dear. Carter, I am positively beside myself to hear about the Montgomery house." She reached for his arm as he came to join her at the door. "The ladies all over town are talking about it. Between your houses and that Miss Shay's dress designs, I scarcely hear any other news."

Carter found it quite interesting to be lumped into the same reference as Miss Shay. He liked the idea but thought it rather strange, nevertheless. Perhaps it was a sign of things to come. He smiled at that thought.

Carter escorted Mrs. Arlington to the dining room and helped her to one of the cabriole chairs. Although at least eighty years old, the mahogany chairs maintained their luster against the gold upholstery. Next to this, a table of the same wood had been set in casual elegance with the family silver and china. Carter knew the pieces, along with the furniture, had been passed down through multiple generations and cherished. Unlike his mother, who preferred new pieces, Zilla Arlington took great delight in the things her family had shared for so many years.

The judge offered grace, and soon the servants were offering a bevy of succulent dishes.

Carter settled on the roasted pork and glazed almond carrots before turning to Mrs. Arlington. "The Montgomery house has been a great challenge. Mr. Montgomery has a strong opinion on how and where he wants each room, each piece of molding and window. However, I found that the more he came to realize my abilities, the less he worried about imposing details and instead listened to suggestions."

"That in and of itself must have been a miracle," Judge Arlington declared. "I've known the man for many years now, and he has never been one to listen."

"Perhaps Carter's impressive talent won him over," his wife replied. "Tell me truly, Carter. Is it to have a bell tower? I heard just yesterday that it will."

Carter laughed. "Not unless the old man has gone behind my back to add one. There is a cupola with a dome, and perhaps it is this which has inspired such unfounded gossip. The dome will have windows all around, which will allow for light in the stairway."

They conversed easily, with Carter sharing details of his efforts to secure talented workmen for the project and Zilla Arlington asking about the number of rooms and fireplaces. Carter took great pleasure in sharing the details. No one at home had even cared to ask, save Winifred.

"I heard many of the materials are to be imported. Is that true?" Leander's mother asked.

"The marble is to be imported from Italy, of course. Nothing but the best. There is to be no blemish in any piece."

"My, but that will be a worry to keep looking its best," she said, shaking her head.

"And what of you, son?" the judge asked, turning to Leander.

Leander shared of his day and the work he was doing to help a local farmer in a battle against the state. The judge weighed in with his thoughts, as did Lee's mother. Carter couldn't imagine his mother taking interest for one minute in the details of his work. By the time dessert had been served and eaten, Carter felt a deep sense of longing. Longing for a table where he might converse with someone who truly cared about his daily tasks.

Longing for a love that equaled what was found in the Arlington family. The realization that should Winifred marry Lee, they would truly be family offered little comfort. No, he wanted it for himself. He wanted to share a home where it mattered not in the least that the furnishings were old and no one dressed in the height of fashion.

After supper Lee and Carter discussed plans for the New York trip. They each agreed now was a good time to get away. They would go immediately, lest the month slip completely away.

"I can make arrangements and leave on the twenty-fourth," Lee stated. "Will that work for you?"

Carter nodded. "Indeed it will. I'll get word to Montgomery that I will secure some of his additional building supplies while I'm there. That should keep him from being overly worried about my absence."

"Wonderful. Shall we take the train?"

"I believe that would be in our best interest. The weather is far too unpredictable at this time of year." Carter checked his pocket watch. "I must go. I'll have Joseph drive us to the station. I'll pick you up at eight."

"I shall be ready. How long do you suppose we should plan to be gone?"

Carter shook his head. "There's no way of telling. Since you don't have an address for the Samuelsons, we shall need time to hunt them down. I'd like to say we'd need no more than a week, but I would plan for two."

Leander nodded. "Very well. I will direct anyone with questions to see my father. He's good to step in when I need to be away."

Winifred was in the foyer to greet him when Carter entered the house. "I missed you at dinner," she told him.

Carter put his arm around her. "I shared supper with the Arlingtons."

Her cheeks grew red as she asked, "Was Leander there?"

"Indeed he was. He asked after you. I told him you were well."

She looked up and smiled. "He is very kind to ask."

Carter laughed. "I think it has little to do with kindness. I believe the man is quite charmed by you."

"What else did you discuss?" She looked away, as if to hide her embarrassment.

"Well, we're to make a trip. We're leaving day after tomorrow and going to New York."

"Did I hear you say that you're going to New York?" his mother asked as they entered the sitting room.

"Yes. I have some business there. Leander Arlington and I might be gone as long as two weeks."

"Oh, you must see to purchasing new crystal while you are there," his mother began. "We need at least another four dozen cups for the punch bowl, and perhaps two dozen wine glasses. There is so much to consider for the party." She pressed her fingertips against her forehead. "I'm quite worried that I will forget something important. The party is only weeks away."

"You always do a wonderful job, Mama," Winifred said, leaving Carter's side to take a chair on the settee beside their mother. She patted her mother's hand. "You will not forget anything important."

"I am glad that at least my children can appreciate my efforts," she said with a sigh. "Your father never knows the lengths I go to in order to keep his name at the top of every social agenda in town."

Carter wasn't entirely sure that was something his father would appreciate or that it truly kept them in Philadelphia's social graces, but he said nothing on the matter. "If you prepare a list for me, I will be happy to see to it while I'm in New York."

"I shall go right to it," she declared, getting to her feet. "I'm sure there are other things. I will check with Cook as well. When do you leave?"

"The day after tomorrow."

"Mercy me. I shall have to work hard to figure it all out in that time." She hurried from the room, calling for Mrs. Colfax, the housekeeper and his mother's lifelong companion. The two had been together since Mrs. Colfax's second birthday, when her mother came to work for Lillian Danby's parents. Carter knew his mother trusted the woman implicitly.

"Must you really be gone two weeks?" Winifred asked.

"I don't know for sure. I plan to return home as soon as possible. Why?"

Winifred shrugged. "I'll miss you. That's all."

He cocked his head to one side as he studied her. "You'll miss me? Or do you really mean that you'll miss having me throw you and Lee together?"

Her mouth dropped open in surprise. "Of course I shall miss you both."

"Well, you shan't get too lonely. I've made some arrangements for you to have Miss Shay's company when you desire."

"But I thought she was much too busy. Mrs. Clarkson needs her to sew the Christmas gowns."

Carter grinned. "Mrs. Clarkson needs her designing talents more than her sewing. A hundred other women can put needle and thread to material. I have given Mrs. Clarkson a sum to hire additional help in Miss Shay's absence."

"You bought me a friend! Oh, Carter, please say it isn't true. I am not so desperate as all of that."

He saw the worry in her expression and shook his head. "My motives were purely selfish. When I return, I shall desire for the four of us to spend a good deal of time together. To put it quite honestly, I would like you to spend time with Miss Shay and learn what you can of her. I find myself completely intrigued—in fact, smitten—by the woman."

Winifred smiled and came to where he stood. "I see how it is with you now. This was no selfless act of love but rather the part of a desperately enamored would-be suitor."

Carter laughed. "Do not mention this to Miss Shay. I wouldn't want her to think so lowly of me as you do."

Winifred took his hand and squeezed it. "I could never think anything but good of you, Carter. You have given me hope for my own future. I will happily help you to secure yours."

He sobered. "It's funny, but thinking of Catherine as a part of my future gives me quite a feeling of contentment. We scarcely know each other, yet I feel as if we've been somehow purposed for each other. Does that sound completely daft?"

Winifred shook her head. "Not at all. It sounds very romantic. I believe Catherine would make a wonderful wife for you. While it's true that we know very little of her past, her kindness and gentle spirit cannot be hidden. She has borne great sorrow, of this I'm certain, yet she endeavors to continue her life in a positive way."

"And it does not put you off that she is a seamstress?" he asked with a smile.

"Not at all, for I am sure to have her first efforts before any of the women in Philadelphia should she marry my brother."

Laughing, Carter put his arm around her. "Then I shall endeavor to do what I can. I would not have it said that I was less than considerate of my sister's needs."

❦

Catherine was waiting, in what had become known as the planning room, for Winifred Danby to dress and return. The gown was coming along nicely, and although Catherine had done very little of the actual sewing, she had been happy with the work done by Dolley and Beatrix.

"I am so pleased with the gown," Winifred declared as she entered the room. "I feel just like a princess in it."

"And it accentuates your assets so nicely," Catherine replied in a teasing tone.

"Yes. Mother likes it very much, but not as much as her own gown. She's still in there fawning over her appearance." Winifred motioned toward the fitting room.

"It gives us a few moments to talk about the final details," Catherine said. "Have you decided about having real flowers sewn into the bodice and sleeves?"

"I think that would be wonderful. It would be like wearing a garden," Winifred said rather wistfully.

Catherine nodded. It was a rather poetic way to express it, but quite accurate. "We shall need to add those at the very last moment. Probably the morning of the ball." She jotted a note to herself regarding the operation.

Just then Mrs. Danby and Mrs. Clarkson appeared. Mrs. Danby rambled on and on about the quality of the work and the appearance of her gown.

"And you are certain no other gown will be made of this material?"

Mrs. Clarkson looked to Catherine, then back to her customer. "There are no other known bolts of this material in Philadelphia. Now, if someone journeyed, say, to New York City, well, I could not vouch for whether the fabric could be purchased there."

"New York City?" Mrs. Danby asked, then nodded. "I feel confident, then. I know of no one, save my son, who has traveled there of late."

"I suppose he has gone on business," Mrs. Clarkson said as a means of small talk.

"Carter left for New York this morning. He had business there and the dear man is going to procure a great many things for my party. I should have given him a piece of my material so that he could search out any other bolts of cloth."

"I wouldn't worry about it, Mrs. Danby. The cloth is quite expensive, as you know. There would be few who could afford it, and even if they did, the design would definitely be different. Now if you'll excuse me, I must see to my other customers."

"Oh, Mrs. Clarkson, there is just one more thing," Winifred said boldly. Catherine found it a pleasant change to see the young woman be more outspoken. "I wondered if Miss Shay might accompany me tomorrow as I shop for shoes and jewelry to wear with my gown. My mother is quite busy with plans for the party, and I would cherish the assistance."

"I couldn't possibly," Catherine replied before Mrs. Clarkson could speak.

"Nonsense," the older woman interjected. "You can have the afternoon to help Miss Danby. What time should she expect you?"

Catherine felt stunned as the entire matter was taken out of her hands. Winifred suggested coming in the carriage around one-thirty, and Mrs. Clarkson agreed. It wasn't until mother and daughter had exited the establishment that Catherine sought out Mrs. Clarkson for an answer.

"I don't understand," she said, finding the older woman in the finishing room. She was showing Martha some pieces of lace they needed for a particular gown. "We have a great deal of work to complete before Christmas. How is it that you would have me go off with Miss Danby?"

Mrs. Clarkson looked up rather surprised. "It's really quite simple. I've been consulted and paid quite well to allow you to accompany Miss Danby whenever possible. The Danbys feel she is quite shy and would benefit greatly from your company. I thought surely they had spoken to you about it first."

"No one mentioned anything to me," Catherine said, feeling even more confused.

Martha went about her business as Mrs. Clarkson came to Catherine. "You needn't look so upset. This will be a wonderful time for you. Mr. Danby said that—"

"Mr. Danby? You mean Carter Danby?" Catherine asked, knowing that Mrs. Danby's husband had never graced their doorstep.

"Yes. Miss Danby's brother. He approached me on their last visit while you were busy with his sister. He told me of her great shyness and how much she enjoyed your company. He felt you had a calming effect, as well as a genuineness that she felt lacking in her other friends. He said that she was hopefully soon to be engaged and if we would cooperate in allowing you to accompany her on various outings, not only would he pay us to hire additional help to fill in for you, but he was certain her trousseau would be ordered from our house."

"Of all the . . ." Catherine let her words trail off to silence. Carter was doing this to ensure she would have to go with them whenever Winifred made a request. But of course, it would really be Carter's request. He was doing this to learn who she was and why she was so secretive.

"I was certain you wouldn't mind." Mrs. Clarkson looked upset. "Have I done wrong by you? I thought you would enjoy the company—the taste of a better life."

Catherine steadied her nerves and nodded. "It's fine. I was just shocked, that's all."

"Oh good. Since you had your dress designs mostly completed, I didn't think it would be a problem. Should there be additional gowns you need to create, we will simply make sure you are available. Now if you'll excuse me, I must see Selma about supper."

Catherine watched the older woman hurry away. She wanted to throw something against the wall in protest but refrained. She had never known a man such as Carter Danby. His determination to manipulate her life was beyond reason, and when he returned from his trip, she would make certain he knew exactly what she thought of the matter.

CHAPTER 12

Carter and Leander found the Samuelson boardinghouse after only a few days of searching. Apparently the establishment was highly regarded for being clean and free of bed bugs. The meals were also praised as being plentiful and delicious. Carter hoped only that the owners would be willing to talk about Catherine.

Deep in thought, Carter was surprised when Lee leaned forward to punch him playfully on the thigh. "What?" he asked, knowing he'd surely missed some comment or question.

"I said you seem a million miles away, but I suppose it's not quite that far, eh?" Lee had a devilish twinkle in his eyes as he added, "Just the distance from this town to Philadelphia."

"I suppose I have allowed this to completely preoccupy my thoughts." Carter stared out the window.

The carriage stopped, and the driver quickly appeared to open the door. "This is the place. Samuelson's Boardinghouse."

Carter paid the man and asked him to wait. "We shouldn't be long." He and Lee then quickly made their way to the house and knocked loudly. Carter felt a sense of excitement that he couldn't explain. It was almost as if he were a boy awaiting Christmas morning.

"Are you Mrs. Samuelson?" Carter asked when an old woman answered the door to the two-story house.

"I am. If you're looking for a room, we have one left and you'll have to share."

Carter noted she was a plump woman with a rather bulbous nose, but her demeanor seemed quite gentle and kind. He smiled as she opened the door a little wider.

"We are not searching for a room," Carter replied, "but rather had hoped to converse with you about something of great importance."

She frowned. "If you're selling something, I'm not buying."

"Not at all," Carter assured. "My name is Carter Danby, and this is my friend Leander Arlington. We're from Philadelphia and have some interest in a young woman you once housed here with her parents."

He could see the woman was intrigued and hurried to continue. "I promise we won't take up too much time."

"Very well. Come in." She stepped back from the door and motioned. "This is the sitting room."

Carter and Leander hurried inside in case she changed her mind. The small sitting room was clean but sparsely furnished.

A settee with well-worn upholstery stood in front of a small fireplace. The fire looked as though it was dying out.

"Please be seated." Mrs. Samuelson pointed.

Carter took a straight-backed chair, while Leander sat on a small wooden bench by the fire.

Mrs. Samuelson positioned herself in a rocker. "Now, who is this young woman you speak of?"

"It would have been back about five years ago," Leander began. "The older couple were called Shay. Dugan and Selma Shay. They were here with their daughter, Catherine. They're from England."

"Oh yes. I remember them well. My husband, God rest his soul, took 'em in. His cousin brought them to America." She pursed her lips as if having said too much, then relaxed. "I weren't to say anything about it back then, but I can't imagine that it would be a problem now."

"Surely not," Carter replied with a smile that he hoped charmed away the woman's fears.

"What do you want to know this for?" the old woman asked, eyeing him to scrutinize his character.

"To tell you the truth, I'm rather interested in courting Miss Shay. I had to be in New York and knew they had come here. I wanted to learn of their time here and where they'd come from."

"Well, my husband's cousin would have to tell you that. He brought them here from England. I got the idea that there was some sort of death or loss in their lives. The young lady cried a great deal. Never knew why. I do know, however, she ain't their daughter. She had a different last name. New . . . Newton . . .

Newbaum. No . . . I believe it was Newbury, and I think she was from Bath in England."

In that instant it all came back to Carter. He remembered the night of the party at the Newbury home. He had been quite intrigued with the beautiful young hostess, scarcely more than a girl.

"That's right," Carter said. "Her father was Nelson Newbury."

Leander looked at him oddly. "You knew him?"

"I had completely forgotten where we had met. I knew I had made Catherine's acquaintance on another occasion. I teased her about how she never smiles, yet somehow I remembered her smile. That is why. We met at a party and she was quite happy."

"She weren't happy here. She must have lost that father of hers. You could talk to my husband's relation. Just so happens he's here. Heads back to Bristol in three days. He could no doubt tell you more."

"Is he here at the house just now?" Carter asked.

"No, but I expect him back shortly. He went to take care of some business matter. Told me he would be back by ten."

Carter looked at his watch. That was only another half hour. "Could we wait here for him?"

Mrs. Samuelson shrugged and got to her feet. "It's no trouble to me. I have to be about my work. You can wait right here."

The men got to their feet. Carter extended his hand. "Thank you so much."

She ignored the gesture. "So the Shays and Miss Catherine are doing well for themselves in Philadelphia?"

Carter smiled and nodded. "Very well. They were in good health last I saw them."

"I hope Miss Catherine is happier now. Sometimes it just takes time to heal the hurt."

Carter nodded. "She still doesn't smile, but I hope to change that." He gave the older woman a wink. "Sometimes it takes more than time to heal a loss. Sometimes it takes something to replace the pain."

She looked at Carter and laughed. "I'm sure a handsome young laddie like yourself could do the job."

Once she'd gone, Carter turned back to Leander. "I can't believe this. How stupid of me not to remember where I'd met her. It's all so clear now. I remember it well. I had even asked my friend, the one who'd taken me to the party, for more information about her family."

"Do you suppose she remembers you as well?"

Carter had started to pace but immediately stopped. "I hadn't considered it. She acts quite uncomfortable around me, so perhaps that is the answer. I haven't changed much in my appearance. When I saw her last, she was a budding young woman but still very girlish in her appearance. Not at all the woman in full that we see now."

"But if she knows who you are, that means she's trying to keep from renewing that acquaintance. Why would she do that?"

"I'm sure it has something to do with her being in America," Carter replied. "And Mrs. Samuelson said something about how she must have lost her father."

"Then we don't need to speak to the cousin. Perhaps we should just return to Philadelphia and you can confront her," Leander offered.

"No, if she does chance to remember me, then there is a reason for her silence. I still can't figure out why she's here, and it's obvious Catherine will not willingly tell me. I recall upon meeting her that we had a conversation about visiting America. Catherine assured me she had no interest in it whatsoever. No, something happened, and given the dates she first arrived here, it would have had to have happened very soon after that party."

At five after ten, Harold Marlowe was introduced to them. The gruff old sea captain eyed them suspiciously, especially after Mrs. Samuelson mentioned why they'd come.

"I can't tell you anything you don't already know." The man waited for Mrs. Samuelson to leave before adding, "We have no common business, I assure you."

Carter could see the man felt protective of Catherine and the Shays. "I know you care about them. I care too. I have come to think quite highly of Catherine and do not wish to cause her harm or pain. Please just sit and hear me out."

Marlowe looked from him to Leander and back. "Very well, but I'm not promising to talk."

"I come from a family of some means in Philadelphia," Carter continued. "Mr. Arlington is a lawyer of great repute and his father is a judge. I met the Newburys while in Bath in late 1850. I was in England—Bath, in particular—studying architecture. While there, a good friend invited me to join him for a party at the Newbury house."

He tried to think of every detail that might put the man at ease and further his attempt to get information. "I met Catherine—Miss Newbury—at the party. We danced and talked. I found her quite charming, albeit very young."

Marlowe nodded. "She's a beauty with a heart of gold."

Carter smiled. "That she is. I left after a couple of days and never had the opportunity to go back and see her again. Then a few weeks ago, I met her by chance. She is designing women's clothing in Philadelphia. Her gowns are quite in demand and she has made a name for herself."

"I knew she would not be one to take life sitting down," Marlowe interjected. He pulled out a pipe and leaned over to tap out the old contents into the embers. Reaching into his pocket, he took out a pouch and began to pack the bowl with tobacco.

"Miss Newbury is going by the name Miss Shay. She poses as the daughter of Selma and Dugan Shay. I know there has to be a reason for this. She adored her father and England. I know she had no interest in coming to America because she told me so. I suppose now I would like to know why she is here and what became of her father."

Marlowe lit the pipe and ceremoniously puffed on it several times before sitting back and crossing his legs. "Before I speak on this, I would like to know why this is of such great importance to you."

Carter nodded. "I can understand that perfectly well. You helped her get away to America and kept her secret all these years. I'm certain that you wish only to protect her. I wish the same, although my motives might be slightly different." He took a breath and continued before he lost his nerve. "You see, I'm losing my heart to Miss Newbury. I would like to help her in whatever way would set her free from the past and allow her to marry me."

Carter saw Leander's startled expression and offered his friend a shrug and a smile. "I didn't know the depth of my feelings myself—at least, not for certain." He gave a sigh. "I think I'm completely done in by her."

Captain Marlowe laughed, and it was the first time Carter felt the man drop his guard. "She's easy on the eyes, but let me warn you, she has a terrible temper if crossed. I've seen her anger in regard to what happened to her father."

"Will you tell me?" Carter asked.

Marlowe nodded. "I can see that you mean well by her. She'll need a strong young man such as yourself to help her let go of the past and its miseries. The sorry truth of it is, her father is in prison. He'll probably die there."

Carter shook his head. "I don't understand. Newbury's in prison? But why?"

"My good friend took a business partner who was less than worthy of his trust. Finley Baker is the man's name. Behind Newbury's back Baker dealt in the slave trade as well as other illegal goods. It was found out when he docked in Bristol the night of the party you mentioned. The authorities were there to meet him to take him to jail, but he would have none of it. He shot and killed the two men."

Carter could see where all of this was headed. "And they blamed Newbury."

"Well, at least for the slaving. They knew he'd not killed the men at the docks, but that was of little matter. They wanted to set an example of him and sent him to prison for the rest of his life."

"What happened to Baker?" Leander questioned.

"He escaped. He came to Newbury that night after the party was over. He demanded money and at least bothered to warn my friend of what had happened. Newbury knew he couldn't run away from such matters, but he had no desire for Catherine to see him ruined. He had his most trusted servants take her and leave as the sun came up. They barely escaped before the officials took Newbury in hand."

He drew on the pipe. "I'll never forget having them show up on my doorstep. Catherine was terrified of what might happen to her father. She didn't want to leave England, but Selma and Dugan made it clear that for her father's sake she had to go. It would have hurt him deeply to watch her be dragged into it all. As it was, I attended the trial and it was ugly. There was no one there whose testimony could help. I spoke of Newbury's good name and reputation, but it was only suggested that he had woven a web of deceit that fooled us all. I knew better but couldn't convince anyone otherwise. His estate and business holdings were confiscated and stripped away. But none of that hurt him as much as the things they said about Catherine."

"What could they possibly say against her?" Carter asked, his anger evident.

Marlowe shook his head. "They suggested she had gone off with Finley Baker as his lover and partner in crime."

"Outrageous. She was seventeen," Carter said, getting to his feet. "No wonder she never smiles. She has nothing to smile about." He paced to the small window and tried to regain control of his emotions. It pained him more than he wanted to admit to imagine all Catherine had faced: the loss of her father, her way of life . . . the shame and stigma of having a father in prison, and for slave trading, no less. Her fierce protectiveness of her past began to make sense.

"What happened to her father?" Leander asked.

"They sent him to prison. First one and then another. He's not allowed any visitors, and last I heard his health was not good."

"I have friends in England," Carter began as he came back to his chair.

"Apparently so did Finley Baker. Some of us are convinced that money exchanged hands to keep him out of trouble. He escaped to France and has been seen as far away as Rome. Some of us, friends of Newbury, went together to fund someone to hunt him down. We thought to force the truth from him."

Carter took his seat. "But you've had no luck?"

Marlowe shook his head. "Every time we get close he seems to sense it and moves on."

"Perhaps the efforts should focus more on getting Newbury out of prison. Surely there are those who would listen to reason. As I said, I know people in high places. Leander, we must get word at once to Lord Carston, as well as the duke of Mayfield."

"You know His Grace?" Marlowe asked with raised brows.

"I do. He is a good friend of my uncle. He will help us, I'm certain."

Marlowe smiled. "Perhaps we will at last see justice done."

"You may be needed to assist in this matter. Perhaps carry the letters with you to England and see to their delivery. Mrs. Samuelson said that you were to return soon."

"Yes, I leave in three days. I will help in any way I can, but I hardly have the funds to make a trip to see the duke of Mayfield."

"I will give you the money myself," Carter declared. "You can go to my uncle and he can in turn take you to the duke. Nothing must hinder this, and nothing must be said to Miss Newbury. She feels enough pain. We must not give her false hope. When her father is free to come to her, then we can let her know the truth."

"I never share news with her," Marlowe admitted. "We thought it best that there be no correspondence between us. I've long wondered what had happened but only knew of little details through Mrs. Shay's sister back in England. I will keep your secret and help you."

Carter nodded and felt a sense of relief and purpose. He could help—he was certain of this. It would be his gift to Catherine . . . and maybe in turn it would free her heart from worry and allow her to fall in love with him.

CHAPTER 13

*C*atherine found herself relieved when Winifred showed up for their outing on the morning of November the sixth. Outside, the air had turned quite cold and there was a threat of snow. Inside, the sewing house was utter pandemonium. The girls were sillier than usual due to celebrating Mrs. Clarkson's birthday, and no one wanted to focus on work.

"I hope I'm not taking you away from anything too important," Winifred announced as Catherine settled into the carriage.

"No, not at all," Catherine said, noting that Carter was not there. She found herself rather disappointed in his absence. "I see your brother has decided to forgo this trip." She hoped her tone sounded disinterested.

"He hasn't yet returned from New York. I'm simply pining away for the both of them."

"Both?"

Winifred nodded. "Leander went with him. I suppose it was some kind of legal business, but I've been deprived of both of them now for far too long."

Catherine shrugged and tried to put it behind her. "I'm certain it must have been important or Mr. Arlington would never have left your side."

"Oh, Catherine, do you really think he might be interested in me?"

The longing in the younger woman's voice reminded Catherine of her own pining heart. "He seemed very interested when I saw him in your company."

"And what of you? Do you miss Carter's company? Is he not the most attentive and kindest of men?"

Catherine startled at the question. "He's very nice," she allowed. "But I hardly know him well enough to miss him."

"Would you like to know him better?" Winifred asked, her expression innocent.

The carriage hit a hole, causing Catherine to jerk hard to the right. She hit her head against the carriage frame and winced. She righted herself, making more of the impact than needed in hopes that Winifred would change the topic of conversation.

"Are you all right?" Winifred leaned forward, letting her lap blanket slide to the floor.

"I think so. I should have been better prepared."

"Father says that the city would do well to spend more money on the streets than worry about improving the dock areas. He says he pays a fortune in taxes and never benefits from a single cent." She smiled and eased back against the thickly cushioned leather. "Of course, my father says a great many things."

Catherine smiled. "Fathers can be that way."

"My father is difficult," Winifred admitted. "He married my mother only for her money and never lets her forget it."

"How sad."

Winifred nodded. "It's made Mother a miserable and hopeless person."

"A life without hope is difficult to bear," Catherine admitted. She knew firsthand how that felt. How hard it was to wait for news from England, only to feel more sorrow upon the arrival. There had been no word of her father in so long, she had begun to fear that perhaps he had died.

"Catherine, I hope you don't mind accompanying me again. Your advice to me on our last shopping trip was so helpful. I know you were paid to join me, and for that I'm sorry. I didn't know that Carter would arrange such a thing."

"Your brother has a way of arranging things whether people like it or not, but I have to admit sharing company with you is a very pleasurable thing. I do worry, however, that you are not spending time with friends of your own social background."

"May I be perfectly candid?" Winifred asked.

Catherine saw nothing but sincerity in her expression. "But of course."

"I am not like them. I care very little for trinkets and finery. I suppose because I've always had those things, they mean less. But when I consider living without them, I know I could be quite happy. Carter and Leander are the two most important people to me in all of the world. But you, Catherine . . . you are rapidly becoming just as precious to me."

Catherine felt the impact of Winifred's words deep within her. She longed to embrace the intimacy and friendship offered, for the toll of shielding herself from others had made her weary. Even Selma had commented about how Catherine never smiled anymore. This, on the heels of Carter's observation, only served to make Catherine realize how dull she had grown.

"You are very kind to say so," Catherine replied.

"The women I have known in my life—the friends and even my mother—well, they are all far too interested in their latest gown or silver setting. My mother has vast books with drawings of her china and silver. She knows it better than she knows me." Winifred bit her lip for a moment and when she looked again at Catherine, there were tears in her eyes.

"She's not bad, and neither are my friends, but they've given their hearts over to pretense. And when that pretense fails them, they become backstabbing and vicious toward one another. Carter likens it to a pack of hungry wolves who turn on each other when other nourishment is gone."

Catherine nodded. "I have known people like that myself."

"Then you must understand why your friendship is so important. I find no pretense in you."

Catherine shuddered. There was nothing but pretense in her life. She felt so wrong in keeping her identity from Winifred that she considered telling her the entire story. Instead, she finally settled on yet another compromise. "Winifred, please do not put me on a pedestal. I have pretense aplenty in my life. One day I hope things will right themselves, and I will be able to share it with you."

Winifred leaned forward and took hold of Catherine's hands. "I would never betray you. I hope you will feel I am worthy of your trust."

The carriage slowed to a stop, and Joseph was soon opening the door, much to Catherine's relief. Winifred dropped her hold and allowed Joseph to help her from the carriage. She waited without moving a step while Catherine did the same.

They did not revisit the conversation, even when they stopped for tea and cakes. Catherine enjoyed the day more than any she could remember since coming to America. Once she allowed herself the liberty of pleasure, she realized just how serious and hard she had grown.

But how can I be happy when I know Father is so miserable and mistreated? What a betrayal of his love for me, should I forget what he has sacrificed on my behalf. No, I must keep my mind on the goal at hand. I must help set Father free and allow no distraction to take me from his cause.

When they were once again parked in front of Mrs. Clarkson's, Winifred took hold of Catherine's hands. "I very much enjoyed our day. I hope you did as well."

"I truly did," Catherine admitted.

"I'm glad. Now, would you do me one more favor? Mother has asked that I remain at home on the eighth. I know we were to have a fitting for my gown, but I'm wondering if you would come to the house for me."

Catherine thought for a moment. With Carter in New York, she wasn't overly worried about running into him. Yet there was a part of her that almost hoped he would have returned by that time.

"I believe I can arrange that."

"Wonderful. I'll send the carriage."

"I would be happy to walk," Catherine said, knowing that there could very well be a foot of snow by that time.

"No. Please let me send Joseph. That way we'll have more time to visit." She smiled and it lit up her entire face.

Catherine tried to remember ever being as happy and carefree as Winifred Danby. There had been a time, she knew full well, but now it felt like it had been a million years ago.

Long into the night Catherine listened to the wind outside. The moans and creaks of the house seemed almost comforting. How could five years have escaped her already? England seemed so far away, so distant in her memories. There had been a time when Catherine knew she would never have left it, but now . . . well, now it seemed foreign, even hostile.

"Oh, Father, how could they have done this to you—to us? I don't understand why you should suffer and spend your days in prison. You were so honored and respected, yet no one came to your call. Not even God."

She thought of that for several moments and hugged her pillow close. How very alone the idea left her. To imagine that even God had looked the other way—had deserted them in their darkest hour of need.

❦

"I'm so happy to have you here," Winifred announced as the butler took Catherine's coat two days later. "When I awoke to the snow, I feared you might not come."

"There isn't that much to contend with." Catherine picked up a large box. "I have your gown. Will your mother want to see it as well?"

Winifred led Catherine into the house. "My mother is busy worrying Cook about plans for the party." She giggled and cast a glance down the hall. "Mother worries Cook on a regular basis, whether there is a party to contend with or nothing but a simple meal to plan. Come, I want to see what you've done."

Catherine allowed Winifred to lead her to a door down the hall. She was rather surprised when they entered a room lined in dark wood bookshelves.

"This is my brother's study. Since he's still gone, I thought we might use it for a fitting room. It has very good light, at least the best we can have this time of year."

Thinking of Carter had nearly driven Catherine mad in the past few days. No matter what she did or where she turned, there were reminders of him. Now, standing here in his domain, she could imagine him behind the desk, smiling at her.

"Will this work sufficiently?" Winifred asked.

Catherine forced her thoughts back to the deed at hand. "Yes. It's perfectly fine."

Winifred locked the door so that they wouldn't be disturbed. "I am so excited. I know the party is still weeks away, but I've only seen the dress in pieces until today."

"I hope you'll be pleased. I think it will be perfect for you," Catherine said as she placed the box atop Carter's desk. She opened it and pulled the gown from inside. "What do you think?"

Winifred grasped the pink fabric and gently trailed her fingers along the cording at the waist. "It's so beautiful. Oh, Catherine, I can hardly believe this is mine."

"I'm glad you like it. I'm quite pleased with the way Beatrix worked the sleeves. She's very talented and yet only ten and four."

"I could never sew half so well. My nurse was appalled at my poor sewing."

"It was my governess who taught me to sew. She died in the same influenza epidemic that took my mother's life," Catherine said. Then realizing what she'd revealed, she stood motionless, waiting.

Winifred recognized the slip as well. "So Mrs. Shay isn't your mother, is she?"

Catherine shook her head. "No. They have adopted me, in a sense."

"And you grew up in a fine house just like this, didn't you?" Winifred pressed.

"Yes. I did. My father owned ships and did quite well for himself. I grew up with every beautiful thing I could want."

"Come and sit with me. We can try the gown on in a moment," Winifred said, pulling at Catherine's arm.

Carefully placing the gown across a chair, Catherine allowed Winifred to lead her to a chair. They sat for a moment before Winifred continued. "I knew there was something about you from the start. You know what it is like to be deceived by those around you."

Catherine nodded. "You must understand something, Winifred. Nothing I've told you must ever be told to anyone else. My father's very life might be in danger if you share this information."

"I swear to you I will not betray our friendship. Others might, but I will not," she said in earnest. "But can you not talk of it at least to me? Is there no one?"

"I talk with the Shays; they are like parents to me and have been with me since I came to America."

"And your father?"

"My father was wrongly accused of transporting slaves. You know what that means in this day and age; people on both sides of the ocean are livid with the very idea that slavery still exists. Shipping and trading in slaves has been outlawed in England for a very long time. I think they meant to make an example of him."

"But how did he come to be accused?"

"His partner, the son of a dear friend that my father took pity on, betrayed him. To make extra money for his own pockets, he dealt in slaves. When he was found out, he went on the run and took much of my father's money with him."

"How awful. Oh, Catherine, I am sorry. What did they do to your father? Is he also on the run?"

"No. They imprisoned him for the rest of his life. I am trying to do what I can to earn money in order to buy him decent legal counsel, as well as someone to hunt down Finley Baker, the man responsible for all of this." Catherine felt such a tremendous relief just in telling the tale to someone. The words poured out of her like an unstoppable flood going over a broken dam.

"I had to take the Shays' name in order to conceal my identity. We feared—even here in America—that finding jobs and even housing would be difficult if others knew that my father was a convicted criminal. There's also been worry that Finley Baker means to do me harm. We've vowed to tell no one of this. At least, I had until now."

"I can see why you keep the story quiet. Some people might try to take advantage of you, while others would surely shun you. I will do neither. I will instead pray for you. I know you are a God-fearing woman. Carter always claims there is great power in prayer. Do you believe that?"

Catherine shook her head. "I don't know. I used to . . . Now I just don't know what to think. I go to church week after week, I read my Bible, and I pray until my knees ache. But my father is still in prison, and I am still . . ." Her words faded. She couldn't bring herself to say the words.

"Alone?" Winifred asked softly.

Lifting her eyes, Catherine shook her head. "Afraid."

Winifred dropped to the floor and knelt beside Catherine. Taking her hand, Winifred held it tight. "Don't be afraid. I know what that feels like, and it is so crippling. You mustn't let the fear overcome you. God has not left you as an orphan or friendless in this time of need. I want to help you in any way I can." Her eyes filled with tears, and the sincerity of her emotion touched Catherine, whose own eyes grew damp as Winifred continued.

"I pledge to you my friendship and help. I will endeavor to pray for you and your father. Catherine, don't lose hope. God has not forgotten you."

After five years of hearing various ministers preach powerful sermons from high pulpits, it was the words of this young woman that gave Catherine strength. She found herself clutching Winifred's hands in gratitude.

"Thank you. You cannot possibly know what you have done for me. I feel ... well ... somehow renewed. Your words have restored me. I do not doubt that God hears me, but I do not understand why He waits so long to act. I do not doubt He cares, but I worry that His way of caring is much different from that which I so desperately need."

"I do understand," Winifred said, nodding. "I have watched my parents live in this loveless marriage and hate each other. My father keeps a mistress that we all try to pretend doesn't exist. We are just four individuals existing in the same house ... not really a family at all."

"What about Carter? I know he loves you dearly."

Winifred smiled. "Yes. He does love me. He has always made life bearable. But I fear he will not be here much longer."

Catherine felt her chest tighten. "But why? Surely he would not desert you."

"He told me it was time for him to set up for himself. When I asked him if he would remain in Philadelphia, he could not say. His buildings are so very important to him, and I suppose he shall go wherever his work is most appreciated."

The thought of Carter's leaving sent a wave of regret through Catherine's heart. Regret for what might have been had she been free to accept his attention. Regret for the deception that she had to maintain to keep him at arm's length.

Catherine forced the thoughts from her head. "I really should get back to work. We haven't even fit the gown, and Mrs. Clarkson will expect me back soon."

Winifred nodded. "One more thing. Carter once told me that we shouldn't fear putting the past behind us. He said that God is about doing new things—creating beauty out of the ashes of despair and defeat. God can and will do that for you, Catherine. I feel confident of it. I want you to feel confident of it too."

Winifred's words echoed in her head long after Catherine had returned to Mrs. Clarkson's. She remembered Bible verses she'd marked in the forty-third chapter of Isaiah and went to look at them once again.

Taking up her father's Bible she read, *Remember ye not the former things, neither consider the things of old. Behold, I will do a new thing; now it shall spring forth; shall ye not know it? I will even make a way in the wilderness, and rivers in the desert.* She gave a sigh and closed the Bible, holding it close.

"I want to believe in a new thing, Lord. I want that more than anything. I want to forget the old things—the bad and ugly things that have sent me here. Please let me see your hand in all of this. Let me see the path through this wilderness."

A knock sounded at her bedroom door, and Catherine immediately recognized it as Mrs. Clarkson and went to open the door.

"I saw the light and had hoped to talk to you before you retired for the evening," Mrs. Clarkson stated. She held some papers in her hand and motioned to the small table where Catherine often sat to sew in private. "May I show you something?"

"Of course. Come in." Catherine closed the door behind Mrs. Clarkson as she made her way to the table and spread out the papers.

"I wanted to surprise you with an early Christmas gift." The older woman smiled. "I want to make you a partner."

"Excuse me?" Catherine was sure she couldn't have heard correctly.

"You have more than tripled my business in the last two years with your designs. You have brought prosperity upon this house in a way no other seamstress could have done. I am growing older, and although my age will not keep me from work for many years, I want to establish the person I want to take over when I am too elderly to work.

"As you know, I have no family, so I must name an heir from someone I trust. I want that heir to be you. When I am gone, you will know how to continue the business. You are an intelligent young woman who knows her own mind. You will not be easily swayed to bad choices."

Catherine went to the table and skimmed the papers. Mrs. Clarkson had gone to a lawyer to have them drawn up, and the contents were quite explicit. It wasn't until Catherine's gaze caught the words *Catherine Shay* that she stopped and shook her head.

"This is all too much for me. I'm sorry. Let us discuss it another time."

Without warning, Catherine fled from the room. She knew she must have appeared to be quite the ungrateful ninny to Mrs. Clarkson, but she couldn't remain there to explain.

Pounding on Selma and Dugan's door, Catherine practically fell into Selma's arms when the woman opened it to see what was wrong. Tears poured down Catherine's face, dampening Selma's robe.

"What is it, child? What's wrong?"

Catherine pulled away. "Everything. Everything is wrong. I cannot bear this charade any longer. Mrs. Clarkson trusts me. She trusts me so much she is ready to leave me all of her worldly goods in a will. She trusts me so much she drew up papers to have me made a partner in this establishment. It is a trust I do not deserve, as we both know."

"Calm yourself, Catherine." Selma drew her to the fire and motioned her to sit. "There is no problem too big for God to handle. If trust is to be mentioned, let us think of Him. There our trust is secure."

"I cannot go on deceiving this good woman. I must find a way to explain."

"Perhaps," Dugan said, coming from the bedroom, "it is time to come clean on our circumstances."

"You mean tell Mrs. Clarkson everything?" Catherine asked.

Selma exchanged a look with her husband as he nodded. "Perhaps it is time to do just that."

CHAPTER 14

*S*o what do you think?" Leander asked, showing Carter a delicate bracelet of gold and coral.

"It's lovely," Carter replied, only half interested. But then he realized Leander had purchased this for his sister. "You're going to give this to Winifred?"

"I thought I would. Look, my time in New York and your declaration of feelings for Catherine have caused me to realize I care very deeply for Winifred. I can honestly say that I love her and want to spend the rest of my life with her. I'm just sorry it took me so long to see."

Carter grinned. "Hurrah! Then soon you shall be my brother." He clasped Leander's shoulder and smiled. "I couldn't be happier."

"Well, we might find your father of a different mind." Leander closed the box containing the bracelet.

"I think Father can be managed well enough. Come to dinner. I will praise you and even mention that you've recently inherited a fortune from your grandfather."

"It is but a small inheritance," Leander countered.

"An inheritance nevertheless," Carter said, grinning. "We needn't tell him the amount. That would hardly be expected, and my father, although ill-mannered, would never ask."

Leander shook his head. "Would that he might be more considerate of his daughter's happiness."

"Or my mother's," Carter countered. "My father only concerns himself with his own happiness. My brother has embraced that teaching in full."

"Then it is up to you to break the mold, and I believe you've already shown yourself worthy of respect."

"Not my father's respect, I'm afraid. But I shall endeavor to put that aside. I know I am doing what I feel is right. Come to supper and we shall see this matter put in order."

❧

Carter watched his father assess Leander from across the table. He seemed preoccupied, but Carter thought that to his friend's advantage. After his father downed his third glass of wine, he leaned back in his chair.

"With the women busy elsewhere, we might as well discuss your proposal to court my daughter. I know your father's reputation and have heard you are doing quite well," Elger Danby began.

"My practice has tripled in less than a year," Leander said, holding Danby's gaze. "I believe it will continue to build."

"Your family has a long history in this town."

"Yes, sir," Leander agreed. "My mother's people settled here in the early 1700s."

"And I'm told you recently received an inheritance from your mother's late father."

Carter shook his head and tossed his napkin on the table, hoping to avert more specific inquiries. "Father, it hardly seems appropriate to discuss such matters."

"This man wishes to court and possibly marry your sister. I have to be certain that he will be able to properly care for her."

Leander continued to fix his gaze on Elger Danby. "I don't mind the questioning. I have received an inheritance from my grandfather."

Danby's questioning was interrupted when Carter's brother made a surprise appearance. "There are problems we need to discuss," Robin said, completely unmindful of the company his father shared.

"Good evening to you too, Robin," Carter said rather sarcastically.

Robin looked at him for a moment, then noted Leander. "I apologize, but this matter is of the utmost concern."

Their father got to his feet. "Mr. Arlington, you have my permission to pursue Winifred. It would serve this family well to have a knowledgeable lawyer in our numbers."

Robin frowned and looked at Leander. Carter thought for a moment he might protest, but he said nothing. Carter breathed a sigh of relief.

"If you'll excuse me now, I'll attend to this matter in my private quarters." Elger Danby left Carter and Lee and immediately began conversing with Robin as they made their way upstairs.

"What a relief," Carter said, pushing back from the table. "Perhaps it's the only time I've been truly happy to see Robin impose himself in such a manner."

Lee nodded and pulled a watch from his pocket. "I should be going. After all, I got what I came for." He smiled and Carter clapped him on the back.

"You'll need to let Winifred know. She had no idea that you meant to talk to Father about this tonight, did she?"

"No. I didn't wish to get her hopes up."

"Probably a wise decision. But now that you've accomplished the matter, she'll be delighted."

Lee allowed Wilson to help him with his coat. "Why don't we have dinner at my house on Sunday. We can invite both Winifred and Catherine. If your sister asks Catherine to come, then we are certain to see her in attendance. I know it would help your cause, as well as mine."

Carter grinned. "I believe I would like that arrangement." He reached out and touched Leander's shoulder. "I pray this works to the benefit of us all. I can think of nothing I would like more than having my sister happily settled with you."

"And Catherine happily settled with you?" Leander said with a smile.

"I don't suppose that would cause me any distress," he laughed, giving Lee a firm pat on the back. "We'll see you Sunday."

Catherine found herself in the Arlington parlor, surrounded by people she didn't really know. The room was small but charming. Done up in hues of red and brown, it gave a warm feeling of comfort and family.

Mrs. Arlington was kind and welcoming, not caring in the least that Catherine was a seamstress. She had commented about hearing Carter and Catherine's names so often mentioned among her friends that she was certain there must be some sort of conspiracy to see them linked. She also mentioned in a hushed tone her pleasure in seeing her son take an intimate interest in Winifred.

Catherine turned and watched Leander take Winifred's hand in his own and smile. The way he watched her and attended to her every need left Catherine little doubt as to his intentions.

"I see you watching my sister and Lee," Carter whispered against her ear.

Catherine startled. Glancing around to see who else might have overheard, she realized that Mr. and Mrs. Arlington had disappeared, leaving only the couples.

"I hope he is acting honorably," she said, trying to steady her voice.

"You will be happy to know, he is in fact asking to properly court her. My father has given his approval."

Catherine smiled at this news and Carter gasped, causing her to clutch her hand to her throat. "What?" She knew she sounded frightened but couldn't help it. Her nerves were raw.

Carter took hold of her hand and gave it a gentle pat. "I apologize. You simply surprised me with that smile. It's the first I've seen from you here in Philadelphia."

She tried to compose herself, but Carter's touch was overwhelming. Her mind could only think of the way his thumb stroked the back of her hand. She felt her breath quicken and tried to pull away.

"Stay," he whispered. "Please. I want to know you better."

Catherine refused to meet his eyes. She knew she'd be lost if she gazed into those dark pools. She'd never felt like this before. What kind of power did this man have over her?

"You must know that I care about you. I would very much like to show you the same attention that Leander is showing Winifred. Catherine, I'd like to court you."

She couldn't help her reaction. Her head snapped up to meet his gaze. "I beg your pardon?"

He laughed. "Don't act so surprised. I've told you before that I intended to know you better—to make you smile."

"Supper is ready to be served," an older blond-haired woman announced.

"Thank you, Marta," Leander said, getting to his feet. He assisted Winifred, and Catherine couldn't help but notice how she was happy to take his arm.

Before she could react, Carter had tucked her arm in his. "Shall we?"

Catherine allowed him to lead her from the room. *Much like a lamb going to slaughter,* she thought. Yet there was a part of her that felt a great sense of pleasure in his touch and attention. No man had spoken of love to her in over five years. She had resigned herself to be a spinster, yet here was Carter Danby suggesting otherwise.

But, of course, if he knew my father was a convicted criminal, he wouldn't be so quick to offer courtship.

Dinner was a festive affair. Catherine was surprised at the lack of formality against the elegant setting. Mrs. Arlington seemed a jolly woman who adored her husband and son. She spoke fondly of two other sons and a daughter.

"Mother believes we can do no wrong," Leander said, laughing.

Catherine had busied herself by cutting a piece of roast on her plate, suddenly yearning to return home to the safety of her room.

"You attack that beef as if you were a surgeon excising a growth," Carter teased in a barely audible voice.

Catherine had been less than comfortable ever since Mrs. Arlington had positioned them side by side at the very small table. She thought to comment but instead put her silver aside and reached for her glass.

"My dear, I am quite impressed with all that you told me about your gown designs. They are quite impressive," Mrs. Arlington declared.

Catherine looked to her left, where the woman was seated. "You are very kind to say so. I like to believe the talent is something God has given to me."

"Did your mother teach you to sew?"

Catherine completely forgot herself. "No. My governess did."

"And is she working with you now?"

"No. She died in an influenza epidemic."

"Oh, my dear. I am sorry. Did you lose any family members?"

Catherine looked at Carter, and he offered her a look that suggested assurance, but for what purpose Catherine could not figure.

She turned quickly back to Mrs. Arlington and in doing so, knocked over her glass. "I am so sorry," Catherine said, jumping to her feet. "Please forgive me."

"Nonsense. Take your seat, my dear," Mr. Arlington said, waving her down. A servant quickly appeared at her side and dabbed at the wet tablecloth.

"No harm done, my dear," Leander's mother added. "We have spills all of the time."

"I wish my mother would be so calm amid accidents," Winifred said with a sympathetic glance at Catherine. "She worries overly much about every little thing." She put her hand to her mouth and shook her head. "I suppose I should not speak out in such a way, for I love her dearly."

"Of course you do," Mrs. Arlington said, giving Winifred's arm a squeeze. "Goodness, but we all have our peculiarities. Now, where were we?"

"I believe I know," Carter said.

His comment put a sense of dread and fear in Catherine's heart. She wondered how difficult it would be to get up and run from the room. Instead she found herself rather stunned when Carter continued.

"Leander, I believe, was about to share some important news." Catherine looked at Carter. He smiled at her and then looked to Leander. "Tell us all about it, Lee."

"I am quite happy to announce that I have asked Miss Danby to allow me to court her. And Miss Danby has agreed."

"Oh my!" Mrs. Arlington gave a squeal of delight. "I can scarce believe it. Oh, this is a happy day."

The conversation went on and on with congratulations and discussions of anticipated outings and gatherings. Catherine knew that Carter had purposefully redirected the conversation on her behalf. The look on his face concerned her deeply, however. He looked as if he knew—as if he remembered where they had met and who she was.

After dinner Catherine allowed Carter to help her with her coat and escort her to the carriage. "Have you given thought about what I said?" Carter asked as he assisted her.

"I . . . I'm not sure what you're talking about," Catherine replied. She shivered against the cold, immediately drawing Carter's attention.

Without warning, Carter crossed from his side of the carriage to hers and pulled a blanket over their laps. It was completely inappropriate, but Catherine found herself unable to speak.

"I was talking about us. About your allowing me to court you."

In that moment, Catherine could honestly say that, save rescuing her father from prison, she had never desired anything more. Carter Danby took her breath away. He was intelligent, kind, and very dashing. Any woman would be blessed to have him for a husband. But the reality of the moment was that she could not confide her secrets to him. Even if he remembered who she was, he didn't know the full story, and she could not go into such a serious relationship without being free to tell the truth.

"I cannot," she finally said. "I'm sorry."

"Why can't you?" He refused to give up.

"I have my work. I have people who are counting on me," she said, knowing it to be true in part. "I have no time for frivolities. I wouldn't even have accompanied your sister had you not paid Mrs. Clarkson."

"So you know about that," he said, sounding rather chagrined.

"I do. It was rather underhanded of you, I must say."

He grinned and leaned very close, his warm breath touching her cheek. "I wonder how much I'd have to pay Mrs. Clarkson to get her to let you court me."

Just then Leander and Winifred arrived at the carriage. Catherine said nothing about Carter's comment, but she couldn't deny she was intrigued. A part of her wished he'd forget she ever existed. Another part hoped he'd go talk to Mrs. Clarkson.

CHAPTER 15

Catherine, I need to be talkin' to ya," Beatrix said in a grave voice. She had come to Catherine's private quarters and looked quite upset.

"What's wrong? Is your family all right?"

"They're fine. 'Tis yourself I'm worried about."

Catherine pulled the girl into the room and closed the door. "Come sit by the fire and tell me what's wrong."

"I overheard Lydia tell Felicia something. She said ya were hidin' the truth, and Felicia said it wouldn't be matterin' much longer. She said ya would soon be gone and she'd be seein' to it."

Catherine frowned. She had no idea what Felicia might or might not know. Right now, however, she knew she needed to appear calm and unmoved in order to put Beatrix at ease.

"Don't worry about it. Felicia has long held me a grudge. She won't be able to harm me. You mustn't worry."

"Are ya sure? I'd hate to be seein' ya hurt."

Catherine nodded. "God is taking care of us, and I know He will watch over me. If you hear anything more, you can tell me, but otherwise, don't be afraid."

"I hope yar right. I don't want to be havin' Felicia for a boss."

"Go on to bed. Everything will work out. You'll see."

Beatrix got up and Catherine followed her to the door. "I love workin' with ya, Catherine. I've learned so much."

"You're a good student and a quick study. It's easy to teach you, and I like working with you as well."

Beatrix looked at her as if wrestling with whether or not to say something else, then decided against it. "Good night to ya, then."

"Good night, Beatrix."

Catherine closed the door and leaned against it. With Dugan and Selma's support, it was clear that now was the right time to entrust Mrs. Clarkson with her secret.

Whispering a prayer for strength, Catherine went downstairs in search of her employer. She knocked lightly on the door to Mrs. Clarkson's private quarters and was relieved when she immediately opened the door.

"I'm sorry to bother you, but I feel we must talk."

Mrs. Clarkson looked worried. "But of course. Please come and sit with me. What's wrong?"

Waiting until they were seated, Catherine struggled with her words. "I'm afraid I've practiced a great deception with you."

"Surely not," the older woman said with a laugh. "I cannot believe that."

"But you must," Catherine said in earnest. "I hope you will hear me out. I pray we might still be able to work together after you know the truth."

"Very well," Mrs. Clarkson said, sobering. "Tell me."

Catherine launched into the full story, explaining in detail the nightmare that had become her life. She was surprised at one point when Mrs. Clarkson dabbed her eyes with a handkerchief. The fear Catherine had harbored—fear of being dismissed because of her father's supposed guilt involving slave trading—vanished.

"I cannot say what might happen in the future, but I assure you that my only reason for this deception was to protect the people I love."

"My dear, I can well understand your choices. My, but how hard it must have been for you to lose your father in such a manner. What can I do to help?"

"At this point, there is nothing to do. I have been working to save money in hopes of acquiring proper representation for my father—that somehow the truth might come to light."

"Well, you should know that I have a nice-sized bonus planned for you. As soon as all of the gowns are paid in full, I will give you that money."

"Thank you." Catherine felt a great sense of relief in having told Mrs. Clarkson the truth. A fleeting thought caused her to wonder if she could offer Carter Danby the same explanation and receive his understanding as well. After all, she was almost certain he remembered her now. His behavior at the Arlington dinner table suggested as much.

"What prompted you now to give me this information?" Mrs. Clarkson asked.

Surprised by the question, Catherine blurted out the truth. "Apparently Felicia wishes to see me ousted. There have been rumors that she knows something and plans to use it against me. I couldn't be certain that she hadn't overheard my conversations with Selma and Dugan."

"I see. Well, you leave that to me. I shall deal with Felicia should the need arise."

Catherine got to her feet, as did Mrs. Clarkson. "You have been very good to me," she told the older woman. "I have enjoyed working with my hands. I never had reason to believe I should ever have to earn a living for myself, but I have not regretted it. Were it not for my father's pain and suffering, I might have truly enjoyed this time in my life."

"My dear, you have been very good to me as well. You have been faithful to your tasks and more than faithful to bring in new clientele. I hope you might remain here and be my partner, but I understand if circumstances develop to take you away. Please just let me know if there is anything I might do to help."

"I will," Catherine promised.

As the end of November approached, Catherine was relieved to see all of the gowns nearly complete. There were details of trim yet to do, but the bulk work had been finished and the Christmas deadlines were now completely realistic. Next would come the New Year's gowns, but they weren't needed until closer to the end of the month.

Catherine told herself that having her work nearly done was the only reason she had agreed to accompany the Danbys and Mr. Arlington to the opera. She convinced herself that this was nothing more than her reward for accomplishing all she had worked so hard to complete.

She thought differently, however, when Carter handed her into the empty carriage and followed up quickly behind her. He tapped the roof for Joseph to go, even before Catherine was properly settled on the leather seat.

As she slammed back against the cushioning, she looked at Carter with a puzzled expression.

"I was afraid you might bolt when you learned that Leander and Winifred plan to meet us at the opera."

Catherine nodded. "You're right. I would have done just that." She righted herself and smoothed the skirt of her gown.

"See, I knew that would be your thought. I'm finding that I know you better all the time," Carter teased with a wicked grin. "But alas, even this knowledge only serves to make me want to know more."

As much as Catherine would have liked to ignore him, she found herself further drawn to him. The privacy afforded them set her emotions on edge, but the feeling wasn't entirely unpleasant.

"Mr. Danby—"

"Carter," he interjected. "Call me Carter, and I shall call you Catherine. At least until that time I might call you mine."

She trembled at the thought, imagining what it might feel like to be in his arms—to feel his caress against her cheek—his lips upon hers. Carter chuckled, as though reading her mind. Catherine quickly looked away and clutched her coat close.

"You don't need to be afraid of me," Carter said, coming to sit beside her. "I only want to help you—to keep you safe. Catherine, I can't help it. I've lost my heart."

"Then you'd do well to find it quickly." She scooted closer to the window of the carriage.

"Why are you afraid?"

"I'm not afraid," she said, trying hard to sound as though she believed it.

"I can be quite charming if you let me," he said, reaching over to take hold of her hand.

Catherine resisted, but he finally succeeded in prying her hand away from the coat. "I know very well how charming you can be," she replied, her voice barely audible. "But we are worlds apart. I am a seamstress and you are a man of great means."

"Come now, Catherine. We both know that our worlds are not that far apart."

She dared to look him in the face. There was a longing in his eyes that was nearly her undoing. It was almost as if, in an unspoken manner, he was commanding the truth from her.

"I am not suited for you," she said and quickly looked away.

"Yes, you are," he replied.

His low, husky voice caused Catherine to shiver. He made her feel things she'd never felt before. How easy it would be to just give in—to agree to be courted and loved by this man.

"Do you have any idea how attentive I can be?" he asked.

She refused to look at him. Drawing a deep breath, Catherine knew she had to resist him once and for all. "I can well imagine."

"I don't think so." He turned her face toward him.

Catherine closed her eyes tightly and clenched her jaw. She would not give in. She would not let him see the way he affected her. Somewhere deep inside she heard the mocking laughter of her own heart.

"Catherine, open your eyes and look at me." She did as he told her. He smiled. "I won't hurt you. I won't impose myself upon you, and if you tell me that you want nothing of me, I will leave you alone."

She couldn't speak. She looked at him and thought of all the arguments she could offer him, but telling him that she didn't want anything of him would be a lie.

He stroked her cheek with his hand. "See, you want to know me, just as I want to know you."

She swallowed hard. "Wanting doesn't mean having. There are a great many things I want . . . that might never be."

He nodded and let her go. "I understand better than you might think. Trust me, Catherine. I only want to help you—to love you."

Catherine bit her lip and forced back tears. She had no words to offer. Here was the man with whom she might have shared her future . . . had her past been different.

Reading the last line of a letter never intended for her eyes, Felicia smiled in a smug, self-satisfied manner. She couldn't believe her good fortune.

Sitting at the back of the church due to a cough, she'd managed to sneak out of church early and now had gone through the contents of letters the Shays had in their apartment. She could clearly see the truth of Catherine's plight. What rich details. What wonderfully damaging information.

The clock struck twelve, and Felicia knew everyone would soon return to the house. She hurried to tuck the letters back in the dresser drawer, then surveyed the room to make sure nothing was out of place.

"So they think you've run off with your father's partner," Felicia said, grinning. "I think this information will merit me a great deal. You've ordered me around for the last time, Miss Shay. Or should I say, Miss Newbury."

CHAPTER 16

Catherine surveyed the finished gown on Winifred and smiled. The pink silk draped beautifully against the younger woman's frame. The darker rose and burgundy trims, along with ivory lace and tulle, perfectly outlined her slender form.

"I have a lovely ivory mask that Mother found for me. It will be perfect." Winifred twirled and let the skirt billow out around her. "I love it. I'm sure it's the nicest gown I've ever owned. Catherine, you have done such a wonderful job."

"I'm glad you like it. You will be the belle of the ball." Catherine put away her small sewing kit. She'd brought it just in case adjustments needed to be made. "I'll send Beatrix over on the morning of the twenty-second to sew on the roses. She'll do a fine job."

Winifred stopped admiring the dress and came to where Catherine gathered the last of her things. "Catherine, I have a favor to ask of you."

"Go on," she encouraged, seeing that Winifred suddenly looked rather nervous.

"Will you promise to say yes?"

"I can hardly do that before I know what the favor might be." Catherine closed her sewing bag and eyed Winifred in earnest.

"It's just that this is very important to me. I am begging you to say yes."

"Then you'd better tell me what it is you want from me."

"I want you to be my guest and companion at the ball." She raised her hand to silence Catherine. "I know it is a great deal to ask, but I'm so very nervous. I think—in fact, I am almost certain—Leander plans to propose marriage."

"Things have certainly progressed rather quickly," Catherine said. "But I am very happy for you."

"That's why I need you. Don't you see? I shall be so very nervous. You have been a dear friend to me, almost like a sister."

"Winifred . . . I cannot come," Catherine said, shaking her head. "It simply wouldn't be appropriate. Your guests would never understand why the seamstress was attending, as if she were someone important."

"But you are important. Please, Catherine. You can come and leave before the unmasking. Mother always has this ritual where everyone pairs up and tries to guess the identity of their partner. It happens at midnight, and you could slip out well before. And, as Mother has always maintained, everyone is equal behind the masks. No one would even know who you are. I'd even have Joseph ready and waiting to take you home."

"I appreciate your invitation; it's been ever so long since I've enjoyed a party. But I cannot come. I have no ball gown and no mask." Catherine remembered well her beautiful gowns she'd once owned. When she left England with the Shays, she had left most of her things behind, taking a few of her maid's dresses instead. They were desperate to draw no attention to their appearance.

"I can resolve the ball gown matter," Winifred said confidently. "You and I are the same size. I have a gown that I've not worn for well over a year. You could remake it."

"There isn't time."

Winifred took hold of Catherine's hands. "Please. You know there is time. You could remake the gown and no one would be the wiser. Please, Catherine. Do this for me."

The clock on the mantel struck two. Winifred had already told her Carter was expected home by three. He had hoped to see her, Winifred had stated with a coy smile.

"All right," Catherine said, knowing she must leave. "You're sure my identity can remain unknown?"

"But of course. It's a masquerade! I'll have an invitation delivered. And wait right here. I have the gown boxed and ready for you to take."

"You must have been quite confident of your ability to persuade," Catherine declared. She waited as Winifred raced from the room.

Catherine shook her head, knowing she would never attend the ball. It was completely inappropriate. She paced the sitting room, noting that it was cold and unwelcoming compared to that of the Arlington home. Winifred had told her this larger room was used for parties and family gatherings. The Niagara blue walls were set off by white crown molding and doors, while every empty spot on the wall had been decorated with gold-framed paintings. Heavy gold damask draperies framed the windows with lighter-weight panels of the same color to allow in some light. The fireplace surround was a cold white marble with gold trim. The clock on the mantel was gold and crystal. It served only to perpetuate the cold, harsh feel of the setting.

"Here it is," Winifred said, panting as she hurried to bring Catherine the dress box. "It is yours to keep. The color doesn't suit me."

Catherine couldn't help but smile. "Is it puce? I'm told you like that color."

Winifred laughed lyrically. "I was told that too, but I find I do not care for puce at all. No, the gown is a shimmering green, like new spring leaves. I'm sure it will look wonderful with your coloring."

"Thank you very much. It's a kind gesture and gift. I won't forget it. But I must go now. I'm expected back at the house."

"I will see you out." Winifred helped Catherine balance the box. "I could have the carriage take you back; this is a lot to carry."

"I carried as much on my walk here. I'll be fine."

Catherine set her things down only long enough to take up her bonnet and secure it in place. The butler assisted her with her coat, then handed Catherine her gloves.

"I hope you will accompany us to supper one night next week," Winifred declared. "Carter has told us of a new dining establishment. He will be so disappointed that you had to leave before he arrived."

"I doubt I will be free to come," Catherine offered as she gathered her things. The box did seem rather awkward, but knowing it had to be nearly the same size and weight as the one she'd come with, Catherine simply adjusted her hold and hoped for the best.

"I will call on you later," Winifred promised, "as soon as I know what evening Leander and Carter are free."

"Very well. Good day."

Catherine hurried through the door and down the stairs before she had to lie again about being willing to attend one of Winifred's affairs. The dress box, however, seemed wont to jump from her arms and very nearly caused her a misstep as she struggled to set it right. Doing her best not to fall or drop the box, Catherine was unprepared when someone took hold of her elbow.

"Might I be of assistance?"

Carter's voice caused her to completely lose the battle. Catherine dropped the box from fright.

Carter easily caught the package and laughed. "It would seem I came along in the nick of time."

"Had you not startled me, I would have managed quite well." She couldn't help but steal a glance as he shifted the box. He was dressed impeccably as usual with a soft wool overcoat to protect him from the chilly day.

"Come. I have the carriage right here. I will have Joseph drive you home."

Catherine thought of the long walk back. It had been easy enough to reject the idea when Winifred offered, but with the carriage right in front of her and knowing the box to be particularly troublesome, Catherine yielded.

"Very well."

She let Carter help her into the carriage but was surprised when instead of merely offering up the box, he climbed in with it and took the seat across from her.

"What are you doing?"

"I'm seeing you home."

Catherine shook her head. "You said nothing of coming along."

"I would hardly be a gentleman if I allowed you to carry this yourself." He leaned out the still-open door. "Joseph, take us to Mrs. Clarkson's sewing house."

"Yes, suh."

Carter closed the door, and the carriage interior immediately dimmed. Catherine put her sewing bag on the seat beside her, hoping there would be no repeat of Carter's previous moves.

He grinned, as if discerning her mind on the matter. He said nothing, however. "So have you transformed my sister into a mysterious creature for the ball?"

"Yes. She looked quite beautiful." Catherine tried to keep her focus on her gloved hands.

"And are you ready yet to give in to my request and court me?" he asked matter-of-factly.

Catherine looked at him and rolled her eyes. "No. I've decided we should forego the courtship altogether and marry by the end of the week." The exasperation was clear in her voice.

"Wonderful!" Carter laughed heartily. "I shall arrange everything."

She shook her head and sent her gaze rolling once again. "Sir, you and your gender are most ... most ..."

"We are quite entertaining, are we not?" He eyed her with an air of amusement.

" 'Entertaining' is hardly the word. I was thinking more along the lines of vexing."

"I haven't even begun to try to vex you, my dearest Catherine. Although perhaps since charm isn't working . . ." He let the words hang and offered her a wink.

"I must say, men in America are far more brazen than Englishmen."

"That's because we're all about life, liberty, and the pursuit of happiness. I'm especially after the latter part at the moment. Speaking of America, how do you find it now after living here for several years?"

For a moment, Catherine lost her ability to speak. The question reminded her of their conversation when Carter had first danced with her in Bath. They had talked of how she had no opinion of America and no desire to formulate one.

Carter watched Catherine's face as she wrestled with the question. He was certain she remembered that they had once discussed this very topic in England. He thought she might then admit to him who she really was, but she didn't.

"I find . . . it has treated me well," she admitted. "But I miss England at times."

"It's a wonderful country. The architecture there is magnificent. I look forward to returning."

"You plan to go to England?" she asked, her tone almost wistful.

"Perhaps. Maybe," he teased, "we could journey there on our wedding trip."

She fell silent and looked out the window, as if to keep herself safe from his advances.

"What were you like as a child?" he asked, hoping she would answer.

"Happy," she replied without so much as a breath. "I was loved, and I was safe. Nothing could hurt me." She bowed her head.

"But you don't feel safe or happy now, do you?"

She refused to reply. Carter leaned forward. "I'd like to help you. I'd like to make you feel safe—to know you're loved." The time was right, he thought. He would tell her that he knew everything. He would share with her how he was working to see her father's circumstance reviewed and righted.

"Catherine, there's something I've wanted to say for some time. I know that you've only been in America for five years."

The carriage came to a stop and Catherine reached for the door, but Carter halted her. "Please just hear me out."

"No," she said, shaking her head. "Please don't. Please." She met his gaze and he couldn't continue. He had no desire to cause her pain, yet that was exactly what he was doing.

Joseph opened the carriage door and offered Catherine his hand. She took up her bag and hurried out of the carriage. She might have run for the door, but Carter called her back.

"You've forgotten this."

She turned and saw the dress box. It seemed she wrestled over the decision to return to the carriage and Carter or simply let it go. Before she could do anything, however, Joseph took the box from Carter and hurried up the walkway. Catherine accepted it from him and wordlessly walked inside.

Catherine entered the house and immediately found Mrs. Clarkson at her side. She seemed quite excited and quickly took the box from Catherine and set it aside.

"Come with me. We have a visitor."

"Who is it?" Catherine asked. She put her bag down and began to unbutton her coat.

"It's Mrs. Sarah Hale from *Godey's Lady's Book*. She wants to feature some of your designs and perhaps a pattern or two in several of their editions. It's all quite exciting."

Catherine had barely removed her coat before Mrs. Clarkson took it from her. "Come along."

Trying to show a positive spirit, Catherine pulled off her gloves and nodded. She followed Mrs. Clarkson down the hall, untying her bonnet as they went. Catherine barely had time to put her gloves in her hat and set it aside on a small hall table before Mrs. Clarkson pulled her into her own private sitting room.

"Here she is," the older woman announced. "This is Catherine Shay."

A beautiful woman, who appeared to be Mrs. Clarkson's age, got to her feet to greet Catherine. "I am Mrs. Hale. I manage *Godey's*." She was dressed fashionably in a walking-out suit of dark plum wool, with a tiny black bonnet and black gloves.

Catherine nodded and curtsied. "I'm pleased to meet you."

"I have long wanted to make your acquaintance. You are spoken of by the best families in Philadelphia. Your gowns have made you famous."

"Catherine has brought enormous success upon this house," Mrs. Clarkson declared. She turned to Catherine. "Mrs. Hale is offering a substantial payment for the rights to print six different designs and perhaps two patterns. Will you agree?"

Mrs. Clarkson gave Catherine a fixed stare, as if to remind her that she was desperately trying to gather money. Feeling there was no choice, Catherine nodded. She hadn't wanted fame. She had, in fact, tried her best to hide away from the world.

"Wonderful. I will make the arrangements for you, dear." Mrs. Clarkson patted her hand.

"I would like very much to discuss your designs," Mrs. Hale interjected. "Perhaps Miss Shay could remain?"

"Catherine is very busy with final gown preparations. You know that there are many upcoming parties. Please forgive her, but perhaps another time?"

Certain her relief was evident, Catherine met Mrs. Clarkson's gaze and nodded. "It's been a pleasure meeting you, Mrs. Hale. I'm quite fond of your work. I believe *Godey's* has offered the common woman great insight into the genteel life of society."

The woman smiled and nodded. "Every woman is a lady at heart. I am certain our readers will delight in what you have to offer. We shall increase your fame across the country now. You will have more than enough work once people know how to reach you."

Her words did little to comfort Catherine. If she wasn't careful, her identity and secret would be revealed. She headed upstairs with this thought on her mind, as well as ideas of what she could do with the payment Mrs. Hale would give. The extra money might very well allow her to get her father the help he needed. Then as soon as he was freed and vindicated, she could go home.

But that thought held some regret. There would be no future with Carter Danby if she returned to England.

CHAPTER 17

$\mathcal{T}$he day before the Danby annual masquerade ball, Carter sat in Leander's office and smiled at the wonderful news. The duke of Mayfield had written to Leander personally.

"He says that the judge is reviewing all of the materials and he soon expects Mr. Newbury to be free. The duke has made special arrangements for Newbury to be moved to his estate. It's unusual, but the duke believes a great wrong has been committed."

"That's putting it mildly," Carter replied. He hadn't expected such good news but was happy for it. What a great Christmas gift this would be for Catherine.

"The duke was also relieved to know that Catherine was safe. Upon studying the entire matter, he was alarmed to hear of threats being issued from Baker for Catherine's well-being. He says there is no doubt, however, that she has had nothing to do with any of this. I shared the matter with Father and he agrees; she should not live in fear. We need to arrange a meeting, Carter. A meeting between you, Father, myself, and Miss Shay. We can give her this information and allow her to know that she is not in danger of arrest."

"But she may be in danger of Baker, the man they clearly want brought to justice. I will not see her used as bait to lure him in. Not unless she can be completely protected."

Leander nodded. "I agree. I would not wish it for her or any woman."

"I'm also hesitant to get her hopes up," Carter said, trying to figure out what was best. "Should something go wrong and her father remain imprisoned, I think it would cause her even greater grief. It would be rather like losing him all over again."

"I suppose you are right. Still, having some hope seems preferable to none."

"Let's pray on it and see what is to be done. I want her to have hope, but I don't want it to be of a false nature." Carter got up to leave, then stopped. "Oh, I thought I would let you know, I overheard Mother going on and on about Winifred's masquerade gown. Apparently it's pink silk with real roses sewn into the bodice. I saw a few of the pieces when it was being designed, but I can't really tell you anything more."

"The roses should make her easy to spot; I'd hate to spend the evening with someone else," Leander said with a smile. "And what of Catherine? Did Winifred manage to convince her to attend?"

Carter laughed. "She nagged her and gave her a gown to make over for the event, but she wasn't at all sure Catherine would keep to her agreement to come. So I have enlisted the help of Mrs. Clarkson."

"I hope it wasn't as costly as setting up Miss Shay's outings with your sister."

"Not quite, but still it was worth every penny."

"And what is she going to wear?"

Carter shrugged. "I haven't any idea, but I'll know her. A mask of lace and wire won't keep me from recognizing her."

❦

The twenty-second of December dawned cold and clear. Catherine worked to see the sewing room put in order. They were finishing with the last of the New Year's gowns, and Mrs. Clarkson had promised a full two days off for Christmas. It had been agreed upon that those two days would be the twenty-fourth and twenty-fifth, and since the twenty-third was a Sunday, they would actually have three days to call their own. With her fingers stinging from hours of needlework, Catherine thought of nothing but delicious hours of idleness.

The last few hours had been focused on the details of cleaning and finishing costumes, and now Catherine performed the final sweeping in the alteration room. She straightened as the clock chimed four.

Three days. Three days to do nothing, if that's what I choose.

She remembered her youth and the boredom she felt in the life of a leisurely young lady. She had often whined and complained only to have Nanny Bryce put her to work with a needle and thread. When Nanny Bryce and Catherine's mother had passed away, Catherine thought her life would end. The emptiness and sorrow she felt were often more than she could bear. There wasn't even the noise of her young brothers to console her. She and Father had clung to each other in their grief. The memory only served to strengthen her resolve to see him set free. Despite Carter Danby's appealing nature and desire to court her, Catherine was determined to keep her mind set on her father's needs. She would simply find a way to put Carter from her life, even though she knew it wouldn't be easy.

Winifred had sent one invitation after the other throughout the month, and Catherine had managed to excuse herself from each event. She hadn't seen Carter since that day at the Danby house and felt quite vexed with herself for even thinking about him. She missed him more than she wanted to admit.

"Nothing can come of it," she muttered.

But that didn't stop her from seeing visions of the handsome dark-haired man in her dreams. Night after night she had tossed and turned while dreaming of Carter Danby. Once when she'd been walking home from town, Catherine had thought him to be following her with the carriage. But when she turned to investigate, there was no one there save a conveyance carrying a woman and several children.

"Catherine?"

"I'm in here," she called.

Selma came into the room and grinned. "We've been looking all over for you."

"I've been working to get things picked up and cleaned so that we might finish early and start our holiday."

"Well, we have a bit of a surprise for you. An early Christmas gift of sorts."

Catherine put the broom aside. "Whatever do you mean, Selma?"

"You'll see. Come with me to Mrs. Clarkson's sitting room. It's quite exciting."

Catherine pulled off her apron and hung it by the door. "Very well."

She walked down the hall behind Selma and tried to imagine what the two women might have been up to. She knew they both worried about Catherine's lack of rest and her refusal to attend parties and outings with Winifred. They had also been concerned about the time she spent worrying over her father. And since Mrs. Clarkson had been admitted to the circle of trust regarding Catherine's true identity, she had constantly fretted over the matter, trying her best to help Catherine find resolution.

For just a moment, Catherine allowed herself a dream. She thought of what it might be like to find her father on the other side of the door. The idea caused her heart to skip a beat. Oh, what glory it would be to see him again. To see him safe and healthy. What if he were here? What if they had caught Finley Baker, and her father had been set free? But when Selma opened the door, it was only Mrs. Clarkson who stood on the other side.

Disappointment washed over her. She silently chided herself for being such a ninny. Had she not guarded herself against just this type of thing for years now? She forced a smile and looked at Mrs. Clarkson.

"Catherine, come in. We have a present for you."

There was little time to advance or even attempt to sit before Mrs. Clarkson clapped her hands and Dolley and Beatrix appeared carrying a gown of shimmering green silk. The neckline had been fashioned in a graceful cut and trimmed in pink hothouse roses. It was lower than Catherine was used to but certainly not overly immodest.

"What is this?" she asked, turning to Selma.

"It's your gown for the party tonight. The masquerade at the Danbys."

"I cannot possibly attend that party, and you should know that better than most." Catherine's stomach knotted at the thought.

"Of course you can. Just as Winifred suggested, you will be completely unrecognizable. With this gown and mask, no one will even suspect your identity."

Catherine thought of one man who might well try. "It would be too big of a risk."

"Not at all, my dear. I have some new white evening gloves," Mrs. Clarkson began. "They will hide the fact that you work with your hands. Not only that, but I also have some lovely jewelry that will cause all present to suspect you a wealthy woman. They were a gift from my dear departed brother, and they match the gown perfectly."

"And I fashioned you a mask of green lace and silk," Selma told her.

"It's all too much to imagine," Catherine said, unable to deny that she would love to attend the party.

"Then don't. Hurry upstairs, where a hot bath awaits you. I will come and help you dress, then Beatrix and Dolley will help you with your hair and such. It's all settled for you."

"I can see that," Catherine replied. "But what of leaving before the unmasking?"

"That's been arranged as well," Mrs. Clarkson announced. "I've hired a carriage to take you to the party. The same man will return for you and be waiting in an agreed-upon place so that you can slip from the house unnoticed and make your way home."

"But what of my—"

"Cease with the excuses," Mrs. Clarkson said with a smile. "You are going to enjoy a party that the rest of us can only dream of. Come home and share all of the details with us, and that will be our reward."

Two hours later, Catherine stood before a mirror as Dolley added final touches to the cascade of curls that she'd created. Catherine could scarcely believe her own appearance. The gown fit her better than anything she'd ever owned. It draped gracefully across her neckline and cinched snugly at the waist before spilling into a full, sweeping skirt. The pale green satin served her well with its inset lace bodice and puffed sleeves.

"I can hardly believe my appearance," she told Dolley. "You've made me look . . . well . . . completely changed."

"I like arranging hair. I had thought to be a personal maid to a lady, but then I came here to live at the sewing house."

"You are very talented," Catherine said, knowing that were her situation different, she would most eagerly hire Dolley to style her hair all of the time.

"You are beautiful and easy to work with," Dolley declared. "I've never seen anyone with such thick and wondrous hair. My own is so thin and mousy. Not at all pretty like yours or even red like Beatrix's."

"Me mum says that red hair is God's way of warnin' folks of the temper that lies beneath," Beatrix piped in.

Catherine smiled at this comment. She was finding it easier and easier to smile these days. She knew her father was still in peril, but the money was quickly adding up, and after Christmas she planned to get word to Captain Marlowe to see if he might locate a barrister to help her father. She felt hopeful . . . something she hadn't felt in a long time. That alone made her happy.

"It's nearly time to leave," Selma said, entering the room. "I've brought the gloves and Mrs. Clarkson's jewelry. I must say you will look like the fine lady you've always been once we finish you off."

Catherine started for a moment, worried that Beatrix and Dolley might wonder at the comment. They seemed unmoved, however, and finished securing the last of the curls. Looking in the mirror, Catherine surveyed her hair from every angle possible. No one would recognize her. She had always worn her hair up and carefully secured to keep it out of her way while working. This arrangement had it sweeping up and then tumbling down her back in an array of curls and tiny ribbon accents. She thought only for a moment of Carter knowing her in England but dismissed her concern. At seventeen, she was only a shadow of the woman she had become. It was little wonder he hadn't recognized her when they first met.

Selma secured the necklace of peridot and gold around Catherine's neck. It draped perfectly against her smooth white skin. Catherine pulled on the gloves while Selma secured matching earrings. "Mrs. Clarkson said this stone of peridot is believed to bring peace and success. It's even mentioned in the Bible."

Catherine gently touched the necklace with her gloved hand. "Perhaps it will help me hide my identity, for surely no one would expect a seamstress to wear such expensive jewels."

"If the jewels don't work," Mrs. Clarkson said, "then surely this will keep you hidden well enough." She handed Catherine the mask.

"Had I not known you since birth," Selma declared, "I wouldn't recognize you now. You'll have no trouble remaining a mystery to all at the party."

Studying her reflection for a moment, Catherine could only agree.

"Here is your cloak," Mrs. Clarkson announced, "and the carriage is waiting for you even now."

Catherine had worried about what she might wear over her gown, but Mrs. Clarkson had already attended to the matter. The hood was carefully fitted over her hair, and Dolley admonished her to take care and not lean back against the carriage seat.

"Remember, the man has been instructed to await you at midnight. He will park and meet you wherever seems fitting and secluded."

Catherine nodded and allowed them to move her toward the door and downstairs. It wasn't until she was being handed up into the carriage that she allowed herself to believe it was all really happening.

"We want to hear all about it when you get back," Mrs. Clarkson called.

"Oh yes," Dolley said with a sigh. "I want to know all about the party. I've never been to a ball. It must be glorious."

"It is," Catherine murmured in the confines of the carriage as the driver closed the door. "It is glorious, especially when someone is there waiting for you."

Felicia watched with Lydia from the upstairs window as the entourage helped Catherine to the carriage. She burned with jealousy.

"It isn't fair that she gets to attend the ball."

"Why didn't you tell Mrs. Clarkson what you know about her?" Lydia asked.

Felicia hadn't shared all of the details with Lydia, but the girl knew that they now had enough information to get Catherine dismissed from the sewing house.

"I don't plan to tell Mrs. Clarkson. Not unless Catherine proves to be less than cooperative. I believe all I will need to do is have a talk with her and she'll leave on her own accord."

Lydia seemed rather intrigued by this and came to Felicia's side. "Can you not tell me about it?"

"Not yet," Felicia said. She moved away from the window and went to sit on the side of her bed. "But in time you shall know it in full."

"I hate having to wait." Lydia plopped down on the only chair in the room and sighed. "I suppose I shall have to, but I wish it were not so."

"Patience, dear Lydia. Patience. Good things take time. I have wanted to see that woman gone for years, but I had to bide my time. Now that time is nearly complete. Perhaps I will speak with her after the party. She will be enjoying the evening's revelry . . . it might be the perfect moment to intrude."

Felicia smiled, feeling rather smug. Ever since learning the truth of Catherine's plight, she had tried to figure out the perfect moment to spring the news on her. She wanted a moment that would have the maximum effect. A moment that would completely crush Catherine's hopes and dreams for the future.

Lydia yawned. "But she won't be back until after midnight. That's a long time to wait, and tomorrow I need to be home early to attend church with my family."

"Stop fretting, you silly goose." Felicia got to her feet and headed for the door. "The time will fly by. You'll see."

❧

The carriage came to a stop at the end of the drive, and rather than head on up to the house, Catherine had instructed the driver to let her off here. He opened the door and assisted her from the carriage.

"I will meet you over there," Catherine said, pointing to a crossroads where the trimmed shrubbery made a perfect hiding place. "I will be here just before midnight, so don't be late."

"Yes, ma'am. I will wait for you there."

Catherine drew a deep breath and headed up the walk, grateful the snow had melted. She was one of the last to arrive and found the party in full swing as the butler took her cloak and pointed her up two flights of stairs to the third-story ballroom. Several men stopped to watch her, and Catherine felt a strange sensation course through her. It was a reminder that harked back to the last party she'd known.

"Good evening," an older man declared as she came atop the final step. He took her gloved hand in his and raised it to his lips. "I don't believe we have met."

"Perhaps we have," Catherine said, pulling her hand away. She didn't care for the way the stranger's gaze roamed her body. "It is, after all, a masquerade."

"True," he said, leaning closer, "but I would have remembered this body despite the mask on your face. You are a stranger here, and quite welcome. I shall look forward to your . . . unveiling."

Catherine shivered and moved away so quickly that she found herself plunged into the arms of another waiting admirer.

"Careful now," the man said as he righted her.

Catherine froze. It was Carter; she would stake her life on it. From the cut of his evening coat to the parting of his hair, the black mask he wore could not disguise the man she'd come to care for.

"Please accept my apologies," she whispered and tried to pull away.

"Nonsense. Join me for a dance."

He smiled at her, and Catherine immediately realized that coming here had been a huge mistake. She looked back toward the stairs and gave serious thought to bolting. But without another moment's pause, Carter was pressing forward into the sea of dancing couples. Her fate had been sealed.

CHAPTER 18

*C*atherine tried to ignore the man who held her. The waltz made intimacy and talk necessary, but she limited her answers to yes and no whenever possible.

"Where do you call home?" he asked softly.

"Philadelphia," she replied, trying to lower her voice. If she could recognize his form and voice, he might recognize hers as well.

He chuckled. "But of course."

"And you?" she asked, already knowing the answer.

"The same. I was born and raised here, but you do not sound as if you were."

"No."

He turned her masterfully in the midst of the other dancers. "And that is all you will say to me?"

"To say too much might reveal my identity."

"Ah, I understand."

They completed the dance and Catherine curtsied deep. Before she could draw a breath, she was quickly claimed by another dancing partner and whisked away without ever being asked if she wanted to dance. Grateful that she would have no need to disguise her voice, she allowed the stranger his indiscretion.

It wasn't until three dances later that Catherine managed to detach herself from the circle of admirers. She had spotted Winifred from across the room and made her way there to announce her presence.

"Good evening."

Winifred looked up but didn't appear to recognize Catherine. "Good evening."

"Are you enjoying the ball?" Catherine asked.

"Yes, it's a lovely party."

"The house has been decorated to perfection. I love the pine boughs and red ribbon. It's quite festive." Catherine lowered her voice. "Your mother has done a wonderful job."

Winifred cocked her head and leaned closer. "Catherine?"

"Yes. Are you surprised?" She smiled.

"I am indeed. You hide your accent quite well. Oh, I'm so glad you're here. I wasn't sure you would come, but here you are and look how beautiful you've made the gown," she said, taking a step back to take in Catherine's profile. "I cannot believe that is even the same dress. You did a wonderful job."

"I didn't do it. Some of the other ladies at Mrs. Clarkson's decided to remake it. I wasn't even sure I would have time to come tonight, but they insisted."

"I'm so glad they did. I've been a nervous wreck. I can't tell which man is Leander. Do you suppose that means we are not truly intended for each other?"

"Nonsense. It's a masquerade. The purpose is deception, but I believe it will be simple. He will be the one who most frequently returns to your side," Catherine teased. "Besides, I'm sure you will know him the minute he comes to you."

"I did not even recognize the gown you're wearing," Winifred said, shaking her head. "I can assure you it never looked like that on me."

Catherine actually laughed. It felt so good to just let go of her emotions and enjoy the night. There was only the tiniest nagging accusation in the back of her mind. An accusation that declared her an unkind, insensitive daughter for enjoying a party while her father rotted in prison.

"I suppose you recognize everyone here," Winifred said with a giggle. "I hadn't considered it, but since you designed most every gown, you'll know exactly who's who."

"Yes, I have a good idea."

"May I intrude?" a man asked. "Would you care to dance?" His voice was very formal and low, but Catherine watched as he extended his hand toward Winifred. She was certain it was Leander.

"Thank you," Winifred said, allowing him to escort her to the floor.

She glanced at Catherine over her shoulder as if to ask if this might be her beloved. Catherine nodded and smiled.

"You have a beautiful smile," Carter whispered against her ear. His warm breath sent a shiver down Catherine's spine. "Are you cold?"

"No." She moved away a step to put some distance between them.

Another man, a portly sort with greasy hair, came to bow before her. "Would you care to dance?"

"I'm afraid," Carter declared, "you are too late. I have just asked for the dance and she has agreed."

Catherine let him take hold of her and lead her to the dance floor. "You, sir, are a liar."

"It's a masquerade, my dear. We are all liars tonight. Some of us more than others. Not only that, but you are clearly the most beautiful woman in the room. Everyone is entranced."

"Including you?" she asked, trying to disguise her voice.

"Especially me. I've not been able to take my gaze from you since you fell into my arms. I can hardly wait to see you revealed so that I might know you better."

"Sometimes such revelations are disappointing," Catherine said, forgetting her determination to answer simply and speak little.

"I'm very certain you could never disappoint," he said with a grin.

The music concluded and Mrs. Danby approached. Catherine thought she looked rather like a pompous peacock. A collection of feathers jutted awkwardly from her head, and more than her share of diamonds dripped from her ears and neck.

"Now, aren't you a lovely couple," she declared. "I think there is not a more handsome coupling in the room."

Catherine felt her cheeks grow hot and bowed her head. "You are kind to say so, ma'am. Now if you'll excuse me."

Winifred came forward and took hold of Catherine. Pulling her to one of the settees along the wall, she sat. "Stay with me for a moment."

"Happily," Catherine said, joining her friend.

They put their heads together as if sharing important secrets. Winifred gripped Catherine's hand tightly. "I hate parties."

"Why? What has happened to grieve you?"

"My mother."

Catherine smiled. "And what has she done?"

"She's making all sorts of inappropriate comments about her daughter having found a husband. I am so very embarrassed. I wish she would occupy herself in another manner."

"So was that Mr. Arlington who took you away?" Catherine questioned, hoping to draw Winifred's attention elsewhere.

She smiled. "Yes. I thought it was him and we cheated. He asked if I liked my new bracelet, and I told him I would always cherish his first gift. After that, we knew."

Catherine nodded. "That's very clever. Where is he now?"

"I'm not certain. He promised to find me later, and when I heard Mother talking about you and Carter . . ." She put her hand to her mouth. "Oh, I shouldn't have said that."

"I knew I was dancing with Carter," Catherine said, leaning back. "I would know him even if he'd hidden himself under a sheet."

Winifred looked at the room full of men and women. "I hardly know how you could figure that. I only knew him because I recognized the mask from last year. How did you know it was him?"

"I'm a seamstress. I have a way of sizing people. Your brother has a distinct way of carrying himself, and his broad shoulders are a certain giveaway. Only your Mr. Arlington comes anywhere close to matching them; but, of course, his hair and eyes are much different."

Her reprieve was soon over as a man approached for a dance. Catherine figured him to be at least twice her age.

"May I have this dance?"

Catherine thought to tell him no but saw that Carter was working his way over. "Of course," she said, getting quickly to her feet. "I'd love to."

The music grew lively and filled the air as she lost herself in the steps. The man attempted to make conversation, but Catherine had no interest. She answered his questions in a curt manner that fell just short of being rude. As the music ended, she was handed over to yet another eager partner. The night continued in that manner until Catherine thought she would surely collapse from exhaustion. A quick glance at the clock proved to her that the evening had passed by with surprising speed. It would soon be midnight.

Desperate to appear unavailable to everyone, she took up a cup of punch and ducked behind a screen that had been positioned behind the table. She pretended to be completely engrossed in viewing one of the nearby paintings and prayed that she would go unnoticed. At least for a few minutes. She had to figure out how to get out of the house.

Sipping the punch, Catherine forced her breathing to even. She had to compose herself in order to think clearly. Before she had to flee her home in Bath, Catherine had been completely capable of dealing with the attention of would-be suitors. Now, however, she felt terrified. A part of her wanted to seek out Carter and beg him to stay at her side. But she also knew the danger that might well come her way should she attempt that action. After all, she was purposefully leaving before the unveiling because she didn't want him to know she'd been at the party.

Seeing the French doors had been opened to allow the chilled night air to cool the heated room, Catherine felt compelled to slip outside. She just might find a means of escape. Perhaps the balcony opened into another room, through which she could slip away. A quick glance revealed no one watching her. She hurried onto the balcony and moved quickly beyond the door.

One young couple stood not ten feet away, so Catherine moved in the opposite direction, seeing that the shadows at the far end of the walkway would conceal her.

The night was quite cold, but she didn't mind. The reprieve from the crowded room seemed more than worth a little chill. She leaned against the railing and stared into the darkness. Thoughts of Carter flooded her mind and once again she considered telling him the truth. Perhaps if she explained the situation, he could help her.

"You're going to freeze out here," he said as if her thoughts had conjured him.

Catherine turned and found Carter only inches away. How he had managed to sneak up on her without her seeing him was beyond her.

"I . . . it was . . . I needed some air." She backed up as far as the stone railing would allow.

Carter was undeterred. He reached out and pulled Catherine into his arms without warning. And she did nothing to stop him.

"You must know the effect you have on me. I want only to be with you."

She shook her head. "You don't even know me."

"I'll be the judge of that." He wrapped her in his arms and lowered his mouth to hers.

Catherine's senses reeled as Carter kissed her with a passion she'd never known. Her hand went up to gently touch the back of his neck. She knew she should stop, but it wasn't until he pulled away ever so slightly that Catherine found the willpower to speak.

"That . . . was uncalled for." She knew the breathless statement sounded very unconvincing.

"Was it?" he chuckled. "It seemed very called for by my account."

"I'm cold. I'd like to return to the party."

"Are you sure? I could give you my coat."

Catherine pushed away and headed for the doors. She longed to stay right where she was but knew it would cause her even more pain. Who had he set his affections on? The lady behind the mask? Or did he know her identity?

She hurried to mingle into the crowd of partyers. The music had stopped and the conversations of at least one hundred people filled the air. Catherine excused herself as she rushed through the room.

I only need to reach the stairs, she thought. Looking in that direction, she was relieved to see that the way was somewhat clear. She recognized the women who had gathered near the arched doorway. One was Mrs. Danby, another was Mrs. Smith, and the third was Mrs. Alger. She approached the women just as the clock stuck midnight.

Panic coursed through her body at the sound. Mrs. Danby turned with a squeal of delight to the gathered revelers.

"It's time to unmask. Choose your partner and we will start in a moment."

Catherine hurried past her, hoping that while Mrs. Danby was preoccupied with her party, she wouldn't question one person slipping out of the room.

By the time Catherine reached the second floor, she was feeling less frantic. Just one more flight of stairs and she could reclaim her cloak and leave. She glanced over her shoulder and breathed a sigh of relief to see that no one had followed her.

"Are you leaving, miss?" the butler questioned as she reached the foyer.

"Yes, I must. Please bring my cloak. It's the black hooded one with the velvet trim."

The man nodded and went in search. Catherine paced nervously, fearing Carter would find her. She heard the chimes of the clock conclude, and the noise from the third floor increased.

The butler finally returned and extended the cloak. "Is this the one, miss?"

"Yes," she replied. She allowed him to help her into it, then turned immediately for the door.

"If you tell me which is your coach, I can have him come round."

"No. That won't be necessary." She heard footsteps on the stairs and startled. "Good evening." She raced from the house and flew down the stairs to the cobblestone drive. Picking up her skirts, she hurried toward the street, the stones bruising her already sore feet.

She reached the street and crossed quickly, heading toward the place the driver had agreed to meet her. He was there waiting, just as she had prayed.

"I feared I was late and you'd given me up," he said, helping her into the carriage.

From somewhere in the distance, Catherine could have sworn she heard someone calling her name. *But that is impossible*, she told herself. *Only Winifred knew I was here.* Yet reason told her that Carter knew her as well . . . knew her well enough to kiss her passionately.

"No," she said quietly, shaking her head. "He's simply a rogue who took liberties with a woman he didn't even know. He knew he could remain unknown behind the mask and simply took advantage of an innocent woman."

The thought grieved her, and pulling the cloak tight, Catherine prayed for wisdom. She touched her lips, unable to forget Carter's kiss.

CHAPTER 19

*C*arter toyed with the idea of running after Catherine and forcing her to come back to the party but decided against it. He watched her cross the street and hurry behind the shrubbery that cornered the Forsythe estate. For a moment he worried that she would try to walk home, but when a carriage very quickly appeared in the intersection and headed south, he felt confident that Catherine was inside.

He pulled off his mask and walked back into the house. He had no desire to return to the party, but he knew Leander planned to propose and felt it was his duty to be at his side, as well as Winifred's.

Upstairs people were laughing and enjoying the embarrassment of not knowing one another. Leander and Winifred stood
together, unmasked, and stared into each other's eyes as if the rest
of the world had completely disappeared. Carter envied them.
They would marry and be happy. They would trust each other
and make a future together. The scene only served to remind
Carter of how far out of reach those things were for him—at
least at the moment.

He hated himself for having kissed Catherine. He'd clearly
offended her. She didn't know it was him, and perhaps that's
why he dared the kiss. Still, it was wrong. He took liberties that
were not his to take.

Leaning against the wall, Carter prayed. *Father, I don't know
what to do. I'm trying my best to help her father and in turn help
Catherine. I love her. You know this even better than I. She's charming and intelligent. She is so kind to Winifred. Show me what I
am to do. Please . . . If she is not for me, then take away this intense
longing for her.*

"Carter, why are you hiding back here?" Winifred asked.
"Are you sick?"

He opened his eyes to see his sister's concerned expression.
"Perhaps lovesick," he admitted. "Catherine has fled."

Winifred's eyes widened. "I had hoped she'd be here. Leander
just proposed. I wanted you both to share in my happiness."

Taking her hands in his, Carter offered her a smile. "I do
share your happiness. Lee has long been like a brother to me
and now he shall be my brother in truth."

"He was wise to propose here. Father could hardly do anything but offer his blessing, especially since he had agreed to

the courtship. In front of all these witnesses, he wouldn't dare take it back."

"I agree. It was a fine decision." Carter dropped his hold as Leander joined them.

"Here you are," Lee said.

Carter embraced him with a hearty slap on the back. "My brother."

"Soon to be." Lee looked around the room. "And where is Catherine? I heard she was to be here tonight."

"She was, but now she's gone. I did something very foolish," Carter admitted.

Leander and Winifred looked at him oddly, but it was Winifred who spoke. "You didn't propose, did you?"

Lee laughed. "So that is what you think of proposals? They are foolish?"

Winifred reddened. "No . . . I just . . . no, that's not it," she stammered. "I just thought maybe it frightened her away."

"I did worse," Carter said. His voice lowered. "I kissed her. I knew it was wrong, but I couldn't help myself."

Winifred and Lee began to laugh. Carter felt only more ridiculous. "All right, all right. Laugh at my expense, but it's not funny. She left without a word. I may well have ruined my chances with her. I only comfort myself in believing she didn't know it was me."

"She knew," Winifred said, then put her hands to her mouth. Both men looked at her, so she managed to whisper, "She told me she recognized you by the cut of your clothes and the . . . well . . . the shape of you. She is, after all, a very talented seamstress."

Carter hit the wall with his fist. "I should have known. I suppose I did. I felt certain she knew it was me, but I didn't make an issue of it."

"So you both knew each other," Lee said with a shrug. "Then you both were willing participants in the kiss. I would say no harm done."

"I'd like to believe that, but if that were the case, why did she run away?"

"She told me that if she came, she would leave before the unveiling," Winifred offered. "She said it was important, because she was only a seamstress and the rest of our company might not understand."

"Catherine isn't a mere seamstress," Carter protested. "She's from a very fine family in England." He realized that he'd said too much, but Winifred was nodding.

"Yes, I know. She once admitted as much but begged me to say nothing. Apparently there is some sort of danger that might befall her family if the truth is told."

"Lee and I have been working to set the matter right," Carter admitted. "It was the reason we went to New York. Say nothing about it, however. I want to wait until I'm certain things can be concluded."

"Carter, how kind. Of course I'll keep silent until you know more," Winifred agreed.

"I don't know about the rest of you," Lee said, "but I'm starving and ready to join the others for the midnight supper. What say you two?"

Winifred looked to Carter and put her hand on his arm. "There is nothing you can do tonight. Perhaps you can go see her tomorrow after church."

"Yes," he said, nodding. "I will do that. I will sit her down and explain that I knew who she was the minute she fell into my arms upon her arrival. Father was paying her a bit too much attention, and as she turned to flee his ogling, she fell against me. Once she knows that I was not merely taking liberties with a stranger, perhaps she will forgive me."

"I'm certain she will," Winifred said with a smile. "Now come. I have no desire to let my husband-to-be perish from hunger. It was much too hard to secure him, and I've no desire to start anew."

The men laughed and Lee pulled her close. "There will be no starting anew. You are mine and I intend to remain at your side until we are old and gray."

❧

Catherine found the entire sewing house waiting up for her when she got home. The atmosphere was one of revelry, and everyone wanted to know about the party.

"Nearly every gown there was one of our creations," Catherine stated. "The women were quite beautiful and the dresses moved in perfect order as they danced."

"Oh, I wish I could have seen it," Martha said with a sigh.

"What did they say when you were unmasked?" Dolley questioned.

"I didn't stay for the unveiling," Catherine admitted. "I was afraid some might have been uncomfortable with that revelation. I didn't wish to offend."

"Oh, but you are so very beautiful, I cannot imagine anyone would be offended," Mrs. Clarkson countered. "You should have remained and showed them all what a graceful and beautiful lady you are."

Selma and Dugan met her gaze but said nothing. Catherine could tell by the set of their faces that something was wrong. Or at least different.

"And how did they go decoratin' the house?" Beatrix asked.

"It was all lovely," Catherine said, still watching Selma. "There were green pine boughs trimmed in red and gold ribbons. There was a large Christmas tree at one end of the room near the huge buffet tables. Following the unmasking there was to be a supper for all to share."

"Oh, me mouth waters just thinkin' of what might have been there." Beatrix closed her eyes. "Food aplenty for everyone. I can just see it."

"Yes, there was plenty. Mrs. Danby plans this party for months in advance. Her daughter once told me that they hold other parties throughout the year, but their Christmas masquerade is her mother's pride and joy."

"And did you dance?" Dolley questioned.

Catherine winced as she moved her feet. "I did. In fact, I danced nearly every dance. My feet are very sore, and I think they are swollen."

"Oh, I would have loved to have danced. How wonderful," Martha declared, then began swaying and pretending to waltz.

Selma whispered something to Dugan, then the two of them got to their feet. "I believe we'll retire. Catherine, do come tell us good-night when you go to bed."

Catherine realized they were trying to tell her that there was news to be shared. She yawned and nodded.

"Look, I want only to soak my feet in a hot tub. I really over-did the dancing," Catherine admitted. "I'm completely exhausted. I promise we can speak more of this in the morning."

"I'll be bringin' ya some hot water," Beatrix told her, getting to her feet. "You just head up, and I'll help you undress as well."

Catherine nodded. "Thank you so much." She eased onto her feet and grimaced. "I might have to crawl, but I'll get there eventually."

The girls laughed, and everyone declared that for Catherine's sake it was good they had three days off.

"You'll need as much for recovery," Mrs. Clarkson teased. "Now, don't forget, girls, I need everyone to meet at breakfast in the morning before going off on your holiday."

Catherine made her way upstairs and waited for Beatrix. The girl seemed to have infinite reserves of energy as she poured a tub of water, then hurried to help Catherine unfasten the gown.

"Ya look finer than any grand lady I've ever seen. Although, I'd have to be admittin' that I haven't seen many." She lifted the gown over Catherine's hair. "Yar hair is still nearly perfect. I love the way it falls. Makes me wish mine were dark and thick like yarself."

Catherine smiled. "Your hair is beautiful. I think the red is far more desirable." She felt a great sense of relief as Beatrix undid the lacing of her corset and helped Catherine from its confines.

"If ya'll be sittin', I'll help ya with the stockings and then ya can be soakin' yar feet," the girl told Catherine as she handed her the well-worn robe.

"No. Just pour the water. I need to go tell my folks good-night. They looked quite ready to go to bed, and I don't want to be the reason they have to stay up."

Beatrix nodded. "I'll be puttin' the tub by the fireplace. Then I'll build ya a right hot fire and by the time ya make it back, yar room should be nice and toasty."

Catherine sighed. It sounded so wonderful. "Thank you, Beatrix. You've been very kind."

"Go on with ya now," she said with a grin. " 'Twas just my good Christian act."

Catherine put on her slippers and left Beatrix working at the hearth. There was no telling what news Selma and Dugan had heard. She headed up the stairs and squared her shoulders. No matter the news, she was determined to be strong. She drew a deep breath and knocked at their door.

Dugan answered and ushered her in. Selma immediately joined them with a letter in hand. "This was misdirected to the house next door," she told Catherine. "They brought it over just after you left for the ball. Apparently it came a couple of days ago, but the family was out of town."

"Who is it from? What does it say?" Catherine asked, suddenly feeling anxious.

"You can read it for yourself." Selma extended the letter.

"No. I'm much too nervous. I can see that something is wrong. Has he . . . is he . . ."

"He's not dead, if that's what you're thinking. No, it's nothing like that. I can't even say if it's good news or bad," Selma admitted. "But it seems good."

"Sit down and we can explain," Dugan offered.

Catherine did as he told her, but her gaze was ever fixed on Selma. "So what does it say?"

Selma continued to stand. She opened the letter and read, " 'Mr. Newbury was moved from the prison, but we have no idea as to who commanded such a thing or where he's been taken. We tried to get information, but apparently his lawyer has decreed that no one speak of it. We fear for him, but at the same time rejoice that he has been removed from such a dreary and desolate existence.' "

"But where has he gone? Who would have taken him?" Catherine asked, panicked. "I can't believe this—of what lawyer do they speak? Father has no lawyer."

"I wish I had answers for you," Selma replied. "There is hardly anything more here, except a promise to try and get information." She folded the letter. "Catherine, it would seem to be good news overall, don't you think?"

"I don't know what to think." Catherine hoped that Father's friends had somehow managed to reach the ear of an official. Or perhaps Finley Baker had been captured and her father's innocence was now recognized.

She got up and began to pace in front of the fire. The pain in her feet kept her awake and focused. "There has to be an answer to all of this. I wish we could get word to Captain Marlowe. He's been diligent in aiding Father and would most likely have additional information."

"Perhaps," Selma agreed. "Maybe Dugan could write him a letter."

"Or go see him. It might behoove us to spend the money to send Dugan by coach to New York."

"That might be a good idea," Selma admitted. "However, we cannot be sure he's in residence. Perhaps we could send a telegram."

Catherine considered it for a moment. "They won't be open on Sunday. We could simply put Dugan on the train and see him in New York in a matter of hours, rather than wait."

Dugan shook his head. "The captain might not be in town, Catherine. It might be weeks before he returns and then the cost of the ticket would be for naught, for I certainly couldn't afford to wait for him there."

Selma nodded. "Dugan's right. We have no way of knowing if the captain would even be there. We should pray about it and see what God directs. He has shown us all along and will no doubt show us now. We have only to seek His guidance."

Pausing, Catherine turned. "I know you're both right, but that doesn't make the wait any easier. I sometimes feel as though God has . . . well, stopped listening. I pray for strength. I pray for help—that someone would come along with the ability to see things made right. But nothing happens."

"Now, you don't know that," Dugan interjected. "Remember Abraham taking Isaac up the mountain to be sacrificed? He didn't see any other way out either. But lo and behold, God was sending a ram up the other side even as Abraham prepared his son to die."

"And when God knew He would destroy the earth with a flood," Selma added, "He made provision for Noah and his family. Not to mention all of those animals."

"I know that God has been faithful in the past . . ." Catherine began.

"But you don't know if He'll be faithful now?" Selma interrupted to question.

Catherine realized how silly it all sounded. "I just don't see the faithfulness. I want to. I really do. It's just so hard to maintain your hope when everything is out of the realm of your influence. I have no chance to alter the course on my own. I have no say in the matter."

Selma nodded. "I know. You're a servant of the Lord. And as a servant, you must trust the Master to guide and do right by you. Dugan and I have done that all of our lives. We've never had any other choice. When the master said we were to go somewhere and do something, we went without asking questions. That's how it is when you are a servant."

"Even when it meant leaving England to come here with me," Catherine said, realizing the impact. "I'm so sorry. I know this has been hard on you."

"But there have been blessings as well," Selma said, exchanging a glance with Dugan. "We love you, Catherine. We love your father too. Mr. Newbury was always good to us. We wanted to honor him and give him something in return."

"And seeing his only child to safety and out of the clutches of misunderstandings or Finley Baker was the one thing we could offer," Dugan replied. "Trusting God in all of this is the one thing you can offer. You can't see where the Master is asking you to go, but you have to trust that He has your best interests at heart."

The words comforted Catherine in a way she couldn't explain. "I will try," she whispered.

"And have hope that He is acting, even when you cannot see it or touch it," Selma offered. "You have no way of knowing how God is at work in this matter, but I assure you, He is."

Catherine thought of Selma's words long into the night. After soaking her sore feet for some time, she finally slipped into bed, exhausted from the day's events. She thought of her father and prayed that he might be comfortable wherever he'd been taken.

But soon Catherine found her thoughts becoming more dark and the images in her mind more bleak and desperate. Resolving not to ponder the worst, she instead replaced them with visions of Carter Danby. The memory of being in his arms—of his kiss—was enough to take her mind from the bad to the good.

When she awoke the next morning to the sound of church bells, she left behind a dream that made those peals the sound of wedding bells. It was hard to put that delightful image behind her, but Catherine knew she had to begin the day.

Breakfast was the usual chaotic affair. The excitement only heightened when Mrs. Clarkson announced that she was handing out the bonuses.

"I wanted you girls to have money as you leave today to visit your families for the holiday." She handed each girl a small drawstring bag. "I have made you each a little purse as my Christmas gift. Inside you will find your bonus for jobs well done. I'm proud of each one of you. You faced remarkable tasks and seemingly insurmountable odds, and came through in victory."

She rounded the table and gave Catherine a very heavy purse. With a smile she made yet another announcement. "Because of the popularity of Catherine's designs, and your hard work to implement her patterns, *Godey's Lady's Book* has decided to purchase several designs for publication. We will probably receive a great many additional orders. Because of this, I plan to expand the sewing house. In the new year, we will take on additional workers. We will bring in some more experienced seamstresses who are looking to give up their current situations, but you girls will always have a special place in my heart, so do not fear I will overlook you. I want this to be the best sewing house in all of Philadelphia."

"How exciting," Dolley exclaimed as she turned to Martha. "Won't that be grand?"

"Experienced seamstresses?" Felicia asked as she toyed with the bag. "I suppose that means none of us shall ever be able to step up in position beyond what we already have."

"It will depend," Mrs. Clarkson replied. "If the other women are more qualified, then you will simply have to wait until such time that your own experience and quality of work can equal theirs."

"That hardly seems fair," Felicia replied. She tossed her purse on the table. "But then, nothing about this place has ever seemed fair. We do all the work and you or Catherine gets all the glory."

Mrs. Clarkson was clearly taken aback, and Catherine felt sorry for the woman. Here she had generously shared her profits with the girls, only to be taken to task.

"I'm sorry you feel that way, Felicia. I truly am. I suppose that occurs when two people do not share the same vision."

"I have a vision as well," Felicia declared. "I have ideas for the design of gowns. Perhaps you should consider that Catherine isn't the only one capable of new ideas."

"If you have designs, you are welcome to bring them to my attention," Mrs. Clarkson answered. "I must admit this is the first I've heard of it."

"Some of us aren't as boastful as others," Felicia said, throwing a smirk at Catherine.

"I believe talent should be rewarded," Mrs. Clarkson said as she took her seat. "When you have something to contribute or offer, make it known. That is not boasting, it is helpful. Your situation here lasts only as long as the business is profitable. Remember that, girls." She addressed them collectively but looked directly at Felicia. "As the house fails, so fails your situation. No one will pay attention to a letter of reference given by a woman whose business fell apart. And without a letter, you will not easily regain employment."

Catherine watched Felicia grimace and turn her attention back to the purse. She hoped fervently that this would be the end of the younger woman's jealousy and anger, but somehow she didn't think it would. No doubt Felicia would do whatever she felt was in the best interests of Felicia, and if Mrs. Clarkson got hurt in the meanwhile, it wasn't of her concern.

CHAPTER 20

*C*atherine was nearly ready to find Selma and Dugan and head to church when a knock sounded at her door. Thinking it was probably Mrs. Clarkson, she opened it quickly.

Felicia stood on the other side. Dressed in a smart blue wool suit trimmed in black velvet, she looked ready to take on the world. "We should talk," she said, pushing her way into the room.

Catherine stared after her, not knowing what the woman was up to. Felicia casually took a seat on the edge of Catherine's bed.

"I'd close the door if I were you. You won't want anyone overhearing what I have to say."

Closing the door slowly, Catherine never took her gaze off Felicia's face. "What do you want?"

"I want a great many things," Felicia said and smiled.

The smug expression left Catherine on her guard. "There is nothing new about that. Why bring it to my doorstep?"

"Because I intend for you to help me."

Catherine shook her head. "Felicia, I'm heading to church. Make your point."

"I know who you are. I know your name is Newbury and that your father is in prison."

She hadn't wanted to react, but Catherine couldn't help it. The shock sent her to take a seat.

"I thought that might get your attention. You see, I have a feeling this news would be very much of interest to a great many people. Especially the police, since the authorities in England believe you might have had something to do with your father's illegal dealings."

Catherine had no idea how the young woman had managed all of this information, but there was no use denying it. Bolstering her courage, Catherine squared her shoulders and met Felicia's comments with a pretense of indifference. "And again I ask, what is it that you want?"

"I want money, of course. I had thought to simply get rid of you. That was my plan all along. I had told Lydia there would be no room for advancement if you were still here. Of course, now that Mrs. Clarkson intends to hire experienced seamstresses to join the staff, there might be no further advancement for any of us. And hence, no great money.

"That got me thinking," she said with a grin. "I might not be able to advance my position, but I could advance my purse.

You received a great deal of money today. And I know you will receive another good portion for the *Godey's* purchase. I want that money. I believe it would also be fitting that you continue to share money with me in the future. After all, we are all about to be made quite busy because of you."

"You're quite mad. I'm not giving you that money. If you know as much as you say you do, then you'd know I intend that money to be used to help my father."

Felicia shrugged. "It's of little matter to me. If the police come to arrest you, I'll simply take your money then. I know you keep it here somewhere, as neither you nor the Shays have a bank account. I checked."

Felicia got to her feet when a knock sounded on the door. "I'll expect your answer by evening." She opened the door and found Selma. "I'll pray for you, Catherine," Felicia said in a syrupy sweet voice. "I know you have difficult decisions to make."

Once Felicia was gone, Selma looked at Catherine for an explanation. "Somehow," Catherine began, "she has found out about us. She's trying to force me to give her all of the money I've made or will make. She's threatening to go to the police otherwise."

"Oh dear. Well, we knew this kind of thing could happen," Selma admitted. "Perhaps we would all do well to go to New York."

Catherine nodded. "I don't think we have much choice. If I turn over my money to her, it will mean Father will go on suffering another five years at least. You'd best tell Dugan. I'll go talk to Mrs. Clarkson."

❧

"I don't understand," Mrs. Clarkson said, her face pinched in an expression of pain. "Why must you leave?"

Catherine shook her head. "It's just better this way. Should the truth get out, you and this establishment will suffer as much as anyone. The revelation that my father is imprisoned for slave trading could ruin you. And while I know Felicia's jealousy and hatred led her here, I don't want her to get in trouble for this. There have already been enough problems in my life. I don't wish to be associated with yet another set."

"She's wrong to do this. She must have snooped around in your rooms. I cannot abide anyone doing such a thing."

"Still, unless you catch her red-handed," Catherine said sadly, "I doubt she would ever admit to it. I think, therefore, this is the only answer."

"But losing you will change everything," Mrs. Clarkson said. "I cannot continue to offer the great Catherine Shay designs. The house will fold." She sat down hard and sighed. "This was why I wanted to make you a partner. I wanted to ensure that you would have a reason to stay."

"I have brought you this," Catherine said, holding out her sketchbook. "There are a great many designs and pattern layouts on the pages here. You won't be without something to offer."

The older woman took the book and held it close. "But it won't be the same. Please promise me that if you have the opportunity or desire, you'll return to us. My offer to make you a partner still stands. Oh, and here . . ." She got up and went to her bedroom.

Catherine heard her shuffling around, and when she returned she held a great deal of money. "*Godey's* hasn't yet paid, but this is the amount they agreed to."

"I can't take it from you if they haven't paid."

"It won't be long before they do," Mrs. Clarkson replied. "I can afford to give you this now, so please do not fret. Also, there is money that I have set aside for you, as I do with each of the girls who come here. I had thought to simply trade it out in a partnership, but I suppose that can never happen now."

Catherine took the money. "I'm sorry our circumstances must cause you such grief. It was never my intention, as you know."

"Where will you go?"

"Back to New York. Captain Marlowe—the man who brought us to America—goes there often, and he can shed some light on what we should do next. He might even have word from my father."

"When do you plan to leave?"

Catherine got to her feet. "Immediately. Selma and Dugan are packing even now. We will each take one small bag and nothing more. It will be less conspicuous that way. If we're quick about it, we can make the afternoon train."

"I want to help. You will, of course, want as much time and distance between you and Felicia before the truth is found out. I can help in that. I will gather what few girls come home from church on the pretense of sharing a cup of Christmas punch before they leave. Have Dugan take the carriage. Leave it at the train station and I will send someone for it."

"Oh, you are too kind," Catherine said.

Mrs. Clarkson hugged her tight. "I am doing only what I can. I wish I could make everything right again for you." She pulled away. "You will be in touch, won't you? I long to know what happens."

"I promise I'll let you know of the changes." Catherine headed for the door. "I'll tell Dugan about the carriage."

"Oh, and Selma may take whatever food she wishes. You must have something to eat on the long journey."

Catherine nodded. "I will. Thank you."

❦

Carter couldn't stop thinking about Catherine all through the luncheon. Leander and Winifred talked about the wedding they desired and of where they might live.

"I would, of course, like for Carter to design us a house," Leander said with a grin, "but I cannot afford to build my own house at this time."

The judge exchanged a look with Leander's mother. She nodded and he cleared his throat. "We had thought to save this for Christmas, but since the subject has come up, we will speak of it now. Your mother and I had planned to buy you a house as a wedding gift. I think it would work equally well to have Carter design something for you."

"But that will take time," Mrs. Arlington said thoughtfully, "so perhaps in the meanwhile, you might live here with us."

Leander looked to Winifred. "What would you say to that?"

She smiled. "I would say so long as I remain at your side, it doesn't matter where we live."

"Ah, spoken from the heart of one truly in love," Leander's mother said with a sigh. "It is a love match, to be certain."

"I would be honored to donate my time and skills," Carter replied. "It will be my wedding gift to you both."

"Oh, you are such a wonderful brother," Winifred declared, getting up to give Carter a hug.

"I'll say. That will save us quite a sum," Leander teased. "I hear you are very expensive."

They all laughed at this as they settled into the music room. Winifred went to the piano and began to entertain them, and Carter thought her playing quite good. He smiled at the way she seemed to lose herself in the music. He couldn't help but wonder if Catherine played in the same style and manner.

He looked at the clock. It was nearly time. Carter had already determined he would wait until four, then make his way to Mrs. Clarkson's. This would give Catherine time to go to church and return for lunch and rest.

After Winifred played two numbers, Mrs. Arlington got up and played. She offered a sweet love song and sang as she masterfully controlled the keyboard.

" 'You are my heart's desire,' " she sang. " 'My reason for morning and night.' "

The words could have been Carter's pledge to Catherine. He determined there and then that when he saw her that afternoon, he would tell her everything. Even if they didn't know for sure that all would work to their desired outcome, Carter knew it was the right thing to do. He would tell her that over the last few months he had thought only of her, and in turn had worked to see her father set free.

When the clock struck four and the women concluded their playing, Carter got to his feet. "If you will please excuse me," he told them, "I have plans to see Miss Shay. I have a great many things to discuss with her."

Mrs. Arlington smiled. "I hope the condition of your heart is one of those things."

Carter laughed. "Indeed it is."

CHAPTER 21

Carter arrived at Mrs. Clarkson's feeling rather chilled. Snow had started to fall, and the temperature seemed to drop as he made his way from Lee's to the sewing house. He had hoped to have Catherine join him for a carriage ride, but since the weather showed no sign of improving, he planned to ask Mrs. Clarkson if they might use her private sitting room.

He grabbed the brass knocker and let it strike several times before standing back. It would have made him happy to find Catherine answering the door, but he was disappointed. The flirtatious blonde he'd met that first day at the sewing house greeted him instead.

"Well, hello. Mr. Danby, isn't it? Won't you come in," she said and curtsied. "What can I do for you?"

Carter gave a brief bow. "Thank you. I would like to speak with Miss Shay, please."

Felicia nodded. "I'm not entirely certain she's here, but if you want to rest in here," she said, motioning to the same room he'd waited in on many occasions, "I'll go see if she's returned." She offered him a coy smile, but her eyes held the look of a hungry lioness. "If she's not here, I'm sure I can keep you company until she is."

Carter said nothing. He took a seat and hoped she would take the hint that he had no interest in her. He toyed with the edge of a book—a collection of poetry, he noted—but made no effort to glance inside. At least the warmth of the fire took the chill from his bones.

Within moments, Mrs. Clarkson appeared at the door. "Mr. Danby, what brings you to our establishment on such a blustery day? My, but it hasn't been this cold in years. Did Felicia offer you something warm to drink?"

He got to his feet. "No, but that's perfectly all right. I actually came to see Miss Shay."

Mrs. Clarkson looked rather confused for a moment. "Well . . . that is . . . uh, the Shays aren't here . . . at present."

"Might I wait for their return?" Carter glanced to the window. "I'm not overly anxious to make another trip out this evening."

"I'm sorry, but I know they do not plan to return for some time. They were to visit with friends."

He thought she sounded guarded in her words but decided to let the matter drop. "I suppose I can just return in the morning. Thank you for your assistance."

Mrs. Clarkson nodded. "I wish you a most blessed Christmas, Mr. Danby."

He smiled. "I wish you the same, Mrs. Clarkson." Carter pulled his hat down tight and headed back to the carriage, now covered in snow. The horse gave a shake of his harness, as if to insist they hurry home.

Felicia found it odd that the Shays and Catherine had stayed away all day. Felicia had no one to visit for the holidays, and the house was eerily quiet. She figured that in time she would make enough of a name for herself that people would clamor to be with her. At least, that was her dream.

Of course, that dream had been easier to imagine before Catherine's success in designing gowns. She thought of the secrets she knew regarding Catherine's past. The knowledge gave her an edge that she hoped would allow for her own success. For now it would come to her in the form of money, but already she was toying with an idea to force Catherine to create designs that Felicia could attach her own name to. It would just be a matter of time before Felicia was able to take the upper hand.

"Soon I'll be as famous as that English tart."

Knocking on Catherine's door, Felicia knew there would be no answer. She quickly slipped into the room and closed the door. The room felt icy without a fire in the hearth. She couldn't suppress a shiver and took up Catherine's shawl from across the back of a nearby chair.

She glanced around the room and frowned. She couldn't put her finger on it, but something wasn't right. Now with the sunlight fading and twilight overtaking the evening, she began to wonder if Catherine and the Shays had gone somewhere for the holidays.

She went to the wardrobe and pulled it open. Clothes were obviously missing, but many things remained. Perhaps the missing pieces were simply being laundered by Selma. Still Felicia frowned, wondering if Catherine and the Shays had fled.

"Surely she wouldn't give up that easily," Felicia muttered, trying to look under the bed to see if Catherine's luggage was gone. There was one large case near the foot of the bed. She straightened, her frown deepening. Had she other bags? Smaller ones, perhaps?

"What are you doing in here?"

Felicia started. She hadn't heard the door open. "I . . . ah . . ." She remembered the shawl. "I . . . ah . . . came to borrow this shawl. Catherine said I might."

"I want to see you downstairs in my quarters," Mrs. Clarkson said, her eyes narrowing ever so slightly. "Immediately."

Felicia nodded and followed the woman out of Catherine's room and down the stairs. She dreaded the encounter, because she'd broken a very firm rule about being in someone else's room. Mrs. Clarkson had always been stern about such matters, and Felicia knew that in order to save herself, she would probably have to turn the focus back on Catherine.

"Have a seat," Mrs. Clarkson said as they entered the sitting room. Felicia sat rather stiff-backed on the closest wooden chair. She bowed her head but gazed upward to watch her employer.

"I'm very disappointed in your behavior, Felicia. It isn't the first time that you've been snooping about, is it?"

"I told you I went there for a shawl. I couldn't find mine. I think maybe Lydia accidentally took it with her."

Mrs. Clarkson crossed her arms. "Felicia, we both know that isn't the truth. I cannot abide a liar."

Felicia tried to think of what she should do next. She raised her head and straightened. "I want to tell you the truth, but I'm afraid it will get someone in trouble."

"Someone?"

Felicia nodded, trying her best to look innocent in the entire situation. "Catherine."

"And why would Catherine be in trouble? You were the one snooping around her room."

"Well, Lydia brought something to my attention. She told me that Catherine was lying about her identity." Felicia watched the older woman for her reaction but was disappointed when the woman acted as though the news meant nothing. "I didn't want to see the sewing house business endangered because of her questionable activities."

"And what activities would those be?"

"Well, to begin with, Catherine isn't Mr. and Mrs. Shay's daughter. Her real name is Newbury, and there are those who believe she might be a criminal."

"I see. And you felt this gave you the right to invade the privacy of others? Even knowing my rules about such matters?"

"I felt the situation merited further investigation. Had I said anything to anyone, the Shays and Catherine might have found a way to hide the truth."

"And what is this truth to you?"

Felicia shifted her weight nervously. "As I said, I didn't want to see any harm come to the sewing house."

"And so you felt it necessary to take matters into your own hands, even if that meant breaking the rules. If Catherine were a criminal, how would you be any different?"

"Looking for information to prove the truth isn't a criminal activity," Felicia argued.

"Perhaps not, but blackmail is." Mrs. Clarkson watched her carefully.

"I don't know what you're talking about."

"Well, my dear, since you refuse to be honest with me, I suppose I shall have no choice but to let you go."

Felicia was uncertain as to exactly what the woman was saying. "Let me go?"

"Yes. You'll have to gather your things and leave. I suppose the morning will be soon enough."

"No!" Felicia declared, jumping to her feet. "You can't do this to me. I . . . I . . . have nowhere to go."

"Felicia, I cannot have you here breaking the rules and threatening the employees. I already knew about Catherine's past. The poor girl was ripped from her home and deprived of the comforts she'd always known. Now you want to further her miseries. It's a most uncharitable and unchristian thing to do. Not to mention illegal. The very thought of anyone using such despicable actions completely offends me."

"But I can't lose my job." Felicia was beginning to see that she was backed into a corner. If Mrs. Clarkson fired her, she would have no letter of reference, and without that, Felicia could hardly expect to get another job. At least not without having to start all over at the bottom.

She dropped back onto the chair, unable to think of what she could do or say that would make matters right. "I'm sorry.

I never meant to hurt anyone. I thought this was the right way to handle the matter."

Mrs. Clarkson shook her head. "It was the selfish way. If you had a concern, you could have come to me and we would have discussed it. Now, because you threatened to take the money Catherine needed to get her father help, she's felt it necessary to go."

"Go?" Felicia asked.

"Yes. She's gone, and without her designs we'll go back to being just one more sewing house in Philadelphia. We will, perhaps, even need to close our doors from loss of income."

Felicia had never thought that the situation could get this far out of control. She had figured Catherine would want to keep the truth quiet and would cooperate with Felicia's demands.

"Where did she go? Can't you ask her to come back? I promise to leave her be," Felicia suddenly declared.

"I don't know where she's gone. Catherine, at this time, is completely beyond my care. What we have to determine is what to do about you."

Felicia knew her only hope was to apologize and plead her case. "Please don't send me away. I have no one. My family, as you well know, are all dead. I need this job—it's all I have."

"Then why didn't you consider this before making such poor choices?" Mrs. Clarkson was still quite stern.

"I suppose I acted out of fear more than anything," Felicia replied. "You always seem to talk of Catherine's accomplishments, and I suppose I felt jealous. I would like to have the opportunity to make designs as well."

"And I told you before that if you have something to show me, I am more than happy to see it. The most important thing we do is provide diversity for our customers."

Felicia sat in silence, fearing that if she said anything she would further damage her chances to stay on at Mrs. Clarkson's.

"If I thought you really cared or were really sorry for the things you did, I might be more open to reconsider. If you weren't given to deception and to imposing your will on others, it might be easier to give you a second chance."

It was becoming increasingly clear that Mrs. Clarkson wasn't about to yield. Felicia felt a deep sense of fear wash over her. Where would she go? She decided to appeal to Mrs. Clarkson's Christian nature.

"But what of forgiveness? The Bible says that we should forgive. I'm asking you to forgive me, Mrs. Clarkson." She tried her best to look contrite.

The older woman shook her head. "And what of repentance? What of being truly sorry for your actions, and not merely because you were caught?"

Felicia fought to control her anger. The woman was completely infuriating. "How can you sit there in judgment of me?"

"Your actions sit in judgment of you." Mrs. Clarkson got to her feet. She produced a small purse much like the one the girls had received earlier that morning. "This is money I have set aside for you. When each girl lives here I take a small amount and put it aside for her in hope that one day she might be able to go out on her own and set up a business for herself. This is your portion." She handed the bag to Felicia. "You may stay until after Christmas Day, but then you must be gone. I cannot have this house further upset."

Felicia looked at the bag and then at Mrs. Clarkson. "I cannot believe you would just send me out like this. I've always been a good worker. I've always done my share."

"Yes, but you've also caused your share of trouble. Felicia, I took you in and cared for you as if you were my own daughter. I understood your hostilities as someone newly orphaned, but that anger has never left you. You would do yourself good to try to find a way to overcome your greed and anger."

Felicia got to her feet. "You'll be sorry for this."

"Are you threatening me?" Mrs. Clarkson asked. "I can still have the police brought into this matter."

"I'm not threatening you, I'm merely stating the truth," Felicia said, her jaw clenching tight. She clutched the bag and headed to the door. "You've lost Catherine and her sewing talents, and now you're sending me away. I'm the Second Hand. You have no other more experienced seamstress in this house, save yourself. That's what I mean when I say you'll be sorry."

"I'll take my chances," Mrs. Clarkson said, sadly shaking her head. "At least I will know I can trust my workers."

Felicia pulled the door closed behind her. A part of her wanted to set fire to the house and burn it to the ground, while another part was resigned to accept her fate. She couldn't change the older woman's mind, and with her luck, Felicia would only end up in jail if she took any kind of action.

Taking sanctuary in her room, Felicia tossed the bag of money to her bed. She had no idea how much Mrs. Clarkson had given her, but it would have to be enough.

"No one's ever cared about whether I survive," she said bitterly. "No one but me." *And that's the way things are likely to stay,* she told herself.

CHAPTER 22

W ell, bless my bows," Mrs. Samuelson said as she ushered the Shays and Catherine into the front room. "I didn't figure to ever see you again, and now here you are standing before me as big as day. And on the day before the Lord's birth."

"Do you have rooms?" Selma asked. "We find ourselves in need of a place to stay."

"I do, I do. I have two and will soon have another," the woman responded. "Just lost a renter last week, and another gentleman is leaving just after New Year's. Said my forgetfulness was starting to affect the quality of the meals around here." She cackled a laugh. "I told him I couldn't help getting old."

"Well, it seems to be to our benefit," Selma said, looking to Catherine. "It might be only a short stay, however."

"Ah, well then, we'll just enjoy our time together while we can." She eyed Selma with a grin. "Would you want to be trading cookin' and cleanin' for rent?"

"I'd like that very much," Selma said. "Dugan can also work around the house to fix things up."

"Oh my, but that would be a blessin'. I have a flue upstairs that's stuck. Causes the fires to smoke up the room something fierce. Since Mr. Samuelson died, I can't seem to get good help. I will let the two of you live here and eat for free if you'll do all of that." She looked to Catherine as if to ask what she might contribute.

"I'll be happy to take in sewing and laundry to pay my portion," Catherine admitted. "I know your boarders are generally men who'd rather not do such things for themselves. I'll give you the cash I can earn."

"Seems settled, then," Mrs. Samuelson said. "I'll show you upstairs. You'll have different rooms than before." She took up a ring of keys from her apron pocket and led the way.

Catherine smiled at the familiarity of the place. She hadn't been here in years, but the same steps still creaked, the banister was still loose, and the place still smelled of lemon verbena and day-old fish.

"Miss Catherine would likely be happy in this room," Mrs. Samuelson said, opening the door. "There's good morning light here for your sewing."

Catherine noted the narrow room and tiny bed. There was a small table and chair beside the fireplace near the foot of the bed, and a trunk in which one could store clothing rested under the table.

"It looks just fine," Catherine said.

Mrs. Samuelson gave her a key and nodded. "The Shays will be next door, and lunch will be served in an hour."

Catherine closed the door and set her bag on the table. The train ride had been arduous and nearly unbearable. The heat stove hadn't been working correctly, so the car was colder than usual. Catherine's feet remained frozen. They'd had to spend the night while en route to New York City due to the snow. She was still surprised they were able to come the rest of the way this morning. Huge drifts had lined the tracks, although the depths had lessened the closer they came to New York City.

She sat down on the side of the bed, not surprised to find the telltale sagging of a rope bed. Already she missed the comfort of Mrs. Clarkson's home. Funny, she used to pine over her home in England, but that seemed like centuries in the past.

Closing her eyes, she tried to remember the look and smell of her house in Bath. The memories were blurred. Five years of pushing them aside in order to keep from wasting away in sadness had taken its toll. The pictures in her mind were faded as a photograph left out in the sun. Worse still, she couldn't even imagine her father's face. She worried that he would be greatly altered from sickness—should she ever see him again.

Carter Danby came to mind. Catherine thought of his kindness to her at the Arlingtons' dinner. She was certain that he remembered her now. But more than this, she suspected he had to have known something of her father's plight. Otherwise, why would he have stopped the conversation and changed the subject?

"He cares about me," she said, gazing across the tiny room. "He'll be upset when he finds out I'm gone."

She could imagine Carter asking Mrs. Clarkson for her whereabouts. He wouldn't like the answer—the fact that she didn't know where they'd gone. Mrs. Clarkson wouldn't betray their confidences.

"So why do I almost wish she would?" Catherine whispered.

Then a dreaded thought came to mind. Mrs. Clarkson might not share what she knew, but Felicia would. Felicia would delight in telling Carter why Catherine and the Shays had gone without saying good-bye.

"She'll tell everyone about my father and the slave trading," Catherine said, shaking her head. "I can never go back to Philadelphia. I can never again design gowns as Catherine Shay." She sighed. "And there can never be a future for Carter and me."

Carter wrestled with the decision, then told the clerk he'd take the necklace. For over an hour he'd tried to decide whether or not to purchase the trinket for Catherine. Well, it was a little more than a trinket. The piece was an exceptional work of gold and sapphires. He knew it was uncalled for. There was nothing official between him and Catherine, and he'd already spent a good portion of his savings helping her father. If he wasn't careful he'd be forced to sell stocks in order to finance his plans to move.

"Here you are, sir. I hope your wife will enjoy the piece."

Carter nodded, not bothering to correct the man. It was indeed the type of gift a husband would give his wife. He tucked the box in his coat pocket and touched his hand to his hat. "Thank you." He left the shop quickly, feeling strangely embarrassed by the transaction.

Outside the shop, Carter nearly collided with a stately older man. "I do apologize, sir. I failed to watch my step."

"Carter Danby? It is you!"

Carter immediately recognized his former mentor, Hollis Fulbright. He was dressed impeccably in a black wool coat and top hat. He hadn't bothered to button the overcoat, and beneath it Carter spied a plum-colored coat, yellow printed vest, and green and yellow ascot against a white shirt. All of this accompanied striped trousers in hues of plum, yellow, and navy. He was the same flamboyant fashion statement that he'd been years earlier when Carter worked with him.

"How do you do, sir? I have often thought of you. I heard that you had moved to Boston?"

"I had. But to tell you the truth, you are the reason I've come back to Philadelphia."

"Truly?"

"Yes. I was just doing a bit of bank business, then it was my plan to come to your house. I thought we might talk."

"I would like that very much. Have you eaten?"

"No. Might we share something together?"

Carter motioned up the street. "There is a reputable spot at the end of the street. Nothing fancy, mind you, but the roast is always fresh and never overcooked."

"Sounds wonderful, my boy. Let us go."

Carter led the way. "When did you arrive?"

"Just this morning. The snows made some of the rails impassable and we had to wait for men to clear them, otherwise I might have been here yesterday."

"How long will you stay?" Carter asked.

The older man smiled. "That is part of the reason I'm here. I have a proposal to put forth. But it will wait until we are seated."

"And what of Mrs. Fulbright? Did she travel with you?"

The older man frowned. "I'm afraid my wife died nearly six months ago. She had a weak liver, the doctor said."

"I am very sorry to hear that," Carter said.

"I miss her dearly. She was God's gift to me, and I made her my earthly focus. I find now I must give work that place, lest I grow discouraged."

They entered the establishment Carter had recommended. A buxom woman immediately greeted them and wiped her hands on her apron.

"Come this way, gentlemen. I have a good table for you. Can I bring you some ale?"

"No, actually, I'd prefer hot coffee. I'm chilled to the bone," Fulbright replied.

Carter smiled and agreed. "That would be good for me as well. I'll also take the roast and potatoes."

"As will I," Fulbright said as he settled at the wooden trestle table. "And plenty of gravy. Oh, and bread. I must have bread."

"Sure, love. I'll bring it right away." She sauntered away, swinging her hips.

Carter turned his attention to his old friend. "So tell me of this proposal."

Hollis Fulbright smiled, his muttonchop whiskers rising along with his cheeks. Carter thought he'd changed very little since they'd last seen each other now nearly seven years past.

There were perhaps a few more pounds and more gray hair, but the twinkle in his eyes gave him a younger man's appearance.

"I want to entice you to work as my partner."

Carter was dumbfounded. His silence caused Fulbright to laugh.

"I never thought I could render you speechless."

"It's just that your timing is rather uncanny. I have been giving serious consideration as to what I should do with my career. I have several clients for whom I'm designing houses, but I must say I'm more than a little interested in what you've offered."

The serving girl returned with their meal on a tray, as well as two steaming mugs of coffee. She put the bread between them, as well as a bowl of gravy, then placed identical plates of roast and potatoes before each man.

Before Carter could offer to pay, Hollis had tossed the girl several coins. "Keep it, and leave us to our discussion." The girl nodded but looked a bit disappointed. She took her tray and strolled away, but not before casting one more enticing look over her shoulder.

Carter ignored her and turned to Fulbright. "So you were saying?"

"I'm glad to hear you say that you're interested. Let me tell you why I'm here." Hollis leaned forward. "But first let me offer grace."

Carter smiled and bowed his head. His mentor had always revealed his love of God in his daily life. Fulbright prayed and asked a blessing on the food as well as understanding and guidance for their conversation. When he finished, Carter truly felt that the meeting had been ordained.

"Washington City is expanding. The government plans this year to contract additional buildings. They've already begun preparations to replace the capitol dome with a fire-proof, cast iron structure. Do you remember the competition in 1850 to choose the designers who would expand the capitol?"

"Of course. Every architect, whether interested in participating or not, remembers the five-hundred-dollar purse that was offered," Carter said.

"Well, there is to be another competition. I believe between you and me, we can win that competition." The older man broke a piece of bread from the loaf and sopped it with gravy before popping it into his mouth.

Carter sat back and looked at Fulbright for a moment. The man wasn't jesting or merely putting out a thought for consideration; he had plans for this competition—plans that had brought him to Carter's doorstep.

"If we won and received the contract," Fulbright continued, "I believe it would require us to move to Washington. Would that be of any interest to you?"

Carter went back to work on his food. The answer for him was very easy. "Yes. Yes, I would find that of great interest to me."

"What of your family? Surely you've taken a wife by now."

Carter smiled. "I'm trying to take a wife but have not yet accomplished that task. I would, of course, want to consider her desires in the matter."

"Of course. However, since the time is so very short, I am suggesting we take a trip to the city and survey the sites already chosen and perhaps sketch out some ideas. I'd like to leave the day after Christmas."

Carter considered the matter for several minutes as they ate in silence. Once he saw Catherine and explained his knowledge of her family—and proposed marriage—he would know for sure where he stood with her. If he could accomplish that much before they left, it would give him a greater ability to make choices for the future.

"I think I would like to come with you," Carter said, forking a piece of potato. "At least by giving the matter some serious specu-lation, we can better tell if the project is of as much interest in person as it is in our minds." He grinned and Hollis laughed.

"It will also give you time to pray on the matter. I've already given it a great deal of thought and prayer, but I know that I cannot take on this project without you. Besides that, I'm nearly sixty years old. I need a partner who can come alongside me. I have always been impressed with your abilities—your style and manner of design."

"Well, you did much to train me. A great deal of my style can be credited to your teachings."

"I appreciate that. But even so, you are to be honored for your own abilities and insight. You are an artist at heart. You see things that are not and dream them into life. I want that kind of partner."

"And where would we set up shop? Washington?"

"Well, I suppose we would have to be there at least as long as the jobs were under construction. Are you averse to moving?"

"No. Not at all." Carter sliced a piece of bread and thought-fully considered what Catherine might say on the matter. "I do have obligations here, however. I have been commissioned to build two houses, one of them quite extensive. My designs will guide the construction, but I will need to oversee from time to time."

"Perhaps that can be balanced between cities. Washington is not that far by train."

"That's true. So tell me what our plan will be."

As they shared their lunch, Fulbright explained they would take the train and stay for several days in Washington. "We should be able to be home by New Year's Eve, so if you have plans, it won't interfere."

"I have no plans at this moment, but perhaps by then I will." Carter thought of Catherine again and smiled. "Yes, if I have my way, I will have very important plans."

❧

Catherine walked along the harbor and felt the cold wind against her face. She thought of her father out there somewhere across the sea. Captain Marlowe wasn't due back in town for a week or more, but Mrs. Samuelson assured them that he was coming. Atlantic winter crossings were always of greater risk, however, and thus the passages were often taken with slower speeds and more consideration to the weather. Catherine prayed the captain might find calm, clear waters. She prayed, too, that he might bring good news of her father's safety—even freedom.

An icy rain began to fall lightly just as she reached Mrs. Samuelson's house. Catherine tried not to worry about the future, remembering a verse that Selma had shared with her only that morning about the Lord giving rest.

She pulled out the piece of paper Selma had given her and reread the words of Isaiah fourteen, verse three. " 'And it shall come to pass in the day that the Lord shall give thee rest from thy sorrow, and from thy fear, and from the hard bondage wherein thou wast made to serve,'" she murmured aloud.

Selma had said the words were given in regard to Israel, but that given God's unchanging nature, she believed them to speak of Catherine's situation as well.

"He might not have had them written specifically for you, Catherine," Selma had told her, *"but because God is faithful and loving, I am certain we can trust them to be true for us. God will give you rest from the sorrows and fears you have known. He will deliver you from a life of running and hiding, of working until you are exhausted."*

Catherine sighed and put the piece of paper back into her pocket. She looked up at the boardinghouse and sighed again. She had come full circle, it seemed. This was where her American journey began, and now here she was again. Had it happened this way to bring her to the end?

CHAPTER 23

"Oh, it's so good to have Mrs. Shay cooking for us," Mrs. Samuelson said as they all ate a hearty meal of fish chowder and biscuits.

There were four other men at the table besides Dugan, and they ate with such an appetite that Catherine thought they might well have been locked away without food for some time. When Selma produced an apple crisp and cream for dessert, Catherine heard a collective sigh of approval from around the table.

When all seemed completely sated, the men shuffled off to various parts of the house. Mrs. Samuelson admonished them as they headed out, "Don't get ashes on my carpet, and if you go out, wipe your muddy boots before coming into my house."

Catherine nibbled at the bowl of crisp Selma had put in front of her, but she had little appetite. She felt more forlorn than she had in years. Being here again only served to remind her of those early days of despair. Here it was, Christmas again. One more Christmas without her father.

"We've managed to get by," the old woman told the Shays. "It hasn't always been easy. There were some moments when I worried about whether we'd be able to make it. There was a bad fire not long after you left. It started about two blocks away. We worried it would spread, but a heavy rain came up and put it out. We were all in church the next day, if you know what I mean."

Selma smiled. "I can well imagine. It looks like you've done all right for yourself. Your husband would no doubt be proud."

Mrs. Samuelson nodded. "He would at that. Despite the trials we've suffered over the years since his death, there's been good along with the bad. Our daughter—you might remember she was a widow?" Selma nodded, and the woman continued. "Well, she remarried and is happier and better off than ever. That husband of hers has a way with money. Seems what little he manages to get hold of he finds a way to double. They've done very well for themselves."

"That must be a comfort."

The chatter continued about Mrs. Samuelson's other children, as well as two elderly aunts who now rested in the arms of Jesus, and a bevy of weary travelers who either blessed or frustrated the old woman.

"And of course," Mrs. Samuelson said, "there were those two gents who came looking for you."

Catherine had barely registered the words as Selma asked, "What men?"

Mrs. Samuelson laughed. "I don't recall their names. Goodness, but my mind ain't what it was." She tapped the side of her head with a finger. "They was both nice looking and well-behaved. They talked with Captain Marlowe. I can't be sure what he told them, but you could always ask the captain when he shows up."

"Where were they from?" Catherine asked. She felt the apple crisp stick in her throat.

"I'm not sure. I'm thinking maybe Philadelphia." Mrs. Samuelson's face scrunched up in a wrinkled but concentrated stare. "I'm almost certain it was Philadelphia." She relaxed and shook her head. "But it could have been New Jersey."

"Please try hard to remember," Catherine said, trying not to sound desperate.

Mrs. Samuelson shook her head and shrugged. "Doesn't do me any good. Sometimes I remember and sometimes I don't. Trying hard at it doesn't seem to change things at all."

Selma began to gather the dishes, but Mrs. Samuelson waved her off. "You three go on up to rest. I'll get the dishes. I'm sure you're tired." She hoisted her stocky frame up and began the work herself. "I wish I could help you more, but I will say the men were quite kind. They seemed very much familiar with you, Miss Catherine. I think they were good friends of yours. Especially the one. He seemed quite taken with you."

Carter came to mind, and in that moment Catherine began to understand. Carter had come to New York back in November. He had seemed to understand she wouldn't wish to speak of her family at the Arlingtons' dinner.

"I am very tired," she said and pushed the bowl away. "I believe I will retire."

She had barely made it upstairs and closed the door to her room when Selma came knocking and calling to her, "Catherine, we should talk."

Catherine reopened the door. "It had to be Carter and Leander Arlington," she said, knowing that Selma would understand.

"Let's not talk here in the hallway. Come to our room."

Nodding, Catherine followed her out, then turned and locked her door. Mrs. Samuelson had said there were plenty of thieves in the area, and a crafty one was often able to slip into boardinghouses unseen. She admonished them to keep their doors locked at all times.

Selma and Dugan seemed less concerned. They didn't bother to lock their door after entering, but Catherine supposed it a rather unneeded exercise. The room was quite small, and if more than two people came into it, they might well have to link arms just to move about. She even found it necessary to remain near the door while Selma motioned Dugan to bring the chair to Catherine.

"Catherine believes the men who came here to ask after her were Mr. Danby and Mr. Arlington," Selma offered as Dugan returned to sit on the edge of the bed beside his wife.

"The thought crossed my mind as well. It seemed quite clear to me that your Mr. Danby had taken a great interest in you," Dugan offered.

"He's told me that he's in love with me. He wants to court me. At least he wanted me to do so then," Catherine said. But if he had come to New York in November, then whatever he learned hadn't changed his heart toward her.

"What do you think he'll do with the information?" Selma asked.

"I don't know. I don't know why he felt compelled to seek it out to begin with or how he found out to start here." Catherine twisted her hands. "Between the fact that he knows and Felicia knows, I don't think we can hope to be safe here anymore. We cannot remain in New York City."

Selma looked to Dugan, and her expression was one of extreme concern. "But where should we go?"

"Perhaps the time has come to return to England," Catherine said firmly. "Captain Marlowe would surely grant us passage. He might not even charge us. He wouldn't take Father's money to bring us here, and maybe he would refuse it to take us back."

"*If* he would take us back," Dugan replied. "If he feels 'tis not in your best interest, he might well refuse."

Catherine hadn't thought of that. "Well, it's possible, I suppose, but it is a chance we can take. It cannot hurt to inquire and present our request."

"True," Dugan said, nodding. "It's not as if he doesn't already know the truth."

"Don't you have family in Scotland, Dugan?" Catherine asked, a thought coming to mind. "I doubt anyone would look for you and Selma there after all this time. You could go there and be safe. No one believes you responsible for anything that happened anyway. I know you only came here because of me."

"And that is where we will stay," Selma replied. "With you. Our promise to your father was to guard you as our own. You are truly a daughter to us."

Catherine gave Selma a hug. "While I do not fear Carter causing me problems, I feel almost certain Felicia will stop at nothing. If she was able to get the information regarding Father and our past, then she most likely will figure out where we have gone."

Dugan turned to Selma. "She makes a good point. Perhaps we could inquire of Captain Marlowe to take us to England, then maybe catch another ship north."

"It might work. From the letters we've had in all this time, no one has indicated that Catherine is being actively sought by the law. They might want to question her knowledge or prove that she's not been kidnapped, but it isn't as if they would harm her." Selma thought for a moment. "It would definitely put us closer to helping poor Mr. Newbury. Now that Catherine has a good amount of money, the longer she waits to put it to use, the more we'll end up spending as we sit trying to decide what to do."

"We must, at any rate, wait for Captain Marlowe," Catherine admitted. "All we can do is hope that Felicia will not know about this place, and that Carter won't try to visit me until well after the holidays. If we can just have the time we need until the captain returns, we should be all right. We can make our way home and find a good barrister who will help Father."

"I'm sorry, Mr. Danby, the Shays and Miss Catherine have gone out," Mrs. Clarkson said with a pleasant smile. "I cannot say when they will return."

Carter fingered the gift in his pocket, frustrated that he'd still not yet seen Catherine. He tried to force the disappointment from his mind. "Very well. Would you please tell Miss Shay that I called? I find it necessary to go out of town for a few days."

"Oh," she replied, sounding suddenly interested. "And where are you bound?"

"Washington. I hope to be back within a week. I'll come back by at that time."

"Very well. Merry Christmas to you, Mr. Danby."

"Merry Christmas to you, Mrs. Clarkson."

She quickly closed the door after bidding him farewell and a safe journey.

Carter stood for a moment staring at the closed door. Something seemed wrong, but he couldn't be sure what it was. Mrs. Clarkson acted quite nervous. He wondered for a moment if perhaps Catherine had become ill or if she were upstairs simply refusing his call.

"I'll send Winifred with a note tomorrow," he murmured. The words did little to comfort him.

CHAPTER 24

*T*his will one day be such a glorious city," Hollis Fulbright told Carter as they walked in Washington. "It will rival any of the other great seats of government."

"If Americans can put aside their differences, it might. The slavery issue is dividing this country. I suppose coming here has really opened my eyes to that matter."

"Yes, it is a sad state of affairs," Fulbright agreed. "One that cannot be ignored, no matter how we try."

"I never thought I'd see the day grown men raise their fists to each other over issues of whether a state should come into the union free or slave," Carter said, remembering a scene he'd witnessed yesterday in a local hotel. "While you were meeting with your friend Mr. Masters, I sat in the hotel lobby to read. Two men, later identified to me as state senators, began arguing over the issue of Kansas coming into the union. One thing led to another and the men were soon pummeling each other."

Fulbright nodded. "Masters told me the issue of Kansas and slavery has consumed the city. It seems that poor territory is suffering a civil war all its own—not to mention whether the rest of the country will fall into that disrepair."

"Yes, but to see gentlemen coming to blows over issues that will need calmer heads to prevail and resolve is worrisome indeed." Carter wondered if the country could survive a war between the states. The South had been threatening secession for years, and no doubt sooner or later they would make good on their threats.

"This year's presidential campaign will tell us a great deal. Should the wrong candidate be elected, we will no doubt see trouble," Fulbright agreed.

"Yet the city builds on, pretending nothing is amiss," Carter said, shaking his head.

"Perhaps that is a bit harsh. I don't think they build on in pretense but rather in hope. The hope that if we invest enough in our country, our government, then we will stand fast to stave off war."

"I pray you are right. I would hate to see war come to America. There are so many blessings that I find it impossible to imagine people can put those aside and focus only on the issues that divide us."

They made their way to one of the properties where it was hoped a new government building could be created. Carter looked at the nearest properties, noting their style and architectural detail. The Greek Revival pieces were highly favored.

"There are plans for a road to be brought through on the other side," Fulbright said, glancing at a paper that detailed some of the information related to the project.

Carter made a quick sketch of the area before they moved on to yet another property. He couldn't help but think of Catherine and wonder if she would like living in Washington. If she wanted to move back to England, Carter knew it would create difficulties for them. Of course, they could always live there part of the year, and in America the rest of the time.

The threat of war was also something to consider. If the issues of slavery and states' rights could not be resolved, then Carter knew the South would secede. No president or Congress in their right minds would allow that to go unchallenged, and there would be war.

If war comes to America, I could always move my family to England, Carter thought. *I could take them out of the ugliness altogether.* He supposed it wasn't a very patriotic thing to think, but at the moment he couldn't help himself. He didn't approve of slavery, but neither was he in support of a war. There was, in fact, a part of him that figured if the South wanted to secede, the rest of the country should let them. Like wayward children, they would come back when they saw what they had lost in shared revenues, protection, and common interests. Still, the matter might be completely taken from his hands. If Catherine moved back to England and refused to stay in America, he might well have to make his way there for the purpose of persuasion.

Catherine was ever on his mind. Even as he sketched and thought of what type of building he might suggest, it was

Catherine's image that rested not far from conscious thought. He had left a note with Winifred, instructing her to take it to Catherine the same day he departed for Washington. With any luck, the two of them would have shared a little time together, and Winifred could explain that Carter was away on business.

The note explained very little but told Catherine it was a matter of great importance that they meet and speak. The matter, he had assured, would be something she would wish to discuss with him at her earliest convenience. He hoped she might read between the lines and realize that he was on her side—that she had nothing to fear from him.

"Your mind seems miles away from Washington," Fulbright said.

Carter looked up from the paper. "I suppose it is. I'm sorry."

"Have you thought any more about the offer to become my partner? I don't wish to pressure you into making a rash decision, but I can't help but be anxious."

"I understand. I have given it some thought, but I suppose I would like to make a decision based partially on what happens with the designs we submit. I would hate for you to feel obligated to take me on if the projects were rejected. I wouldn't want to see you saddled with a partner you could no longer use."

"My boy, I have more than enough work in Boston to keep us both busy. Of course, my decision about taking on those projects will also be based on what happens here in Washington. I suppose I can understand your concern and desire to take matters slowly, but I beg you to let me know at the first opportunity."

"When do we need to have the designs submitted for the competition?" Carter asked. He secured the sketch in a satchel and joined Fulbright as he began walking in the direction of their hotel.

"The deadline is the first of February. I know it's short notice, but they hope to break ground in late March."

Carter thought again of his great desire to spend time with Catherine. "It will be difficult but not impossible. I will help you with the designs, but I would want to work from Philadelphia. Can you somehow accommodate this?"

"I can. I will stay with my sister, who resides in Philadelphia, until the designs are complete."

"I greatly appreciate that, sir. I promise not to keep you waiting for an answer too long. Once we hear back from the competition, we can decide how to move forward."

❧

Back in Philadelphia, Carter was quite anxious to visit Catherine. He had barely stepped from the train before turning his attention to that very matter. Joseph was waiting faithfully with the carriage, and to Carter's surprise, Winifred waited with him.

They gave Hollis Fulbright a ride to his sister's house on Seventh Street. The house was a fashionable three-story brick with elegant but simple marble stairs to the front door. Joseph saw to the man's luggage while Carter bid him farewell.

"I will be in touch just as soon as I've sketched out some designs. I've taken good notes on what you suggested, and combined with my own thoughts on the various purposes and locations, I'll come up with something useful. I promise."

"I've no doubt you will, my boy. Why don't you plan to come see me on Monday the seventh, say around noon? We can share lunch and discuss any further concerns you have. I am certain my sister will not mind my arrangement."

"I would like that," Carter admitted. "I will see you then."

"Very well. Good day to you," Fulbright said, then turning to Winifred, he smiled and bowed. "And a very good day to you, my dear. You are quite pretty, and were I a young man, I might attempt to court you."

"Then you would have to fight my dear friend," Carter threw in, "for he just proposed to my sister only a little more than a week ago."

Fulbright laughed and put his hands over his rather round belly. "Well, I am too late in years and days, it would seem. Never mind. It does not change the fact that you are beautiful and quite worthy of such attention."

"Thank you, sir." Winifred blushed, and Carter thought it only served to make her all the prettier. "You are very kind."

They left Fulbright still chuckling at the door as the carriage pulled back onto the street. Carter was quick to move the conversation in the direction he desired.

"Tell me of Catherine."

Winifred frowned and toyed with her bonnet ribbons. "There's nothing you wish to hear, I'm afraid."

Carter sat back hard. "You mean she'll have nothing to do with me?"

Winifred met his gaze. "No. I mean that she is gone."

"Gone?" Carter shook his head. "What are you saying?"

"I went to see her at the sewing house. Beatrix told me she and the Shays had gone. So I asked if I might speak with Mrs. Clarkson. The woman came and seemed quite upset that Beatrix had shared any information. She said only that the Shays had been called away unexpectedly."

"Did she say why?" His mind whirled; perhaps word had come from England. Maybe her father had already been set free and she'd gone to him.

"She said only that there was no thought of their returning. At least not right away. I'm so sorry. I asked Leander about it. He doesn't have any idea of what happened."

Carter hit his fist against the side of the carriage. "This is all my fault. If I hadn't kissed her, she wouldn't have gone."

Winifred smiled. "I seriously doubt that. I'm sure that your kiss was the one thing that would have kept her here if she could have stayed. I'm thinking something else must have happened. And, furthermore, I believe Mrs. Clarkson knows exactly what that something might be."

"Very well. Then we shall go straightaway and visit her." He tapped on the roof of the carriage and waited for Joseph to bring it to a stop. Carter leaned out the door. "Take us to Mrs. Clarkson's sewing house."

"Yes, suh. Right away."

Carter secured the door, then looked at his sister. Winifred was smiling rather smugly. "What is that grin all about?"

"I knew you would do this," she said. "It's part of the reason I came along. I could have waited for you to come home, but I knew it would mean that Joseph would simply have to turn around, and that seemed a great waste of time."

He smiled, but the rest of their journey was silent, as Carter's fears of what Mrs. Clarkson would say grew.

When Joseph brought the carriage to a stop, Carter looked out and saw the familiar sign over the doorway. "We are here," he said in a tone that almost sounded regretful. If Mrs. Clarkson told him that Catherine left because of his actions at the ball, he wasn't sure he could bear it.

He waited for Joseph to open the door, then allowed him to help Winifred down first. Carter soon was at her side and together they made their way up the walkway.

"No matter what," Winifred said, patting his arm, "God has everything perfectly ordered. Always remember that."

"I'll try." He let go the brass knocker several times and waited for the door to open.

Mrs. Clarkson was the one to greet them, and her expression told him she was not at all happy to see him. "Good afternoon to you both. What can I do for you?"

"We need to talk. It's quite important."

Reluctantly she allowed them in and motioned for them to follow her. Carter could hear work going on in the various rooms. "Please be seated in here. These are my private rooms," Mrs. Clarkson told them. She opened the door and led the way. Once they were all inside, she closed the door and took a seat.

Carter waited until Winifred was seated before taking his own place between the two women. "I've come because of Catherine Newbury. My sister tells me she has gone."

Mrs. Clarkson nodded. "I'm sorry. I did not feel at liberty to tell you sooner."

"I understand," Carter replied, trying hard not to be angry. "You wished to protect her."

"Yes. She's a dear girl who has suffered much."

"So you know about her past?" Carter questioned. "About her father?" He could tell by her reaction that she did. She looked away but nodded nevertheless. "I found out as well," Carter continued. "She doesn't realize that I know, but I do. I've been working for some time now to see her father freed."

"Is this true? Why did you not tell her?" Mrs. Clarkson looked at him in complete surprise.

Carter shook his head and shrugged. "I don't know. I suppose I honestly felt it would be wrong to get her hopes up until I was certain of the outcome. I suppose it was silly, but I didn't want to see her hurt any more, and I worried that my meager efforts might result in more pain."

Mrs. Clarkson's expression softened. "You love her very much, don't you?"

Carter nodded. "Did she say why she had to go?"

"I'm afraid one of the other girls here learned the truth and threatened her," Mrs. Clarkson replied.

"What?" Carter looked at Winifred, who only shook her head.

"I'm afraid it's true. Felicia managed to learn the truth and threaten Catherine. She tried to blackmail her into giving Felicia all of her savings—the money she was working so hard to collect for her father's legal counsel."

Carter hadn't realized he'd balled his hands into fists until Winifred leaned over and put her hand atop one of his. Her gentle touch caused him to relax.

"Felicia then told Catherine that if she didn't do as she was told, Felicia would let the police know the truth and she would be arrested."

"For what?" Carter spat out the words. "Catherine had done nothing wrong."

"Well, apparently Felicia believed Catherine was somehow considered under suspicion."

"Not to any real degree," Carter replied. "There was more concern that she had been kidnapped. Catherine has never been in trouble. Her father sent her to America to avoid having her exposed to the shame he knew his imprisonment would cause her. Are you familiar with Judge Arlington?"

"Yes," Mrs. Clarkson said, nodding.

"He knows the full story. He's been helping us with Mr. New-bury's situation. He assured us that Catherine was not wanted by the law." Carter got to his feet. "Mrs. Clarkson, if you have any idea where Catherine has gone, I pray you tell me."

"I don't know. I wish I did. I would have you tell her to come back. Felicia is gone. I dismissed her as soon as opportunity presented itself, but it wasn't until after they had gone."

"So they said nothing?"

"I do know they planned to take the train to New York City," Mrs. Clarkson said with sudden enthusiasm.

"New York City? Are you certain?"

She nodded. "Yes. They took the train last Sunday afternoon. Just before you came here to ask after her. Though I don't know where they were headed once they reached New York City."

Carter remembered Mrs. Samuelson's boardinghouse. "I might have an idea, but since it's been over a week, it might be too late."

"I'm sorry that I didn't say something to you sooner. Catherine's like a daughter to me, and I didn't want to see her hurt."

"Neither do I, Mrs. Clarkson. Neither do I. I promise you I will do what I can to find her and keep her safe." He looked at Winifred. "Come."

"What do you plan to do?" Winifred asked, getting to her feet.

"Go after her. What else?" He grinned and gave Mrs. Clarkson a brief bow. "Thank you for your help."

CHAPTER 25

Carter sent for Leander and together the trio tried to figure out the best plan for going after Catherine. Grateful to find his parents preoccupied with several New Year's Eve parties, Carter arranged supper with Cook. They sat down to the meal at exactly six-thirty, none of them really able to focus on the food.

"It's too late to go yet tonight," Winifred declared. "I don't know what the train schedule might be, but the trip takes hours and snows may cause further delays. You wouldn't get into New York City until the early-morning hours at this rate. I think you should wait and take the morning train. That will allow you to be well rested."

"Hardly," Carter said. "I doubt I will sleep a wink tonight. I don't know where she is or if she's safe. How could I sleep warm and comfortably in my bed without being sure of her circumstance?"

The servants offered them roasted lamb and mint jelly, along with creamed peas, baked squash, and a bevy of other delicious foods. Carter took an ample portion, but his heart was far from the meal.

"Still, I think Winifred makes a good point," Leander replied. "Better to arrive in the afternoon. We will have better luck with transportation to the boardinghouse."

"I suppose so." Carter pushed the food around his plate.

"It will also allow me to have a little time with Winifred," Leander said, smiling. "After all, if I'm to leave for England as soon as Captain Marlowe is ready to return, I will be gone for some time. I want to have every possible moment with my betrothed." He gave her a wink.

Carter tried not to allow the feelings of jealousy to overtake his sensible mind. He needed to plan wisely for Catherine's sake. "When is Marlowe due back?"

"He told me he would dock in New York on or around the fourth, barring complications. He plans to leave again on the seventh and will take me with him."

"I can hardly bear to think of your being gone for so long. Weeks and weeks," Winifred said with a sigh. She pushed back her plate as if she'd lost her appetite. "I'm blessed that you care enough to do this for Catherine, but I'm selfish enough to wish it already said and done."

"Travel is much faster these days," Leander said, trying to encourage her. "You needn't fret. There are good trains in England,

I am told. And if all goes as well as we hope, Mr. Newbury will be near the western coast and ready for his trip to America."

"But what if he doesn't wish to come here?" Winifred questioned. "What will you do then?"

"Remind him that his daughter is in America," Lee said with a smile.

"But if Catherine knows you are going to England to bring her father back, she will insist on going with you," Winifred said with conviction.

"Then perhaps we will not tell her," Carter replied. He knew he sounded selfish, but he didn't want her exposed to more pain and misery, should the duke have been unable to complete the matter of setting Newbury free.

"Better still, we'll just be honest with her and remind her that her father could be on his way to America without waiting for my arrival. It's a possibility, and if she accompanies me and that happens, there will be no one here to greet him."

"That's true enough." Carter imagined the fight Catherine would give, but he knew this explanation would also calm her.

"I'll pray for you all without ceasing," Winifred said, shaking her head. "I'll pray first and foremost that you will find Catherine and the Shays and that they are safe. Then I'll pray that you be wise in your choices of words and deeds. I don't want anyone to suffer because of further deceit or secrets. We've seen where that has gotten us."

"I didn't mean to suggest we would be less than honest with Catherine," Carter said, feeling a little guilty. "I just . . . well . . . I don't want her to go. For myself, as well as the situation Lee stated."

Winifred nodded. "I know. Just as I wish for you both not to go." She smiled. "I suppose I shall just busy myself with plans for our wedding."

"That would be a very worthy project," Lee said with a wink. "That way we can marry as soon as I return."

"Then that is what I shall do," she said, not sounding at all like the shy young woman she'd been just a couple of months ago.

Catherine finished mending a shirt and put it aside. Her neck ached from hours bent over the pieces. The men in the boardinghouse had been happy to have her help in repairing their clothes, even if they had to part with a little of their drinking money. Two of the men staying at the house were fishermen, whose clothes were more ragged than any Catherine had seen in a long time. She worked her skills to see the shirts put into better order, but it hadn't been easy. One of the other gentlemen had actually asked her to make him a new shirt, and she had immediately gone to work on that project. Now the creation was nearly done.

Getting up, she stretched and suppressed a yawn. It was New Year's Eve, and once again it served only to mark yet another year without her father. Now they didn't even know where he'd gone, and Catherine had no idea where to get answers.

Downstairs there was a bit of a party going on. Mrs. Samuelson encouraged the revelry, telling everyone that 1856 was destined to be an exceptional year. Why she felt that way, Catherine didn't know, but she hoped it might be true.

"Catherine?" Selma's voice called from beyond the door.

"Come in," Catherine called back. She turned to greet Selma. "It sounds like the party is going quite well."

Selma nodded. The sounds of music filtered up from downstairs. "Dugan is playing his fiddle and the men seem to enjoy the entertainment."

"I wish I could be more enthusiastic. I just feel so overwhelmed with my emotions." Catherine sank to the edge of her bed.

Selma smiled and pulled up the chair Catherine had only recently vacated. "Is this about your father or about Mr. Danby?"

Catherine met the older woman's eyes. "Both. Oh, Selma . . . I believe I've fallen in love. Carter Danby has managed to worm his way into my affections."

"What a romantic way of putting it," Selma said with a laugh.

A smile crept onto Catherine's face. "All right, so it isn't a very complimentary way of stating the fact, but it is true. I didn't want this complication. I never intended to remain in America one second longer than it took to get Father the justice he deserved, but now I feel torn. If I go, I know I will leave my heart behind."

"And if you stay?"

Catherine's brows knit together. "If I stay? How can I? Father is in England, and that is my home too."

"But America has been your home these last five years. And they have been good years overall. Hard years, but good."

"It's true," Catherine admitted, "but I never considered staying . . . until now."

"Child, you have borne a tremendous burden for such a long time. It started with the loss of your mother and brothers and continues right through to this moment with your father's whereabouts still unknown. You needn't bear this alone. God has now provided true love for you; why be afraid of that?"

Catherine got up and paced the tiny space. "Because when Father is freed, he will need care. He might be sick by now. Prisons are notorious for consumption and other diseases. His constitution might have failed him. If I were to allow Mr. Danby's attention and affection, would I be sacrificing my father's well-being?"

"Your father was not a man who would ever want his only daughter to forgo the love of a lifetime for the sake of tending to him. Besides, America might well be the best place to bring your father. If you can find a way to see him set free, he may want to put England behind him."

"I suppose all these years and the betrayals done to him by his friends may well have that effect. We shall see in time, but for now, I don't know what to do. Carter Danby wants to court me—to marry me."

"And what do you want?" Selma asked.

Catherine wrung her hands together. "I think I would very much like that, but I cannot allow myself that liberty. Not with Father having such a great need. Not only that, but Carter has no idea of what's happened. Even if he remembers me and where we first met, he doesn't know about Father. That's a great deal to expect any man to bear for the sake of love."

"Perhaps Captain Marlowe told him the truth."

Catherine nodded. "Perhaps."

"What if you were to tell Mr. Danby everything and allow him to be the judge of what happened and what it means to him?"

"What if I told him the truth and he decided to take me to the authorities?"

Selma chuckled. "Do you honestly believe Carter Danby would do that?"

Catherine searched her heart and immediately knew the answer. "No. No, he would protect me. I know that."

"Then why not be honest with him? Tell him what happened and let him decide if he can bear the burden. Two sharing the load is much easier than one. Remember, the Bible speaks of such things in Ecclesiastes."

"I do remember. It says something about how it's better because if one falls down, the other can help them back up, right?"

Selma nodded. "Mr. Danby wants to come alongside you and offer you his shelter and protection. And from what you say, you would very much like to have that attention from him. So why not allow your love to grow—to bring you to a place of matrimony?"

"But what of Father? Surely I should consider him in this and what he might want for me."

"I think your father would want you to be safe and happy, but above all to be loved. He never planned to dictate your union or arrange your marriage. I believe he would be pleased to see you happily wedded to Mr. Danby, even if he couldn't be a part of it."

Catherine knew in her heart that Selma was right. The thought of finding Carter and telling him the truth was almost overpowering. "So should I write Carter a letter? Surely I cannot go back to Philadelphia."

"I think a letter would be appropriate. Maybe remind him of the past and where you met, even though you're sure he now remembers. Then tell him why you came to America and why it was necessary to remain so secretive. I would also tell him how you feel about him. Leave no question of it—play no game. If you toy with his affections, you might well lose them altogether."

"Very well. I will write to him."

"Good. Now do you feel better?" Selma asked.

"I do." Catherine came to Selma and gave her a hug. "Thank you for your counsel. You always seem to know just the right thing to say."

Selma pulled away just a bit to see Catherine's face. "You are dear to me, child. You always have been and always will be. My most fervent desire, outside of seeing your father freed, is seeing you happily settled."

"You and Dugan have been so good to me. My pain is cut in half in light of your tender love." She hugged Selma one more time, then released her. "I think I'll write that letter now."

Selma smiled. "It's a very good start to the new year."

Carter heard the clock chime midnight. He sat in front of his bedroom fireplace, and the loneliness he experienced was so intense it nearly caused physical pain. Catherine was out there somewhere. Somewhere far away from his care and watchful eye.

The flames danced in the grate as the logs shifted. Carter stared at the fire, but it was Catherine's face he saw.

"I cannot even imagine life without her by my side."

He remembered their first meeting. Her outlook on life had seemed sweetly naïve. But life had hardened her. Now all he wanted for her was the best. He wanted Catherine to have hope—to know true happiness. And he wanted to love her and to have her love him in return. He knew she felt a great deal for him—he could tell by her response to the kiss they'd shared. But he knew, too, that she was afraid. Afraid of the future and of what sorrows might yet betray her hope.

Running his hands through his hair, Carter stood and went to the window. "I promise you, Catherine," he whispered against the frosty pane, "I promise I will ease your suffering. I will help you in every way possible, and I will love you always."

Tomorrow he would go to her—he would find her—and if he had anything to say about it, he wouldn't come home without her.

"Oh, Father, please help me," Carter prayed. "I want so much to see her safely returned. To see her father set free. To see her happy . . . even if that happiness cannot include me." But the very thought was like a knife in his heart. "But, please, let her love me."

A light knock sounded on his door. Carter startled at the sound. He had no idea of who it might be. "Come in."

The door opened and Winifred peeked inside. "Happy New Year, brother."

"Happy New Year. I thought you were with Lee."

She smiled and her joy lit up the room. "I was. He kissed me at midnight and then departed. Then I came up here to see you. Are you all right?"

Carter wasn't sure how to answer. "I doubt I will be all right until I see Catherine again—until I convince her of my love for her and hear her consent to be my wife."

Winifred came to stand behind the fireplace chair. "I think once she knows what you've done for her father, there will be little difficulty for her to believe in your love for her. You've put aside your own interests and needs to see to hers. What woman could ask for more?"

"I just want her happy. Of course I want justice served, but more than anything, I want to see her smile—a smile she feels all the way to her toes. Just as you do when I mention Lee's name."

Laughing, Winifred came from behind the chair and crossed the room to where Carter stood. She took hold of his hands. "And I want to see you as happy as I am. I have prayed for you, brother dear. I have prayed that God would prosper your business and send you a wonderful mate. I believe He has already accomplished both things. I feel certain once Catherine knows the truth of her father's freedom from prison, then she will feel free to turn her heart toward you and the future."

"I pray you are right." Carter leaned forward and planted a kiss on his sister's forehead.

❦

Catherine looked at the blank piece of paper and tried once again to start her letter to Carter. In her heart she wanted to tell him how important he'd become to her—how much she missed him now that they were far apart. But the words sounded trite. With each salutation she considered, she felt even further from accomplishing her task.

How can I just tell him that I love him? How can I spill the past in all its ugly truth across the pages of this letter, and then conclude it so neatly with my adoration and ardent desire to be his wife?

The blank page seemed to mock her. *How dare you believe in love when there is so much uncertainty in your past and future?* Guilt washed over her. What if Carter thought her less worthy of his attention and affection when he knew the truth of what had happened to her father? Worse still, what if he believed her father truly guilty? She could never love a man who would openly condemn her father for actions that were not his own.

With a sigh, Catherine deserted the empty paper and went to her bed. The revelry had long since quieted downstairs and one by one the partiers had gone to bed. She blew out her lamp and eased onto the bed.

"Maybe tomorrow the words will come to me," she whispered into the darkness. "Maybe tomorrow . . . my heart will speak for itself."

CHAPTER 26

*C*atherine sat at the dining room table of the boardinghouse and considered again what she might write to Carter. The house was otherwise empty. Selma and Dugan had gone with Mrs. Samuelson to share in some of the local festivities, while some of the men were off to work and others had gone out to enjoy the day. Catherine had offered to remain behind to watch over the house. There was soon to be a room to let, and Mrs. Samuelson had already placed an ad. She didn't want to miss a potential renter, and Catherine had happily volunteered to fill in for the duty. But so far no one had come and everything remained calm and still.

The silence was actually a welcome relief. Life at the sewing house had always been fraught with noise and anxiety. The work load was also much lighter compared to Catherine's previous job. While sewing and repairing clothes for the men in residence took time and effort, it was nothing compared to the long, tiresome hours Catherine had spent working for Mrs. Clarkson.

The brass knocker clattered against the front door, momentarily startling Catherine. She left thoughts of letter writing behind and went to answer the door. Finding Carter Danby on the steps was the last thing she ever expected, but even as she stared into his eyes, stunned, it seemed like the most natural thing in the world that he should be there.

Without a word he took her in his arms and held her. Catherine didn't resist. A sense of relief poured over her. It left her warm and peaceful inside. He had come. He had come for her.

His hand gently cradled her head while his other arm went around her back. Catherine melted against him, wrapping her arms around him. Tears came to her eyes. She loved him. She truly loved him.

He pulled back as if reading her thoughts. Smiling down at her, Carter reached up and wiped away a tear. "I have missed you, Miss Newbury."

She stiffened at the sound of her own name. Fighting to calm her fears, the past rushed at Catherine in a bevy of images she couldn't force into order. She had so eagerly wanted to tell Carter of her past and explain the truth of why she couldn't tell him how they first met, but now that he was here, the truth seemed so hard to speak.

"Come. I need to speak to you," Carter said. He gave her a little nudge to push her back into the vestibule. "I should have told you about this long ago."

He led Catherine to the sitting room. "Sit here," he told her and motioned to the well-worn settee. "This will take a bit of time."

Catherine wanted to speak but didn't trust herself. She sat as instructed and focused on spreading her gown in an orderly fashion around her.

"I know who you are, as you must have guessed by now. I re-member your party in Bath and the dances we shared. I've known it since visiting New York in November. All Mrs. Samuelson had to do was mention your name and it all came flooding back. You were so young and charming then." He smiled. "But you're a beautiful woman now, and the weight of the world disguises that young girl's innocence."

Catherine started to comment, but Carter held up his hand. "I know, too, that you were the lady behind the mask at my mother's masquerade ball." He gave her a rather roguish grin and shrugged. "I couldn't help kissing you and would happily do it again, but perhaps that should wait until I complete my explanation. If I offended you then, I apologize. I have never taken such liberties with a woman, and never will again."

"I knew it was you," Catherine whispered. "I would not have allowed the kiss otherwise."

"I know," he said, sobering. "Winifred told me. I felt horrible after imposing that kiss upon you, but as I considered the matter these last few days, I felt certain that it must have been received with the same fervor and desire in which it was delivered."

Catherine felt her cheeks grow hot and looked away. "I acted in a wanton fashion."

He laughed, and in the empty house it seemed to echo all around her. Catherine's glance shot back to Carter. "You laugh at me?"

"I laugh at such a silly statement. You were no more wanton than I. We are two people in love. It is that simple. Deny it if you must, but the truth of it will stand."

Catherine said nothing. She couldn't deny it, but to admit such a thing would mean declaring her heart before she was ready.

Carter didn't wait for an answer but merely pushed ahead. "I digress. I have known for some time about your circumstance— about your father and the wrongs done him."

"You know? But how? Did Captain Marlowe tell you?" Catherine asked. Her heart beat wildly as anxiety coursed through her body.

"I made it my job to know. I wanted to know more about you so I put Leander on the job. He began to seek out information on when you had come to Philadelphia and where you had come from. Once we knew about the Samuelson boardinghouse, we made a journey here, as you know. At least you know about our trip to New York City."

"Yes. I suppose I do." She shook her head. "I honestly had no thought of your coming here on my account. Mrs. Samuelson mentioned it, and . . . well . . . I've been trying to write you a letter."

Carter took the seat beside her and took hold of her shaking hands. "Catherine, please know that I only wanted the best for you. Captain Marlowe wouldn't even speak to me until I convinced him that I cared deeply for you—that I wanted to make you my wife."

She couldn't speak. The words stuck in her throat. Carter was here—beside her—holding her hands. The very thought of it was more than she could comprehend. "What . . . what did . . . Captain Marlowe say?"

"He told me about your father. About his being imprisoned."

"He was falsely accused!" Catherine declared, pulling her hands away. "He's innocent. Father would never have traded in slaves. It was all Finley Baker. He's the only one who profited from it."

"I know," Carter said soothingly.

"If you know, then you also realize that you must say nothing to anyone. If it were to be revealed that my father was found guilty of slave trading, my reputation and future would be ruined."

"I cannot make that promise."

"Please. I left Philadelphia for that very reason."

"But you are as innocent as your father. You did nothing wrong and no one holds you accountable. The authorities already know about this matter. They have for several weeks."

"What?" Catherine could hardly believe what he was saying. "How could you have involved them?"

"I've been working with Leander to see your father set free. Judge Arlington has also worked with us, as well as Captain Marlowe."

"You've what?" Catherine could scarcely believe what she was hearing. Could it even be possible?

Carter looked at her rather sheepishly. "I wanted to make you happy. I wanted to help. I have friends in England—the duke of Mayfield has been particularly helpful."

"His Grace?"

Carter laughed. "Yes. He was one of my sponsors while in England. I have to say I found him to be quite without pretension or airs. My uncle lives in England part of the year. He is good friends with the duke, as well as with Lord Carston. Both proved to be useful in our pursuit to see your father set free."

Catherine's hand went to her throat. "And is he . . . is he free?"

"I believe so. Last word I had, they had managed to get him released to the duke's personal care. We are hopeful that he will soon be cleared of the charges, his record expunged, and his properties returned to him."

Tears streamed down Catherine face. "I don't know what to say. I cannot imagine better news. It's been five years, and I've yearned to find a way to help him."

Carter put his arm around her. "I know. I wish that we might have met again sooner."

"I must go to him. I must go to England."

"No." Carter held her fast as she tried to jerk away from him. "Please hear me out, Catherine."

She stilled in his arms. "I owe you that much."

"I cannot say where your father might be at this moment. It is our hope that he will be cleared quickly and released completely, but I do not know where that process might take him. Leander will go to England on your behalf. He's even now awaiting Captain Marlowe."

"Then I will go with him. Do you not see? Father will be comforted by my presence. He will need me."

"Catherine, I know that you want to be at his side, but I'm begging you to do this my way. It's really for the best."

"But why? Why can I not go to him?"

"Because Finley Baker is still free. And he's never hesitated to slander your name—and he'd do far worse. If you were to go to England, you might well fall into the hands of his cohorts. Your father has ample protection, but you would not. Imagine his heartbreak if something were to happen to you."

Catherine well understood the situation. Finley Baker was dangerous. She'd said so many times. Despite her longing to see her father safe, Catherine knew she could end up being more of a liability than an asset.

"Not only that, but Lee will bring your father here to America. Imagine the complication of missing each other while en route. Your father might arrive here to find you gone to England. He might leave before Lee makes his way over."

"I hadn't considered it, I suppose. It's hard to imagine his being free and not being there with him."

"Look, I understand how difficult it is for you to remain here," Carter said softly. "I hope to ease that by keeping you company. I want to take you back to Philadelphia."

"I never considered that it might be possible." Catherine moved away from Carter and turned to face him. "I can hardly believe any of this." She put her hand up and boldly touched his cheek. "Carter, you cannot know what this means to me."

He covered her hand with his own, his dark eyes meeting hers. "I think I do. My heart is yours—it beats with yours, it longs with yours."

The front door opened and Catherine could hear Mrs. Samuelson's cackling laughter. She jumped to her feet.

"Selma! Dugan!" She rushed for the vestibule. They looked at her with expressions of fear.

"What's wrong, child?"

She shook her head. "Nothing. Nothing is wrong. Come." She reached out for Selma. "Mr. Danby has come and there is good news. We have the miracle we've prayed so long to see."

Carter felt a sense of relief as the evening wound down and everyone was in agreement that they would return to Philadelphia. Leander joined them for supper and answered their additional questions about his part.

"Captain Marlowe told me that he planned to be in the city on the fourth. That's just three days' time. He plans to leave again by the seventh—earlier if his return cargo can be loaded. I will go with him."

Selma shook her head. "I can't begin to tell you what wondrous new this is for all of us. This young lady has been so brave." Tears came and she drew her handkerchief and dabbed at them. "I've never seen anyone work as hard as Miss Catherine has, and all to save money to buy a lawyer for her father."

Dugan patted his wife's shoulder. "It's true," he said. "Catherine has been tireless."

"I'm certain of that," Carter replied. He had watched her for months now. He knew her determination.

"And poor Mr. Newbury. What he must have suffered," Selma said, putting her handkerchief away.

Catherine pushed her plate back and looked hard at Leander. "You will do what you can to see to his comfort, won't you?"

Leander smiled. "You know I will, Miss Newbury. I'm happy to be a part of this worthy cause. Winifred was less enthusiastic, but only because it would take me from her side."

"Actually, Winifred was very supportive and she sent her best wishes. She, too, longs for you to return to Philadelphia," Carter said.

"And no doubt Mrs. Clarkson would love to see you back at work," Selma said, regaining her smile.

"No," Carter interjected. "I don't want Catherine to have to work anymore."

All eyes turned to him and then refocused on Catherine's face. Before she could speak, Carter offered an explanation.

"Catherine has, as you've already stated, worked much harder than she should ever have had to work. My desire for her is that she rest and prepare for her father's return." He couldn't bring himself to add that he hoped to spend the time before her father's arrival in courting Catherine.

"Carter makes a good point. There really is no telling in what condition we will find your father," Leander agreed. "I will endeavor to put him in the best circumstances on the return journey; however, it would be wise to do as Carter suggests."

"And where would we stay?" Catherine asked. "I have some money set aside, but that truly belongs to Carter for the money he's already spent in helping my father."

"I don't want any of your money," Carter said. "But I can help you find a place."

"We have more than enough room at my house. My parents would no doubt be happy to help," Leander offered.

"Dugan and I could return to Mrs. Clarkson's. I'm certain she could still use our help," Selma offered.

"If I don't have to work, you shouldn't have to either," Catherine protested.

Selma patted her hand. "Goodness, but Dugan and I wouldn't know what to do with ourselves. You might not have been born to work, but we were. No, Dugan and I will go back to Mrs. Clarkson's, and you will go stay with the Arlingtons."

Catherine considered it for a moment. "Very well. It seems that you have decided this matter for me." She straightened, and for a moment Carter thought she might be angry, but then she smiled. "Perhaps I should trust that you know my needs better than I know them myself."

Carter felt his heart soar. He grinned and slapped Leander's back. "I told you she was an exceptionally smart woman."

CHAPTER 27

*So let me get to the heart of why I came today," Winifred began
as she and Catherine shared tea in the Arlingtons' parlor. "Lee
and I are to be married upon his return from England."

"Goodness! You were only just stating an interest in the man
a few weeks ago."

"It's been nearly four months," Winifred protested.

Catherine laughed. "I suppose four months should be suf-
ficient. Especially when you have harbored deep feelings for
him for years."

It was Winifred's turn to laugh. "Of course, Leander did not
know about such feelings. He thought of me only as Carter's

little sister. And why not? I was so much younger and not always very pleasant to those two young men."

"Now, that is something I will not believe," Catherine replied. "You have always presented yourself the very epitome of a kind and genteel woman. Surely you were never any trouble whatsoever."

"Oh, I think the men would disagree, but we shan't give them the chance. Now, here is what I wanted to talk to you about. I know that Carter wants you to take a break from work, but I wondered if I could entice you to design my wedding gown?"

"Of course! Oh, how exciting." Catherine immediately went to the corner desk and pulled out a sketch pad. "Tell me what you have in mind."

"Well, that's why I came to you. You know me better than I know myself, it seems. You created the perfect ball gown for me."

Catherine considered the situation for a moment. "I think we should make the gown in white silk barège." She began sketching. "This will be so much fun. I'm quite excited to have something to do—something with which to occupy my mind."

"It's so very exciting," Winifred agreed. "Mother is beside herself to have the wedding be so quickly completed. She longs for us to wait until June and have a large wedding in the garden, but I assured her I had no interest in such things. A small gathering at the church would suffice for me, but not for Mother. So we compromised."

Looking up from her sketch, Catherine raised a single brow. "And what might that have been?"

"We will have a large wedding in the ballroom on the third floor," Winifred declared. "That way there will be room for everyone Mother intends to invite."

"That sounds reasonable." Catherine grew thoughtful. "I think we should do a pointed corsage. We'll bring the neckline to a V, like this." She showed Winifred what she had in mind. "Then we'll have folds of lace from the shoulder to the waist. It will be quite beautiful, I assure you."

"And it will show off my assets," Winifred said, to which they both broke out laughing.

"But we will not show too much. We'll keep the skirt one length and full, with a trailing train behind. We can trim the train with the same folded lace as the bodice. See?" Catherine quickly drew what she had in mind.

"I love it. I knew you would think of something very appropriate." Winifred put aside her tea and glanced past Catherine. "So where is Carter today? I thought he would be here with you."

"No, he had work to do. Apparently he was to have had sketches to Mr. Fulbright last Monday. Since we did not return until then, he sent word and made arrangements to see the man today."

"He's quite excited, you know. The prospect of creating a lasting monument that people will credit to him ... well ... I think that's important to Carter. He wants to leave his mark on the world—to create beauty that will last."

"I can understand that. I have very much enjoyed my own time of creating. It's enjoyable to give other people pleasure. Your brother no doubt feels the same way."

"I would hate to see you move to Washington," Winifred said with a sigh. "I know it's not very far away, but I would miss you both terribly. I had thought it would be very pleasant for the four of us to spend time together once we were both married."

Catherine was rather taken aback by the news. "Does Carter plan to move to Washington?"

Winifred frowned. "Has he not told you about the project?"

"Well, I knew there was some sort of competition that he and Mr. Fulbright planned to join in. I did not realize it required a move to Washington."

"Oh dear. I fear I have said too much, perhaps. Of course, the contest has not been won, but it is my understanding that if Carter and Mr. Fulbright's drawings are chosen, they would have to relocate to oversee the project."

"What of his work here?" Catherine asked, setting the sketch pad aside. "I thought he mentioned Mr. Montgomery's house taking some three years to complete."

"He plans to come back as needed. At least, that was the last thing I was told. Still, I would imagine he plans to speak to you more on the matter. Has he proposed?"

"Not exactly. He has teasingly asked me several times to marry him, but it has never been seriously offered."

"Oh, don't be so sure," Winifred replied, getting to her feet. "My brother would not even joke about such a thing if he were not quite serious."

The thought warmed Catherine and she smiled. "I'm glad. I'm glad he would not toy with my affection in such a manner."

Winifred shook her head. "He will never be insincere, I assure you. He loves you."

Just then the housekeeper appeared. She curtsied quickly and announced, "Mr. Danby to see you, miss."

Catherine stood and smoothed her skirts while Winifred moved toward the door. "I'll be leaving now," she told Catherine.

"You needn't—"

"Carter will want to spend time alone with you. With the Arlingtons out for the afternoon, it will prove a perfect time."

"A perfect time for what, little sister?" Carter asked as he bounded into the room. He caught Catherine's gaze and smiled. Giving a slight bow, he turned to Winifred.

"I was merely telling Catherine that I needed to go and that now seemed a perfect time for you two to have a chance to be alone."

"I quite agree." He kissed her on the forehead. "You are very wise, Winnie."

"Yes, well, I hope you continue to think that way when you learn what I've done." She moved to the door and smiled. "I've asked Catherine to create my wedding gown. I know you didn't want her working, but I could think of no one I would trust but her."

"And I want very much to accommodate her trust," Catherine replied.

"I suppose I always knew she would not sit idle," Carter said, laughing.

With that, Winifred took her leave and Catherine watched as Carter studied her. "It hasn't been that long since you saw me last," she declared.

"I suppose not, but it seems like an eternity." He grinned and crossed the room to take hold of her hands. "You are quite beautiful, but these simple dresses will no longer do. You really should create some gowns for yourself instead of just slaving away for my sister."

"As a matter of fact, your sister has just brought me three gowns that she no longer has use for."

"Well, I suppose that is fine for now, but soon I intend to see you more appropriately dressed in gowns of your own."

Catherine grew flushed under his scrutiny. She pulled away and went to take up her sketchbook. "How did your meeting go?"

"Very well. I believe Mr. Fulbright was pleased. He'll work with the designs and we'll meet again next week."

"Will you move to Washington if you win the competition?"

"Time will tell." He came and took hold of her hands again. "Come and sit with me. I want to talk to you about the future—about your father and England."

Catherine allowed him to lead her to the fireplace. She took a seat while Carter leaned back against the fireplace mantel. She folded her hands and looked up.

"I'm wondering what you desire to do once your father's reputation is restored. Will you want to return to England?"

"I don't know," Catherine said, surprising them both. "I had once thought that my one and only desire was to return to Bath, but I cannot say I feel that way now. I have no idea what Father will want to do. He must come first—at least until he is well and happily resettled."

"I agree."

Catherine loved him all the more for that comment. "I want to see Father return to shipping if that is his desire. He's lost everything. I have the money I saved, but of course, I know that will hardly purchase a ship."

"It is our plan that the Crown return the property they con-fiscated from your father. I have no way of knowing how that might be accomplished, but if the courts are willing to see the error of their ways, then perhaps they will also return your father's wealth."

"I . . . I . . . never thought it possible." The very idea caused Catherine to see an entirely new future for her father.

"We shall just continue to pray that it will come together. Leander is a very persistent sort, and with the help of the duke and others, we should see the matter quickly resolved."

"I can't thank you enough. You have been so generous—so kind. You had no reason to care." She met his gaze. "I owe you everything."

"You owe me nothing. I want nothing from you that isn't freely given. When I learned of your father's plight, I knew it was the right thing to do. Knowing it would please you . . . well . . . that did make the decision easier." He grinned.

"We are still in your debt."

"Put it from your mind."

She could see the subject made him uncomfortable and took pity on him. "I will need to do some shopping for your sister's wedding gown. Perhaps you might be willing to accompany me."

"I would be delighted."

"Ah, here you are," Mrs. Arlington declared as she opened the door to the parlor. "Carter, what a pleasant surprise. Look, my dear, Carter is here."

"But of course he is," Judge Arlington said, then went to Catherine. "And how are you, my dear?"

"I am quite well, thank you."

"Did you enjoy your visit with Winifred?" he asked.

"I did. We planned her wedding gown."

"Oh, how wonderful. May I see what you designed?" Mrs. Arlington asked, hurrying over and leaving Carter's side. "I suppose I should not be too deeply wounded that I've been cast aside on the behalf of a Catherine Shay gown."

"Newbury," Catherine corrected. "My name is Catherine Newbury."

"Not for long," Carter murmured. "Not if I have anything to say about it."

❦

A few days later Carter had settled in to work on the design changes suggested by Fulbright, when he heard his father and brother arguing. They had just returned from a meeting at the mill, and Carter knew the news had not been good by the tone of their exchange.

"At this rate we'll be in the poorhouse by summer," his father declared.

"The money can be made back. It's hardly my fault that the arrangement fell through."

"I left you in charge. That was a mistake. Had you not focused your time and attention on your mistress, this wouldn't have happened."

"Do not bring her into this. Elsa is gone and it's your fault."

Carter shook his head and got to his feet. As long as his father and brother insisted on bellowing at each other, he'd get very little done.

"Would you just forget about her!" his father commanded. "We have a very real problem here. If there isn't a way to repair the damage, you won't be able to afford a mistress, much less that wife of yours."

Carter stepped into the hall and saw his father glare. "What are you doing here?" he asked.

Carter shrugged. "I live and often work here. What's the commotion about?"

"None of your concern," his father retorted.

"Why not?" Robin questioned. He unbuttoned his coat. "Why shouldn't Carter know of the situation? After all, you're always after him to take an interest in the family business. Maybe he can design a miracle." Robin's sarcastic tone was not lost on their father.

Carter crossed his arms and leaned against the wall. "I take it there are financial problems at the mill."

"Your brother managed to lose us everything."

"We will get another investor," Robin protested.

"But when? It won't come in time." Their father slammed his fist down on the hall table. "I'll be the laughingstock of Philadelphia."

"I don't understand," Carter said. "Why is time a problem?"

"There is a large note due," Robin said without waiting for their father to speak. "And if it is not paid, we stand to lose everything."

Carter shook his head. "Everything? Can you not sell some stock or other assets to meet the need?"

"If it were that simple, it would already be done," his father said. "I've sold off everything that I could. This deal was going to help us get back on top, and now there's nothing."

"Could you not speak with the bank and ask for an extension?"

"And admit that we've failed?" his father asked in disbelief.

"Wouldn't a temporary failure be better than a complete collapse of your business?" Carter asked. He found his father's attitude to be out of line.

"You know nothing about business. Just stay out of this." His father stormed off, muttering and swearing all the way up the stairs.

Carter looked at Robin and could see by his ashen expression that the situation was not over-exaggerated. "You'll need to convince him to at least try to extend the loan," he told his older brother.

"Don't think I haven't tried. He's determined to be thought a huge success, but my guess is that most of the town knows full well the details of our problems." Robin ran a hand through his hair. "I don't know what I'll do if this disaster continues."

"Have you prayed for guidance?" Carter asked.

Robin met his gaze. "No, but I suppose it would be a good idea. I've not done a good job on my own."

Carter nodded. "None of us does."

CHAPTER 28

*atherine sat across from Mrs. Arlington as they finished a
light lunch. The judge sat between them at the head of the
table and regaled them with tales of various happenings in the
city. Catherine liked the couple immensely. They were kind and
gentle in nature but also quite amusing and entertaining. They
reminded her very much of her own mother and father.

"My dear, you look radiant today. Is that a new dress?"

"Actually, it's a gown Winifred Danby gave me. She had
several that she didn't need and wanted me to have."

"Well, it suits you very well," Mrs. Arlington continued. "That
color of blue suits your complexion."

Catherine looked at the powder blue color and nodded. "I like it very much. The construction is done quite well, and the material is of the utmost quality."

"You know so very much about sewing. I can do enough to get by," the older woman declared, "but I was never gifted with the needle."

"You are gifted in many other ways," the judge said and picked up his coffee cup. "There is none that can hold a candle to your china painting."

Mrs. Arlington smiled. "Thank you, my dear. You are so kind to say so."

"What plans have you today?" Judge Arlington asked Catherine.

"I am going to buy supplies for Winifred's wedding gown. I will probably visit Mrs. Clarkson first, however. She has ample supplies of pattern paper, and I'm certain she will lend me some. Carter has offered to take me this afternoon. I thought I would visit with Mrs. Clarkson and let her know all that has happened since we were last together."

"Well, I hope you will give her my regards," Mrs. Arlington said.

"I will." Catherine slid her chair back. "If you will both excuse me, I need to finish preparing. Carter should be here shortly."

"But of course." Mrs. Arlington nodded enthusiastically. "Be sure to invite him to supper tonight."

Catherine had just gotten to her feet when the judge added, "I hope you know that your father is welcome to stay here with us. We want to do whatever we can to assist in his recovery."

"That is so kind of you both. I know he will be touched by your generosity." Catherine started to go, then paused and offered the couple a smile. "You both remind me of my parents. They were always laughing and happy. I have seldom seen two people more suited to each other than my mother and father, but you match their joy of life in every way. It is refreshing and pleasant to see."

"I'm sure you'll find the same once you and Carter are joined in marriage," Mrs. Arlington said with a coy smile.

"Well, that might be true," Catherine said, "but he has yet to truly propose."

"Surely you jest," the judge said, putting down his cup. "That young man is wasting valuable time."

"Perhaps you should propose to him," Mrs. Arlington teased.

Catherine laughed. "Perhaps I shall."

❧

"My dear, you cannot know how happy I was to hear you were back in town. I do wish you would have returned to me, but I understand Mr. Danby's desiring you to rest. Still, I would have allowed for it here," Mrs. Clarkson said.

Catherine sat in Mrs. Clarkson's private sitting room, explaining all that had happened since she had fled to New York. "You have been more than generous already. I know Selma and Dugan are happy to be back. I talked to Selma before coming to see you."

"They are very good to me," Mrs. Clarkson admitted. "I hope to entice them to stay no matter what the outcome is with you and your father. But I'd also like to revisit my earlier proposition to you. I'd still like very much for you to become my partner."

"That's very kind," Catherine said.

Mrs. Clarkson got up and went to a small sideboard. "I had the papers changed. See here, it says Newbury in place of Shay." She brought the contract to Catherine. "We are already having requests for your designs, and in a few weeks when your patterns and drawings appear in *Godey's*, I know we will have more than enough work to keep all of us busy."

"You cannot know that for sure," Catherine protested.

"I feel it," Mrs. Clarkson said. "It is what my heart tells me. Not only that, but I am certain others can be hired to do the sewing. You could simply design the gowns and oversee their creation."

"I will think on it, Mrs. Clarkson, but until my father is returned to me and I know what his desires are, I cannot commit to anything. You understand, of course."

"Certainly I do, my dear. I only hope you will continue to consider it as you and your father make decisions. I must say I was more than a little pleased when Selma told me what Mr. Danby and Mr. Arlington had done to help you."

"Yes, it was a tremendous surprise," Catherine replied, nodding. "My heart hasn't been this light in years. I can scarcely stand to wait for word from Mr. Arlington."

"When did he leave for England?"

Catherine sighed. "Only a week ago. He's not even made it to England yet. I fear it will take so very long before I even know for certain Father has been set free. Supposedly he was released to the duke of Mayfield, but I cannot say for certain."

"My dear, we will simply continue to pray for his safety. Do not lose hope or allow yourself to fall into despair."

"No, I will not. That's one of the reasons I plan to busy myself with Winifred Danby's wedding gown."

Mrs. Clarkson clapped her hands together. "How wonderful. It will be all the more special because of the closeness you two share. Is there anything we can help with?"

"Just the pattern paper, as I mentioned earlier." The clock chimed and Catherine got to her feet. "Oh, you'll have to excuse me. Mr. Danby promised to pick me up at three, so I should go now."

"Please come and see me again soon." Mrs. Clarkson embraced Catherine and kissed her lightly on the cheek. "You are such a dear. I have missed our talks and your company."

"I have missed you as well. I promise to consider the partnership."

They walked to the front door, where Catherine reclaimed her coat from Beatrix. "Do ya have to be goin' just now?" the girl asked.

"I'm afraid so. Mr. Danby promised to come for me at exactly three." Catherine pulled on her coat and did up the buttons before taking a stack of pattern paper. "Thank you for this. It will help me as I work on Miss Danby's wedding dress."

"But of course, my dear. You come back if you need any further assistance."

Lydia appeared and stood in the doorway to the planning room. She looked rather forlorn, and Catherine couldn't help but feel sorry for her. Lydia probably didn't know what to do with herself without Felicia badgering her.

Catherine offered a smile. "I hope to see you all again very soon." She opened the door to see Carter's carriage waiting for her. He quickly exited the carriage and came up the walk to claim Catherine.

"Good afternoon, Mrs. Clarkson."

"Good afternoon, Mr. Danby. Thank you so much for bringing Catherine to see me. I hope you will bring her again soon."

"I'm certain she will see to it," Carter declared, giving a bow. He looked to Catherine and extended his arm. "Shall we?"

Catherine nodded and let him lead her down the steps. Once they were inside the carriage she could see that Carter was deeply troubled. Putting the pattern paper aside, she turned to face him. "What's wrong? Have you had some bad news?" Then a horrible thought came to mind. She put her hand to her mouth. "Is it Father?" The words came out in a muffled whisper.

He frowned and patted her arm. "No. At least not your father. Mine, however, has caused more than a few problems for the family."

"I'm sorry to hear that. Your mother must be quite upset."

"She doesn't know. At least not yet. Father would never allow her to know anything about his business. I wouldn't know myself, but I overheard him the other day. Then today after dropping you off for your visit, I returned home to find him in a rage. Apparently Robin went behind his back and asked their banker about the possibility of an extension on a loan."

"And what was the result?" Catherine asked, rather confused as to why that would cause problems for Carter's father.

"The result is my father learned of this and lost his temper. He didn't want anyone to know about the problem. He prides himself on being a leader in business. To admit the need for help deeply wounded him. He would never have done it on his own, but Robin knew the risk was too great to ignore."

"I am sorry." Catherine could see that Carter was more than a little worried.

"Were it not for Mother, I wouldn't care. If Father lost everything it would serve him right. He's broken the law and caused great harm to so many people. He deserves whatever happens to him, but my mother is innocent in this. She brought a part of her family's fortune into the marriage, and now it's gone."

Catherine put her hand over his. "Since the night I had to flee my home, I have struggled to trust God in every circumstance. I knew such fear from my loss and didn't understand why God would allow such things to happen to me. I still don't, but I do trust Him. You need to trust Him in this matter as well. Hopefully your father will make the right decision."

"I doubt it. He seldom does." Carter looked away and squared his shoulders. "I apologize. I didn't intend for our day to turn to this. Where are we headed?"

"To pick up the things I need for Winifred's wedding gown. I want to get to work right away. I have the paper I needed, and now I want to go ahead and purchase the material for the dress."

He smiled. "Very well. I shall accompany you and carry your packages."

She couldn't help but laugh. "And I shall let you."

"Maybe you should buy some extra material," Carter said with a wink. "Just in case you wanted to make yourself a wedding gown."

Catherine pretended exasperation and rolled her eyes. "I have no need for one, Mr. Danby. Your sister is the one getting married. Remember?"

Carter tried not to think of his father's rage while he waited for Catherine to find the things she wanted. He left her looking at several bolts of cloth and turned his attention to the traffic outside. He still hadn't managed to formally ask Catherine for her hand in marriage, but he intended to rectify that tonight.

Yet there was the matter of her father. Catherine wouldn't want to marry without knowing he was safe and well. She would probably seek her father's blessing, and while that would add to the time before they could be wed, Carter would have it no other way.

He glanced back to see if Catherine needed any help, only to realize that Felicia stood behind the counter. Only moments ago an older woman, whom Carter presumed was the owner, had been assisting Catherine. Now the same blonde who had caused Catherine so much grief at the sewing house was obviously at it once again. She was talking to Catherine and looked quite menacing. From the way Catherine's expression had tightened, Carter knew there was trouble. He snuck around the aisle and came upon the women without either one seeing him.

"I will tell the police," Felicia stated quite clearly.

"You'll tell them what?" Carter asked, coming up behind Catherine. He put his hand protectively on her elbow.

Felicia looked quite taken aback. Carter glanced at Catherine and back to Felicia. "Will you tell them how you tried to blackmail Miss Newbury?"

"I . . . I . . . did nothing wrong!" Felica declared.

"The authorities are in a better place to judge that," Carter replied. "And since they already know about Miss Newbury's situation, including how her father's former partner could prove to be dangerous to her welfare, I think they would be interested to hear how you have threatened her. Better still, perhaps your employer would like to know about it first."

"No!" Felicia sounded rather desperate. She leaned forward on the counter. "I need this position. Mrs. Clarkson turned me out without thought as to what I would do."

"Perhaps you should have thought of that before striking out yet again to harm Miss Newbury."

He turned to Catherine. "What shall we do? Would you like me to send someone for the police?"

Catherine looked at Felicia and then back to Carter. "No. She has no means to cause me harm. Not anymore."

Felicia seemed to be holding her breath as she met Carter's gaze. He shook his head. "Very well. You don't deserve Miss Newbury's mercy, but I shall comply with her wishes."

"Thank you." Felicia took up the bolt of material. "I'll add these things up for you." She hurried toward the front of the store, her arms full of various materials and trims.

"Are you certain you wouldn't like to see her pay for her bad deeds?"

Catherine shook her head. "No. I lived in fear of the law for so many years. I don't wish that to be anyone else's fate."

"But she deserves it—you didn't."

"Perhaps, but just as you mentioned, I will show mercy."

Carter surprised Catherine by paying for the purchases. He told her his father could make it right at a later time. He would probably never see a single cent from his father, but it could be a gift to his sister. She deserved that much and more.

He helped Catherine from the store, carrying the stack of materials and sewing notions. Joseph waited faithfully to take the purchases and put them into the carriage before Carter handed Catherine up.

"Mrs. Arlington told me I should invite you to stay for supper. Would you like to do that?" Catherine asked.

Carter joined her, sitting beside her, while the purchases were carefully resting on the opposite side.

"I'd like to, but perhaps I should wait to decide until we have a chance to talk."

"And what would you want to speak to me about that would negate an invitation by Mrs. Arlington?"

"I want to talk to you about our future."

"I see."

He thought he heard a tremor in her voice, but he pressed on. "You know I've been working on designs for new government buildings in the capital. What I didn't tell you was that if our designs are chosen, it would require me to relocate to Washington."

"I suppose so." She looked out the window as if the matter was unimportant.

"That's all you have to say about it?"

"I'm uncertain as to what to say. You should know that Mrs. Clarkson would like to have me as her partner. She wants me to design the gowns and oversee their creation. If I agreed to do that, I would most likely move back to the sewing house."

"What of your father?"

"I told Mrs. Clarkson I would need to wait and see what was best for him. If, as you said, the Crown returns his assets, then that will need to be considered. If he desires to remain in England, that is yet something more for me to think about."

Carter felt a sense of frustration. The discussion wasn't going the way he'd planned it. "Look at me," he said in a voice barely audible.

Catherine turned and met his gaze. It was nearly his undoing. Her beauty was intoxicating. "You have no idea what you mean to me."

She smiled. "Perhaps I do."

He laughed. "Perhaps you do. Still, I'm not entirely sure how I feel about married women working."

"What are you talking about?"

"Mrs. Clarkson's offer."

"But I'm not a married woman," Catherine said, raising a brow.

Carter pulled her into his arms. "If I have my way, you will be." He kissed her without waiting for any further comment. Catherine put her hand on his cheek and returned the kiss.

Pulling away, Carter grinned. "Is that a yes?"

She gave him a rather blank look and shrugged. "I don't recall being asked a question."

"Perhaps this will refresh your memory." Carter pressed his lips to hers once again. Wrapping her in his arms, he pulled her closer still and let his kiss deepen. He heard Catherine sigh and couldn't help but smile. Ending the kiss he looked at her, surprised to find her already staring back.

"Oh, that question," she said rather breathlessly.

Carter released her and leaned back against the carriage. "I love you more dearly than I can even say. When I came back from Washington and found you were gone, I could hardly think for the need to know that you were safe."

He looked at her and found that she was smiling. "I want to spend the rest of my life with you. I realize we don't know what the future will hold, but I love you and I want to take care of you. Please say you'll marry me."

Catherine nodded. "I will. I love you and, with exception to seeing my father again, cannot think of anything I want more than to marry you."

He laughed, knowing no greater joy as he pulled her back into his arms. "I told you that you should have bought extra material."

Her laughter joined his as she slipped her arms around his neck. "I did."

CHAPTER 29

$\mathcal{T}$৩৫৻

*I*t's been six weeks," Catherine protested. "We should have had some word by now."

She and Carter sat in the carriage outside the Danby house. It had snowed throughout the day and even though it had stopped, the winds gusted from time to time and rocked the carriage. "Try not to worry. Lee won't take one minute longer than is necessary. He knows how hard this is for you. He is a man of great compassion."

"Are you certain we shouldn't wait and talk to your family later?" she asked.

He thought she looked frightened. Today they planned to tell his parents that they were engaged. Carter had refrained from telling them until his father's crisis at the mill had passed. Once his father reluctantly agreed to an extension on the loan, the tensions eased, and now there was even a new investor interested in pledging great support. Things were looking up for the Danbys.

"They won't attack you, I promise." He grinned and put his arm around her. "When my mother realizes the great gown designer is to be her daughter-in-law, she'll soon overlook our delay in letting them in on the secret."

"I hope you're right. I would not wish to cause further problems in your family."

"My family is quite good at creating problems all by themselves. You really needn't worry about interjecting any help in that area."

Catherine smiled. "I think I shall be very happy as your wife."

He nodded. "I know you will be, because I will make it my job to see that you are more than content. Now come along. The sooner we greet them, the sooner we can be on our way."

Wilson was there to faithfully meet them at the door. He took their coats and informed Carter that the family was assembled in the large drawing room.

"I told them I was coming by with someone and that I had important news."

"Will you tell them the news about the design competition first?"

Carter shrugged. "I'm not sure. We'll see what kind of mood they are in."

He ushered Catherine into the blue-and-white room. His mother sat by the fire, bent over her embroidery stand. She seemed quite intent on working at her pattern and didn't even look up. Carter's father sat on the opposite side of the room, reviewing some papers, while Winifred read a book on the settee.

"Sorry we kept you waiting," Carter announced. "The snows were quite deep."

"Is it still coming down?" his mother asked. Still she did not look up.

"No, but the winds are still a bit strong and the snow has drifted in the streets."

He led Catherine to the settee. She took the seat beside Winifred, who grasped her hand affectionately. Carter was glad for their friendship. His family would never be easy to live with, even from Washington or England.

"Mother, I believe you know Catherine. Although I daresay you know her by the name Shay. Her true name is Catherine Newbury." At this his mother glanced up.

"Miss Shay! How delightful."

"Newbury, Mother. Miss Newbury." Carter turned back to wink at Catherine. He knew she'd rather be anyplace but here. "Catherine, you know my mother, Mrs. Danby, but this is my father."

"Mr. Danby," she murmured in acknowledgment.

"So, what is so important that you gathered us here today?" his father asked, putting aside his papers. He eyed Catherine intently, and Carter could see that it made her uncomfortable.

"There are two announcements I wish to make. First, Mr. Fulbright and I received word just this morning that we are to be awarded two of the competition projects in the capital."

"What does that mean?" his mother asked anxiously. "Will you move to Washington?"

"Yes. It is most likely that I will."

"Oh, but that's so very far. I could hardly bear it. Would you come home often?"

"I would come to Philadelphia on occasion to oversee the current projects I have designed. Mr. Montgomery's house won't be completed for another few years, and I have been asked to design a new house for Leander and Winifred." He smiled at his sister, then looked back to his father, who had now come to stand by the fire.

"He must be quite well off if he's building a new house," his father said, rubbing his chin. "Perhaps we could interest him in an involvement with the mill."

"Lee is a lawyer, Father. He keeps quite busy with his work," Carter replied. He looked to Catherine and met her gaze. He lost himself for a moment in her expression. She smiled at him and broke the spell.

"There is also a second announcement I wish to make. Catherine has agreed to become my wife."

"But she's a seamstress," his mother declared.

"She is also the woman I love, and so much more," Carter said. He stood behind Catherine with his hands on her shoulders. "Catherine comes from a well-to-do family in Bath, England. Leander has gone there, in fact, to accompany Mr. Newbury to America, where he can rejoin Catherine and be a part of our wedding."

"Why is she working as a seamstress if she is well-to-do?" his father questioned.

Winifred looked at Carter and he nodded. She jumped up to interrupt. "Did I tell you that Leander and I plan to marry as soon as he returns?"

"What?" their mother exclaimed. "But that is too soon. You said he might return any day now. What of our plans? You haven't even picked out a gown."

"But I have. Catherine and I have worked together and she designed a beautiful dress. The final fitting will be tomorrow. You should come and see it, Mother. I know you'll love it."

"But you've said nothing about this," their mother said.

"And I'll not have it said my daughter rushed into marriage as though it were necessary," their father countered.

"I thought we would plan a dress together," their mother said, sounding very disappointed.

"I wanted to surprise you," Winifred said.

" 'Surprise' is hardly the word for it. Weddings take time to arrange," Mrs. Danby said, shaking her head. "How can I possibly have the matter concluded in such a short time? What if Mr. Arlington comes home tomorrow?"

"We want a very small wedding. There is no need to make a big fuss. I already told you we could marry in the ballroom."

Their mother fanned herself with her hands. "Yes, but there are flowers to order and invitations to be sent. You truly have no idea."

Carter was relieved to see his mother's focus turned from his own engagement to Winifred's wedding. He knew Catherine had tensed when his father had questioned why she was working as a seamstress. They had agreed to tell the truth if absolutely necessary but otherwise planned to refrain from bringing up the past. If Mr. Newbury wanted to remain in America, after all, there was no need having his reputation put into question because of the past.

"Oh, this is all so much to consider," Mother said.

"When will you leave for Washington?" Carter's father asked.

"By the middle of March. They want to break ground by the end of the month, provided the temperatures are warm enough."

"And will you marry before then?"

"Yes. As soon as Catherine's father arrives, we plan to arrange the wedding."

"Two weddings in such a short span of time!" his mother declared. She got to her feet and began to pace the floor. "It's quite impossible."

"Mother, no one is asking you to do anything in regard to our wedding," Carter said. "We want a very simple arrangement. A private ceremony without any pretense."

"Pretense? I'm sure I do not know what you mean. You are a Danby. Society will demand you marry very publicly. Surely you won't shame your family this way. If you marry in secret, people are sure to talk."

Carter shook his head. "There will be no shame in our wedding, I assure you, and people will talk whether we marry in two weeks or two years. Now, if you'll excuse us, the Arlingtons are expecting us to join them for supper." He helped Catherine to her feet.

Winifred embraced Catherine. "I'm so glad that you will be my sister."

"I am too," Catherine answered.

A new idea seemed to dawn on his mother. "Oh, I will be the envy of every woman in town. I will have the most sought-after dress designer as a daughter-in-law." She clapped her hands together. "What great fun this will be."

Catherine had never been happier to leave a place in all of her life. She got into the carriage and sighed in relief as Carter closed the door and took a seat beside her.

"I thought it all went rather well," he said, taking hold of her gloved hand.

"Your father was not happy."

"My father is never happy unless he's in control of a matter. He's just looking for ways to bolster his bank account. But enough of them. We will put the matter behind us for the time." He drew her hand to his lips and kissed her fingers.

"I wish Leander would return," Catherine said, leaning against Carter's arm. "What if something has happened to them?"

"We would have heard," Carter replied. "Stop fretting. Instead, tell me what kind of house you would like to live in. We shall have to find a place to live in Washington."

"Carter, I have to see to my father first. You know that," Catherine said, straightening. She turned to eye him very seriously. "He might need a great deal of care. It may be the reason we've not yet seen them return. He might be too sick. Leander might even return alone and tell me I need to go to England."

"And the stars might all fall from the skies tomorrow," Carter said, smiling. "You really do worry too much."

"I am simply trying to be realistic about this. Father is important to me."

Carter nodded. "And to me. You know that very well."

"You are so good to me. I never thought I could be so happy. My life seemed over before it had begun, and yet God had other plans."

"I'm just glad I'm a part of those plans, Miss Newbury."

They reached the Arlington house and waited for Joseph to open the carriage door. To Catherine's surprise, lights seemed to blaze from nearly every window. "Goodness, but it seems the entire house is glowing."

Carter alighted from the carriage and noted the appearance as well. Snow thickly blanketed the lawn, but the servants had cleared a path to the door. "Well, come along. We shall see what awaits us."

They didn't have to wait long. Just then the door opened, and Lee came bounding down the steps. Catherine's breath caught in her throat. Leander had returned. She looked to Carter as if for reassurance.

"Carter! Catherine! We've been waiting for your return." He embraced Carter briefly, then turned to Catherine. "We were beginning to think we should send out a search party."

"We?" Catherine asked softly. "My father?"

"Yes." Lee nodded and gave her an enthusiastic hug. "He is here. See for yourself."

Catherine glanced up to see her father standing in the open doorway. "Father!" She forgot about the slippery walk and hurried to greet him. Rushing up the stairs, she threw herself into his embrace. "I can't believe you are finally here."

"Oh, Cat, is it really you?" He held her tightly and sobbed. "I thought I might never see you again. Oh, my despair nearly caused me to give up all hope."

She pulled away, tears streaming down her face. "I nearly gave up as well."

He smiled. "But now we are here—together."

Studying him hard for a moment, Catherine was amazed at how well he looked. She could only pray that he had suffered no permanent harm. "Are you well, Father?"

"Yes. The duke treated me very well, and in his care I recovered from all sickness. When Mr. Arlington showed up to take me to you, I must say I was in better shape than I'd been in five years."

"Do you suppose we could take this inside—preferably by the fire?" Leander questioned. "The wind is chilling me to the bone."

Catherine smiled. "I'm sorry. I suppose I got a little caught up in the moment."

Her father put his arm around her as they moved inside. "You look so much like your mother. My, but you have grown into a beautiful woman. Mr. Arlington told me you were sewing for a living when he first met you."

"It's true. I worked in a sewing house here in Philadelphia, and I designed gowns. I've earned quite a reputation. My employer expects my work to become as popular as any French designer's creations."

He shook his head and laughed. "I can scarce believe it. I knew you to be an industrious child, but who could have expected this?"

They went into the brightly lit room, and Catherine got a better look at her father. He seemed to have aged considerably, but his color was good. "How I have missed you."

"And I you."

Catherine thought of their home in Bath and of her father's business. "Did the Crown return our home and your ships?"

Her father's expression seemed strained for a moment. "They gave me a healthy sum of money to allow me to make the decision as to where I would live and what I would do for a livelihood. The ships have long since been sold to service elsewhere, as was our home. I thought it better this way."

"I suppose so."

"The duke did offer me my choice of several properties, but I wanted to speak to you before making further decisions."

Someone cleared his throat behind Catherine and it startled her. She turned to find Carter grinning at her. "Why don't you give your coat and gloves, and then introduce me to your father."

She smiled and began to unfasten the buttons. "Father, this is—"

Her father stepped forward to take Carter's hand. "The man who wishes to marry you," he interjected. "Mr. Carter Danby, if I'm not mistaken."

CHAPTER 30

"The duke had cleared much of the way for Mr. Newbury by the time I arrived," Leander told the gathering of people in his parents' sitting room. "He had managed to track down the crew and other witnesses. Not only that, but with his help, Finley Baker was captured."

"Did he confess?" Catherine questioned.

"No, but he didn't have to. The mounting evidence was revealed, and witnesses came forth to bear testimony that it had been Baker all along who had masterminded the slave trade onboard the Newbury ships. Further evidence revealed by your father's bookkeeper showed the double set of records. The man was given immunity from charges if he would willingly testify to being bribed by Baker and paid to keep the matter from Mr. Newbury."

"And all of it under my nose," Newbury said, shaking his head.

Catherine gripped her father's hand to remind herself that he was really there—really safe from harm.

"Your father is free and his reputation has been restored to him," Leander added.

"It's a happy ending to a horrible nightmare," her father told them.

"I should say so," Mrs. Arlington said, shaking her head. "A more fragile person would not have survived. You are a remarkable man, Mr. Newbury, but that does not surprise me. Your daughter is also quite impressive."

Catherine saw him smile. His pleasure was evident. "She is that," he murmured.

"Lee, Carter . . . let us go and give Catherine some time alone with her father. We can come together again for supper," Judge Arlington suggested. Even now he was reaching for his wife's hand. "Come, my dear."

Catherine was grateful for the judge's sensitivity to her need. She waited until everyone had gone and the sitting room door had been closed before falling into her father's arms.

"I missed you so much," she sobbed, unable to stop the tears. "I worried every day about what they were doing to you and what horrible conditions you might have to endure."

"It was not easy, I will not lie. However, it is not something we should dwell on either. I will not tell you stories of my time in prison, for it is not for such delicate ears. But I will say this: My freedom is so much more precious than ever before."

Catherine sniffed back tears and raised her head from his shoulder. "And what would you like to do with that freedom, Father?"

He smiled. "Live my life to the fullest. I don't want to waste even a moment."

She frowned and looked away, uncertain of how to broach plans for the future. Would he expect them to return to England? Or did he even plan to return?

"You seem troubled, Cat. What is it?"

"I . . . well . . . you know about Mr. Danby—Carter."

He smiled. "That he wishes to marry you? That he was responsible for seeing me set free?"

"Yes." She bit at her lower lip. "Father, I've already told Carter that we needed to wait and see what your situation turned out to be. If you were sickly and needed help, I wanted to make certain you knew I would be there to care for you. I also wanted your blessing."

"Cat, you always have my blessing. Mr. Danby seems to be a remarkable young man. Mr. Arlington tells me that your Carter's faith in the Lord is quite strong. He also tells me that Carter is a man of determination and sensibility. Would you agree?"

"Oh, most assuredly. Carter is very considerate and attentive. There have been so many ways in which he's come to my rescue. He is a good man, Father, and I love him so dearly."

Her father smiled. "Then that is all I really care about. Life is far too short and unpredictable to play games where the heart is concerned. What I wouldn't have given for another twenty years with your mother. I miss her more than I could ever express." He sobered and took hold of Catherine's hands. "You are so very much like her. You have her dark eyes and heart-shaped face. I feel as though I'm looking at a living painting of her when we first met."

"I hope that gives you pleasure and not pain," Catherine said softly.

"It does. It pleases me greatly. It pleases, too, to hear from the Shays how industrious you were for my cause. I always knew you to be a survivor. When I sent you away with Selma and Dugan, I knew you would find the separation painful. But I also knew you would bolster your courage in the Lord and stand fast."

"There were times when I was not that courageous, Father. Times when I despaired, I'm sorry to say."

"We all have those moments, but the important thing is to move beyond them. I had to do that as well, and now here I am. And here you are."

"And where do we go from here?" Catherine asked.

"Well, you will marry your young man."

"And you, Father? What do you desire to do?"

He smiled. "I'm not such a young man anymore. I will perhaps invest my money and live a quiet and comfortable life spoiling my grandchildren."

"Carter has a job awaiting him in Washington—not far from here. He plans . . . well, it would be necessary to move there. Would you be opposed to remaining in America and living there also?"

"Not at all. I have put England behind me, at least for the time. There may come a time when I will return—perhaps as my age advances, so that when I die I might be buried beside your mother and brothers."

"Don't talk of such things. I've only just gotten you back," Catherine said.

"Don't fear such things," her father countered. "God holds the future for us. We needn't fear it—especially not death. Christ overcame the grave that we might have eternal life if we but put our faith in Him. We have done that, and there is no need to be afraid—whatever the future holds."

"I know you are right," Catherine said, nodding. "Still, I would like to know that you might remain close by in the years to come. At least for a little while."

"Then I will," her father replied. "I will come with you and Carter, but I will find my own place to live. Newly married people need time alone, and I will not impose upon you."

"You could never be an imposition, Father. My future is so bright—with the two men I love most."

❦

Three weeks later, Catherine married Carter in a double wedding ceremony with Winifred and Leander. She could not have imagined anything more perfect. The Danby ballroom was filled to capacity with well-wishers and the curious. Mrs. Danby had made the wedding a remarkable social occasion despite having so little time to accomplish the feat.

Catherine felt like a princess in her own gown of white silk barège. The style was cut somewhat differently from Winifred's gown. Catherine had designed the creation with a gently rounded neckline and basque waist, but Mrs. Clarkson and her girls had been the ones to bring the gown to completion. They were even on hand to help her prepare, including Dolley, who dressed her hair in the same cascading manner that she'd fashioned for the masquerade. A veil of antique French lace, given to her by Mrs. Clarkson, adorned Catherine's head with a beautiful comb of pearl and gold—a gift from Carter's mother. And around her neck Catherine wore a delicate necklace of sapphires and gold, a belated Christmas present from her new husband.

Upon the conclusion of their wedding vows, Carter smiled. "Well, Mrs. Danby, there are no masks between us this time. Shall we share a kiss without all of the secrets that kept us apart?"

"Most assuredly, Mr. Danby." Catherine abandoned herself to his kiss despite the gathered congregation watching them most intently.

The rest of the day passed as if in a whirlwind. Catherine knew more happiness than she'd ever imagined. She couldn't help but smile at the way her father seemed to take an interest in Mrs. Clarkson. Perhaps there was a future for the couple.

"Are you ready to go?" Carter asked as she descended the stairs after changing her clothes in Winifred's old bedroom. "Lee and Winnie are anxious to get to the train."

"Let me say good-bye to Father," she said. "I could not leave on my wedding trip without being reassured that he has been seen to."

Carter laughed. "I think he's being very 'seen to,' if you ask me." He motioned to the side. "Mrs. Clarkson seems to hold his attention quite nicely."

Catherine caught sight of her father laughing at something the widow had said. Selma and Dugan were not far away, and they, too, smiled as they met Catherine's gaze. Selma raised her eyebrows and nodded in Mr. Newbury's direction as if to suggest the matter bore great consideration. Catherine nodded rather enthusiastically and laughed.

"I think you're right. Maybe Father won't be moving to Washington with us after all."

"Perhaps not," Carter replied. "Perhaps we shall have to find ways to keep each other company without him."

Catherine looped her arm through his. "Perhaps we shall."

EPILOGUE

Two years later, Catherine stood in front of the half-finished structure in the heart of Washington. The day was warm and pleasant, with new flowers blooming and birds twittering in the trees. People were everywhere as they enjoyed their Sunday afternoon. Women passed by, and Catherine couldn't help but smile as she recognized one of her own designs.

"They've made great progress," Carter stated. He smiled with pride at the accomplishment of his plan. "The craftsmen are some of the finest available, and I have been very pleased with their execution of my design."

"It is a wonder," Catherine said, noting the three-story Greek Revival building. "I can hardly wait until it's complete. I'm so proud of you, Carter. What a marvelous mark you will leave on the world."

"Well, perhaps on this city," he said. Only the day before, Carter and Mr. Fulbright had received a commission for yet another building. Not only that, but they were often consulted and commissioned to design homes for those in and around the city.

"You will leave your mark as well, Mrs. Danby. For there is probably not a woman in the entire area who has not either coveted one of your designs or who even now is wearing one. *Godey's* has done much to see your fame increased."

"And Mrs. Clarkson is quite content with the volume of work given her to reproduce my designs and increase the number of girls she employs to sew them." Catherine pressed closer to Carter despite the warmth of the beautiful spring day. "It would seem that we make a most creative team, my dear husband."

"Someone is very tired, and perhaps hungry," her father declared.

"Ah," Carter said, smiling, "yet another proof of our creativity."

Catherine turned to find her father coming toward them, the fussing Zachary Danby in his arms. His howls of protest only increased when he caught sight of his mother's face. At nine months of age, he was very nearly as demanding as his father, Catherine had determined.

"I believe this young man to be God's creativity," Catherine countered. Her dark-haired son only began to cry harder when she did nothing to ease his misery. "Poor baby. I suppose we should make our way home."

She started to reach for him, but Carter took the boy from his father-in-law instead. He began to talk to the baby in a low, soothing voice. The boy immediately calmed and smiled, even though tears still dampened his cheeks.

How blessed Catherine felt. Her father was happy and prosperous in his life in America. He had taken an interest in helping to manage Catherine's designs. Not only could he benefit his daughter, he had told her, but it also put him in the company of a certain Mrs. Clarkson, whom, Catherine had on good authority, was soon to become her stepmother.

But even more so, she had her son and Carter, for whom her love knew no bounds. No longer was her past hidden, her future uncertain. Instead, her life had become an intricate design by the Master Creator—a Creator who loved her and had never left her, even in the darkest hours of her life.

More Exciting Historical Fiction From Tracie Peterson

Mia Stanley has a knack for matchmaking—and for trouble. When her job at *Godey's Lady's Book* opens her eyes to the plight of the seamen's wives, she uncovers a scheme that puts her life in danger. But her heart is on the line as well. Have her determined matchmaking ways driven away the one man she loves?

A Lady of High Regard
LADIES OF LIBERTY

New Series! Bestselling authors Tracie Peterson and Judith Miller team up for another dynamic series. A sudden, large inheritance leaves seventeen-year-old Fanny Broadmoor surrounded by opulence, wealth...and hidden motives. And her secret love with the family boat-keeper only complicates matters. In a society where money equals power, who does she dare trust?

A Daughter's Inheritance by Tracie Peterson and Judith Miller
THE BROADMOOR LEGACY #1

From her own Big Sky home, Tracie Peterson paints a one-of-a-kind portrait of 1860s Montana and the strong, spirited men and women who dared to call it home. The rich, rugged landscape of the prairie frontier presents a dangerous beauty that only the boldest can tame. Join Peterson in the Montana Territory with all the history, drama, and faith you come to expect from her books.

HEIRS OF MONTANA
Land of My Heart, The Coming Storm, To Dream Anew, The Hope Within

Be Sure to Check Out Tracie's Moving Contemporary Fiction Too!
After her husband's betrayal, Jana McGuire is left with only one choice: to humbly seek refuge with a mother she barely knows yet longs to understand and connect with. But Eleanor has firmly shut the door on the past. As the heartache of Jana's situation heightens, her need for her mother compels her to seek out the truth of that past. But will Jana's search bring back a pain that was better left alone?

What She Left for Me

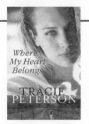

As their father lies on his deathbed, estranged sisters Amy and Kathy Halbert are forced to care for him—together. Honoring his dying wishes, they try to walk the road of reconciliation. But twelve years of separation and secrets lie between them. How can they even begin to overcome the layers of bitterness and betrayal?

Where My Heart Belongs

Looking for More Good Books to Read?

You can find out what is new and exciting with
previews, descriptions, and reviews by signing up for
Bethany House newsletters at

www.bethanynewsletters.com

We will send you updates for as many authors or
categories as you desire so you get only the
information you really want.

Sign up today!